Love is

There is nothing more terrifying than a first kiss, even if you know it's a sure thing.

"Press play," she said.

But I ignored her and leaned in to catch her lips instead, grabbing her head with both my hands to press her closer to me. Had a fortune teller been present, she could have laid out the trajectory for my entire life with this girl. All the weight of the world was lifted from me and our lips were entangled for ages. I was lost in the ebb and flow of our kiss. Her mouth pressed harder into me, as if she weren't close enough, and I was unable to detach from her any more than a disoriented swimmer can escape the rending nature of oceans. She was like the relentless stirring of water in a merciless storm. Without warning, she broke away, leaving me gasping, robbed of breath. Briana sat bewildered, speechless, still facing me, and then without a word she stood and began to undress. She stripped and threw her clothes to the floor, exposing the full curvature of her body. Strength was etched into her every limb from years of dance. I had never met a woman with such a tidal design.

What They Are Saying About
Love is a Cheerleader Running

Liam, R.F. Gonzalez's character, takes his readers on a journey that essentially belongs to one's soul. Gonzalez's debut novel, *Cheerleader*, abounds with moments filled with throbbing adrenaline rushes that showcase moments of dark abysmal despair, to heart-tearing pulsating love, to what we hope is his final salvation. Liam is doomed to fall in love and suffer as much as he's prone to making those he doesn't love suffer. It's a very slice-of-life novel with myriad shades of gray. This is no Greek hero who shall conquer and win. This is a truly Shakespearean protagonist who has flaws caused by his own hamartia. An enriching reading experience created through dexterity of language and mindfulness, *Cheerleader* will not disappoint its readers. It's an awesome start to an adventurous journey!

—Parul Bhatia
Author of *My Gypsy Dreams*, writer and director of the film *My Father's Daughter*

To paraphrase many, the course of true love does not run smooth. And it doesn't run smoothly for Liam, our hero and narrator. *Cheerleader* is a tale filled with sex, attempts to love, pain, and ultimately resolution, told with wit, depth, and sparkling dialogue. Liam tries to find his way, thinks he has, loses it, and ultimately, drawing from a depth of experience he shares with the reader, catches up with that elusive cheerleader he's been chasing for years.

—John Paulits
Author of *The Sad Case of Brownie Terwilliger*

In Liam, R.F. Gonzalez creates a narrator that's reminiscent of every boy's quest for love...a quest filled with pain, joy, and everything in between. *Cheerleader* takes its readers on a witty journey through the roller coaster that is life. Filled with detailed dialogue and skillful writing, Gonzalez's debut novel, *Cheerleader*, will leave you anxiously waiting for his next release.

—Leigh Macneil
Author of *SPAZ: The True Story of my Life with ADHD*

Love is a Cheerleader Running

R. F. Gonzalez

A Wings ePress, Inc.
New Adult Novel

Wings ePress, Inc.

Edited by: Jeanne Smith
Copy Edited by: Christie Kraemer
Executive Editor: Jeanne Smith
Cover Artist: Trisha FitzGerald-Jung

All rights reserved

Names, characters and incidents depicted in this book are products of the author's imagination or are used fictitiously. Any resemblance to actual events, locales, organizations, or persons, living or dead, is entirely coincidental and beyond the intent of the author or the publisher.

No part of this book may be reproduced or transmitted in any form or by any means, electronic or mechanical, including photocopying, recording, or by any information storage and retrieval system, without permission in writing from the publisher.

Wings ePress Books
www.wingsepress.com

Copyright © 2019 by: R. F. Gonzalez
ISBN 978-1-61309-613-0

Published In the United States Of America

Wings ePress Inc.
3000 N. Rock Road
Newton, KS 67114

Dedication

To Corinne, Sahara, Sabian, Everest, Yuumai, and Mom and Dad, for revealing love's unconditional conditions.

Part One: Never is Just One Path

One

Twelve Hours Left

Love had stripped her to the bone.

"Don't kill us," she'd said six months earlier during our fallout. Her volume peaked as she panicked. "Aren't we worth saving?"

"Stop," I said, evading her question.

Liz wrestled with a fit of sobs before crying out, "I don't want to forget how we feel." But she was already forgotten.

She was wounded, bleeding out words, and all I could muster was a bland, "Just leave."

"Not like this," she begged, swollen and red from the gush on her face. "Come back to me." When I didn't respond, she lowered her head and wept into shaky hands. Suddenly, she shivered in one spasmodic wave before roaring, as if possessed, "Do you want me to forget you forever?"

"Yes," I said, flatly, like only a mean bastard could.

"What are you running from? Tell me."

I was out of answers, and my blank stare made her turn around, and go for the door. She'd finally had enough. Her fragrant breath filled my nostrils before she disappeared.

~ * ~

Six months later, we were on a plane. She still knew me better than anyone, despite our separation, and her innuendoes were cast to gauge my thoughts. Secretly, I think she hoped I wasn't resentful anymore.

I was shocked when she said, "Let's join the mile-high club." Liz knew it was on my bucket list. Her baby blues were locked on me, and my brow furrowed from being teased with the impossibility of plane sex with a hot girl. I almost missed the fluid coloring that ran through her eyes. I'd forgotten how they were speckled with amber and green, as if brilliant coins or sparkly gems had been thrown into a wintry stream. When she was mad, it was as if the sun had burst in her eyes. They were bedazzling. I may not have been in love with her, but she was so stunning—blessed with curves delicately accentuated by wavy auburn hair.

It's every guy's dream for a girl to suggest that on a plane, but she wasn't being sincere. Plus, it would have been bad for us. There are few things more destructive than ex sex, so I said, "No. Did you even try to get a refund for this flight?"

Of course not. It was written all over her face as she folded her arms and sulked. Our elbows grazed, and we both drooped like shameplants into our seats. We had been on this flight for two hours. Twelve hours left, and we were already at each other's throats.

She didn't wait long to make it more awkward. "I absolutely loved you," she whispered into my ear, "and, I would have married you if you hadn't been such a coward."

I turned my head sharply toward her again and whispered back in the lowest, raspiest tone I could manage so as not to startle the other passengers, "You sure you want to do this now?" She maintained a blank expression, nervously fluttering her eyelashes, hoping the next words would catapult us into a relationship again. Our time together had been no saga. "It was fake, Liz. We were fake."

Her lip quivered, and I barely heard her say "Ok" as she turned away again and hugged herself tightly. She slumped so hard into her seat that she nearly disappeared.

~ * ~

We had met at the university where I studied five days a week, six hours a day. My life was about books back then. To Liz's credit, she had been brave to approach me, especially since I hadn't given off any signal or vibe, or followed her to see where she studied, or taken a class because she was in it. I did nothing, but she tried anyway.

I was buried in my studies when her words cut through my trance. "Excuse me, do you want to be friends?" Worst pick-up line ever, yet it worked on me.

Liz was crouched next to my table…barely out of peripheral range. Her crystalline eyes could have made God himself doubt his choice of color for the oceans. She seemed encumbered by an overeager, optimistic anticipation, and her small, pointed nose complemented her geisha lips. At first, I thought she was flexing but, after some time, it became obvious that her mouth was designed this way. Natural selection has a funny way of making women sexy. She saw the confusion on my face, and then giggled while coyly covering her mouth, as if to hide her teeth, though they were bright white and perfectly straight.

"What?" I responded. "Do I know you?"

"Kind of. We're in the same math class."

"We are?"

"And the same anthropology class."

"Oh, I've never seen you around," I said, slightly embarrassed at my oversight.

"Well, I've seen you," she said.

I was unsure where or how to take the conversation, until she said, "You want to go to a movie?"

Accepting the invitation was my first mistake with Liz. At the time, it didn't feel like a mistake, but that's always the most dangerous kind of relationship...the kind that sneaks up on you. Case in point: She said *I love you* over the phone one evening, months after our first movie. I had gotten stuck in a blizzard at a rest stop in North Carolina. One minute we were at a theater, and the next, she was surrendering herself to me. She followed up those three damning words with, "I know you can't say it back, but I do, and it's okay if you don't." We didn't talk long, and the signal dropped, so I wasn't clear as to whether she meant it was okay that I didn't say it back, or that she knew I didn't love her. Either way, I didn't want to say it because I didn't feel that for her. I wasn't *in love*. I mean, I did care, but I also cared about not graduating on time, finding a job, recycling, and the starving children of the world. Everyone outside our intimate life painted us as the perfect couple with realistic and obtainable goals and potential for a harmonious future. Really, we were like an hourglass clock with its layers of sand gradually thinning down to nothing. This timepiece had whittled down to its last grain over the course of two years.

~ * ~

As the hours passed on the plane, the brutality of the journey was taking its toll. Beijing was too many hours away. Liz eventually passed out and slept for most of the flight. She gave up talking to me...no more whispers, no more innuendoes, no chance of checking anything off my bucket list. Being stuck with Liz for the next four days wasn't comforting at all, and screeching through the sky at abominable speeds while strapped to a hunk of metal made it worse.

I hated flying. Adrenaline tended to overfeed my imagination, turning gravity into a monstrous octopus whose sole purpose was to snatch planes from the sky and crash them into the water. I hadn't slept in two days, and the exhaustion of prepping for the trip finally hit me. As the ocean below resonated into the boundless midnight, I thought, *If we die today, then we both may go to heaven due to the ironic tragedy of the entire situation...since I would be dying next to the woman who loved me unconditionally, and she would be dying next to the man who would not love her under any condition.*

Two

Pain is a World Away

"No bags," said the adolescent Asian girl behind the customer service counter at Beijing Capital International Airport. We had exited the plane and intuitively made our way to baggage claim. There were no signs, and if there were, I couldn't read the Mandarin very well, anyway. My conversational abilities were not much help either, but we were lucky English language learning was mandatory in Beijing.

"Where are our bags?" I pressed the question to the agent. "Can I speak to a manager?"

"I'm manager." No way was this teeny bopper the manager, but I didn't insist. "We will deliver to you when found. Write address and phone number down," she responded.

"What do we do?" Liz said, growing more upset by the second.

"Relax. They'll find our bags." I didn't think we'd ever see our bags again, but I wasn't going to tell Liz that. "We still have our backpacks and emergency clothes and toiletry. It'll buy us an extra day," I said. I put my hands on her shoulders and locked my eyes on hers. It was my habit of reassuring her after being together for so long. I did it reflexively, but then she brushed me off and glimpsed around the airport.

"And how will they know where to deliver the stuff?" her voice cracked. Back to panic mode. *Leave it to me to solve our problems, as usual.* Liz tended to overplay the helpless damsel. When we began dating, I suspected she faked this role to get me to like her, but her norm was to function as a compulsive dependent. She was limp without someone there to hold her up—whether it was a friend, parents, or me.

After scanning the list of a dozen hostels I had picked before leaving the States, I chose the first one, gave the customer service agent the phone number and address, and filled out the required paperwork. "Do you know where the bags are right now? And how long will it take for you to deliver them?"

"Yes, sir. They are in New York by accident," she answered, typing and talking at the same time. "In two days, we deliver them to this address," she continued, pointing to the form I'd filled out, and maintaining her composure so I wouldn't create a scene. Liz and I left the customer service desk and, after the final immigration checkpoint, we exited through cheap turnstiles into a maze of hallways. It was 9:30pm, and the airport was busy.

Liz was acting more nervous than usual, if that was possible.

"Now, what do we do?" she said.

"Now, we venture into this strange land," I responded.

"I mean, where do we go? How do we get to where we're staying?"

Ah, the panicked maiden. I could have easily ditched Liz. Not only was she tagging along without my consent, she was my ex, and I wasn't obligated to stick with her. But she had done it all to be with me. The guilt, of course, got to me again…making me feel responsible for her. Thankfully, it was only for a few days.

Half a dozen policemen scrutinized the crowd of passengers bustling down the hallway to our left. "Let's go that way," I said, and we hustled into the crowd. As we moved forward, the officers worked to usher us further down the hallway. No loitering allowed.

We veered left at the corner and ran into a cramped ticket booth with a mob attached to it. Everyone was screaming and shaking money at the three cashiers. Opposite the booth, to our right and beyond two large glass doors serving as the main exit to the airport, were a dozen buses ready for departure. We had to get tickets and find our bus soon or else sleep in the street. After standing in line for a while and being shuffled around to the back a couple times, it was apparent there was no queue, and we would have to push our way forward alongside everyone else. Later, I would discover that no matter where I went in Beijing, nobody knew what patient, orderly, linear waiting was. Even cafeterias resembled scenes from the New York Stock Exchange, and getting on and off the underground felt like someone had yelled, "Fire!" But instead of fleeing, we would sardine ourselves inside a train. Buying tickets to the center of the city was madness; yet, by sheer luck, we made our bus seconds before it departed.

After forty-eight hours of total travel time, including hours of awkwardness on the plane, and two confusing bus rides, we dragged ourselves out of the downtown main station a few blocks from our hostel. It was 11:30pm on a Wednesday, and the streets were surprisingly deserted, despite the rumors I'd read online that this place was another New York, a mini-city that never sleeps. Everyone we passed on the street was smoking, and every fifty yards we had to make our way around a row of mopeds and a pile of tangled bikes. Surprisingly, no owners were nearby, and the bikes weren't secured to anything. *This wouldn't fly in the States.* The map and pictures of landmarks I'd packed were easy to follow. As we approached the address on my list, the words "crime syndicate" came to mind. Liz trapped my right hand with her left and squeezed it tightly, signaling me to keep her close. We hadn't touched each other in half a year, but now we felt the fear, so I squeezed back. To reach the front door of the hostel, we had to enter an alley flanked by shady men scattered along the sidewalk who peered at us as they leaned on the chained entrances of abandoned shops. They leered like they'd struck gold.

Bracing ourselves for the worst, we were surprised when they continued to puff away as we passed by, granting us passage to the shoddy hostel entrance without any trouble.

The frame of the entrance was desperate for repairs and, above us, the chipped letters of a sign that read "Homely Haven" did not conjure up any sense of warmth or safety. It didn't help that the whole entrance was lit up by a weak twenty-five-watt bulb. Because it was a known foreigner spot, everything was Romanized. We got up to the fifth floor of the seedy tenement, and I knocked on the manager's door. He barked, "No room," and slammed the door in our faces. On our way out, a younger man who introduced himself as Bruce peeked his head out of the same apartment and assured us his belligerent uncle was a nice man, just not at that moment, and that we should return tomorrow morning for rooms.

"I'm so tired, I'm about to collapse," whispered Liz. I motioned for her to be quiet while I sorted things out. I was on the verge of crashing, too.

"Do you know where we can stay tonight?" I said to Bruce in a hopeful tone.

Without saying a word, he closed the door and came out. All three of us were downstairs in the street when he said, "I take you to very nice hotel. Very nice hotel. Tomorrow, you come back here, and I give you room."

"See," I said to Liz, "the man is taking us to a nice hotel."

She was apprehensive about the spontaneity of the entire situation and, true to her character, she whined, "Why didn't we stay in the hotels I suggested?"

I glared at her for being a four-star snob and wanted to shout, *Shut your privileged mouth.* As we followed Bruce down the street, the night thickened, as if there were a blackout in this sector of town.

"You don't have luggage?" said Bruce as we walked.

"Airline lost it."

He didn't say much else until we reached the "very nice hotel" which appeared to be more of a rundown motel found off a suspect highway exit. But once we were inside, it was evident I had granted it too much credit. It was a crumbling, roach infested, near condemnable establishment. Bruce went ahead to the receptionist and said something to her. He then motioned us over, and we approached the desk.

"Do I pay now?" I inquired.

Bruce reiterated what he had said to us earlier, "Tomorrow, you come back to Homely Haven and find me for rooms." He then handed us the key and exited the building. The receptionist nodded at us but said nothing...perhaps too shy to show off her fragmented English.

We walked past the desk and began to climb a creaky, balding wooden staircase leading to the rooms, when Liz shrieked, "Ew, roach," and turned around to face me. Her heels synchronized in a cartoonish rapid mini-march as she spoke. "I don't want to stay here." Her voice trembled at the prospect of bugs crawling on her. I wasn't privy to the idea either, but sleep deprivation had reached a critical point. If we didn't get into a room, we'd surely begin hallucinating. Plane sleep was not enough.

"It's the street or here," I said.

She breathed profoundly, turned around, and kept climbing. Once we entered the room, I was surprised to see that there was a private shower, but when I peeked my head in, I saw it hadn't been cleaned in months. The vibrant black mold lodged in the tile grout was testament to that.

"So gross," said Liz.

"Suck it up for now, and tomorrow we'll see if we can get a better room at the hostel."

We had quick showers, brushed up, and lay down in two separate twin beds. The next eight hours were a coma-like sleep.

~ * ~

It was early morning, and I sat at the edge of the bed listening to the toylike honks of compact car horns in the distance. Liz was sound asleep in her bed. I blamed myself for everything—for permitting our frail friendship to escalate into a serious and committed relationship. I'd done nothing to stop it until it was too late, until we were too far gone.

~ * ~

The next mistake I made with her, after we went to the movies, was to accept her invitation to help her housesit. She was dog sitting and, late afternoon on my birthday, she called me up and asked if I wanted to help her out. It was rare, but I wanted company. Usually, I hated celebrating my birthday. Two weeks had passed since our movie, and we were well on our way to a platonic union.

"I'll text you the address," Liz said excitedly over the phone. "Oh, and I have a surprise for you."

"No birthday stuff, alright? I'm not coming over if it's going to be like that."

"It's not a gift or anything. I made us dinner," she said. "It's a meal. Nothing weird."

"Okay, dinner. No cakes or candles."

"No birthday stuff. Promise. It just happens to be your birthday, and we are going to eat together," she said matter-of-factly. She was a terrible liar. I suspected she was suppressing a slight giggle and imagined her hand covering her perfect teeth which was something she did when she felt she was being clever or mischievous.

I knocked on the townhouse door and heard Liz holler, "It's open." As I walked through the strange entryway, it felt like I was breaking and entering. Less than ten feet from the entrance stood an awkwardly placed white staircase spiraling up to the second-floor suite. I heard movement, shuffling, the thumping of feet above me, and then she peeked her head down from the railing above. "Hold on. I'm coming down. Have a seat." But I didn't have a seat. I stood between the doorway and staircase admiring an eclectic collection of Native American artifacts, all scattered on tables and hanging on walls in loose geometric order. She began to walk down the stairs in what appeared to be a bikini, but it was fall so it didn't make sense. Liz was flaunting red underwear and a blue bra. Pale skin began at her bare feet, ran up her legs, and spread itself over a toned expanse of flat stomach accentuated by a belly button ring. Her blue eyes resembled gems, and the hair on the back of my neck stood up. Liz was a voluptuous beauty, but fit, a Venus eager to share her curves with the world. Her thick auburn hair bounced with every footstep yet remained perfectly combed behind a silver hairband. She paused halfway down, looking delighted, as if having discovered something.

"This is my surprise," she said, throwing her delicate hands up in the air and shimmying. I was speechless. This was a first. Of course, I had seen other women in their underwear, but none had ever made it an accessory to cooking me a birthday dinner.

She strutted by me and grazed my face with her hand as she entered the kitchen directly to my right. I stood and observed her rummaging for pots and pans for a minute, until she said, "Relax." I snapped out of my trance and went to sit at a stool that would allow me to continue enjoying the show. I must have been gawking a lot because Liz chuckled each time she glanced over at me.

She walked on the balls of her feet, keeping her back unusually straight, and it occurred to me she would make a hell of a dancer. "Are you a dancer?" I blurted out. Liz set a large pan down on a burner and turned around to face me. My eyes were forced to scan her physique from head to jet painted toes. This was the kind of girl that guys fantasize about.

"I am," she said as if reading my mind. "Why do you ask?"

"You move so gracefully on the balls of your feet." I felt stupid for answering so pragmatically.

Liz batted her eyes at me.

"Um, thanks?" she said confusedly.

"I mean, you have nice feet considering you're a dancer."

"What? Are you saying you like my feet?" she snorted.

"Uh, yeah," I said with obvious discomfort in my choice of words.

Liz leaned her butt on the stove behind her and crossed her arms and legs. "Seriously? You're gawking at my feet while I'm standing here slaving away, cooking dinner for you in lacy underwear?"

There was an awkward pause before I said, "Kind of, but—"

"If you think I'm sexy, then say that," she interrupted, a bit cross that I couldn't or wouldn't divulge everything that was on my mind. I was uncertain what she expected, since we'd barely met a couple weeks ago. Liz acted as if we'd known each other forever. Up to this point, she'd worn clothes so baggy, she looked like a performer on a 90's revival show. Had I known that underneath all the garb was a body built for porno, things may have started differently. She turned back around and tossed in a couple tender steaks. Thankfully, the awkwardness subsided as the meaty aroma filled the air. If she hadn't been the sexiest cook on the planet at that moment, I would have left.

There was some small talk as she turned steaks over in one pan and threw veggies in another. She was a decent cook. We had dinner, drank beer, and shared life stories for hours, but after thanking her for a great time and motioning to leave, she said, "Don't go. Come on, let me show you the upstairs."

"I should go," I said, purposely playing coy to test her intentions.

"But it's too early," her voice begged as she grabbed both my hands and led me up the staircase.

Being a guy, my first thought was *Freak! She likes to freak in strange houses!* But as soon as we were upstairs, she climbed into the bed and began to jump.

"Come on," she said in the air, her crisp voice disembodied. "Jump with me."

I kicked my shoes off and jumped with her until I felt the steak she had cooked was about to make a reappearance in the upstairs toilet.

Our voices ping-ponged around the room as we tried to have a conversation between our jumps:

"This...is...my...first...bed...jump...ing...date," she said.

"I'm...not...sure...but...this...may...be...my...third...or...fourth," I said.

"L...i...a...r!"

After a while, I collapsed on the bed and she said, totally out of breath, "Wh-wimp. You have no endurance for bed jumping."

"I guess not," I said, struggling for air. I should have said, *I have endurance for other things*. Right then, a tornado of clothes should have shot from our bodies and settled onto the floor, followed by *Top Gun*-like romancing, but it was wishful thinking.

"That's the first laugh I've heard from you in a while," she said, exaggerating to make her point, as if she'd never seen me in any other state than morose. Perhaps she hadn't. "You're too serious," she continued as she flopped down next to me and began to scan my face. She was three inches from me, the closest we'd ever been. "You can kiss me if you want," she said. "I won't mind." Her eyelashes fluttered like a manic butterfly. I leaned into her, but it was sloppy. We couldn't find the spot where our lips would settle comfortably into the weight of a first kiss. She would pinch my lower lip and make me jump as I tried to press softly into hers, or we would bump our teeth as we dove for a wide-mouthed kiss, like two berserkers desperate to knock down walls, or I'd feel her tongue block my airway, and I'd choke.

"This is how clowns kiss in clown porn," she said. I could barely make out the words "Kiss fail" through her giggling. I was a tad embarrassed as we playfully jabbed at one another, until we finally shifted our talk from ridiculous to mildly fun, and then to sad and serious topics.

"Happy twenty-first birthday," she sang gently, caressing my face. "I can't wait to be there."

"Don't be in such a hurry. Besides drinking legally, it's a pointless age."

She rolled her eyes and fired back sarcastically. "Oh, how wise you are. Teach me more."

I realized how ridiculous I sounded and tried to change the subject. "Tell me something nobody knows about you," I said.

The covers, sheets, and pillows were scattered about the floor by that time. We both scrunched into fetal positions as the ceiling fan chopped the air above us and filled the room with gusts of cool air which poked at our skin like ghostly fingers. Liz didn't speak for a while, then began kissing me furiously in a futile search for that spot.

She broke away to say, "We need to practice so we can get better."

I didn't protest, and we kept going.

Of course, it was intense, and at the point when we trembled in anticipation—a consequence of making out while carelessly grinding our bodies together in nothing but lacy underwear and thin boxers—Liz disengaged and said, "I'm a virgin."

I sat up, and she sat up next to me. "Seriously? Are you messing with me?" I said.

"I've never met anyone I wanted that much. It never happened." She paused and waited for me to say something in response, but I had nothing, so she continued. "There's no restart button for virginities, and I want it to be with someone who wants to be mine forever. I want it to be perfect. I want the fairytale."

"Okay," I said dumbfounded. Liz's response was romantic, cliché, and potentially tragic. I felt the immense pressure, the burden, that would come with getting involved with her. Her expectations of love were still glittering with fairytale dust, and mine were stashed in a dusty tomb somewhere.

"But we don't have to stop now," she suggested as she ran her hand down my chest and over my thighs. "We can still have fun, if you want." It wasn't fun anymore, though.

I recoiled at the idea of ruining this girl and began to back away from her. "I need to go," I said, feeling as if running away were the answer. She lunged forward and held me in place as I got off the bed. "No. Don't. Please, stay. Sleep here with me. It'll be worth it. I promise." Liz was urging me to climb back in. She was delicate about it, and afraid that if she tempted any harder, she'd crack me in half. "I can't be alone anymore," she whispered as we lay back down.

Maybe it was the way she trembled from loneliness that made me want to console her, or it could have been her pitiful words, or because I liked her. Whatever it was, Liz was more alone than anyone I'd ever known. Loneliness kept us fettered to the bed, and I stayed with her for a long time after that.

Three

Homely Haven

"Liam!" I heard Liz's voice echo into my icy shower. Hot was not part of the plumbing in this hotel. I jumped out, grabbed a towel, and stepped into the bedroom.

"What is it?" I said.

"I couldn't find you," she said. "I didn't hear you showering. Sorry."

"Jesus, Liz. You scared the hell out of me. I thought a rat bit you or something. Plus, my stuff is still here. I wouldn't leave without it."

She was sitting up in bed with the sheets over her chest when I mentioned the rats. Not that I'd seen any rats, but the place was likely crawling with them. "Asshole," she said, searching the room for rodent clues. Then she threw off the sheets, hopped out of bed, and kicked my bags aside. She had slept in her bra and panties but didn't care that we were practically standing there naked together, like old times.

"Ugh, this place is so putrid. We aren't eating here."

"You're here for four days. Relax, okay? Let's get through this without the dramatics."

"Rats are so gross," she cried, and then tiptoed toward the shower door where I was standing. "And that's not me being dramatic either."

I rolled my eyes at her. *Why the hell did I mention rats?* She shoved me out of the way and slammed the door.

"Hey, I'm not done in there," I said.

"Screw you!"

I gave up the fight. It was pointless to argue. After breakfast, we would need to find our way back to Homely Haven hostel and secure rooms—four days for Liz's stay, and then another month for me. That's what we needed to focus on. Screw the rats. Screw Liz.

We packed our stuff and headed downstairs. Still irritated, Liz waited outside while I settled the bill. At the receptionist's desk, I asked in broken Mandarin how much we owed. It was a different attendant there, a skinny college kid, who answered in English. "All paid for," he said, grinning through unfortunate bifocals. He resembled a nerdy, acne riddled Jackie Chan.

"But I haven't paid," I said, suspicious of a foreigner trap unfolding before me, one where I walk out content that things are *paid for* and then cops throw me to the ground, haul me to a desolate construction site, and extort money from me by teasing my passport with fire. This had happened to me before.

"Homely Haven man already pay for you this morning," said the attendant.

"Bruce? But it's 9am. When was he here?"

"Very early," he responded, his face beginning to show signs of fatigue from my questions. As it dawned on me that he'd reached his zenith in the English language, I asked him to direct us to the Homely Haven hostel. He handed me a copy of the receipt where he drew a simple map to guide us.

Though I embraced the new sights, while Liz resisted, we both struggled to ignore the smells as we made our way to the hostel. And damn, were there smells. Beijing was a clashing of two worlds. We'd pass a fully stocked Americanized teeny-bopping internet café, and then later, on a crumbling sidewalk, we'd see a wizened man dressed in a potato sack shirt and secondhand cotton shorts cooking eggs and mystery soup on his rickshaw stove. Weary from our travels and short on bravery, we grabbed two crescent bacon and egg sandwiches from a café, and ate as we walked. Street vendors eyed our sandwiches and leered at us as we walked by, as if we'd stolen from them. Liz didn't catch the looks and gobbled her food down. There were three McDonald's in the city, and I predicted we'd be dining there often.

"Why would he pay for our room?" said Liz as we continued down partially cobbled streets. Every dozen feet or so, we had to step over a hump of patched cement where cobbles had been pried out. Her face grew tense with concern.

"He's trying to be nice," I said, sensing a fit approaching.

"I don't like that. We don't know him."

I rolled my eyes at her and ate some egg that was dangling off my crescent.

After munching on bacon, she gasped, and her eyes nearly popped out of her skull. "Oh my god, what if it's like the movie *Hostel*?" Her crescent sandwich almost fell apart in her fingers as she swung it at me.

"Calm down. I'll pay him back when we find him later. It was only twenty-five bucks, Liz."

"That's a lot of money here," she said. And it was. Even a poor university student like me was well off in this country. I was a hundredaire. Liz was the millionaire equivalent.

As we approached our destination, we saw three distinct buildings making up a hostel complex. The gray structures resembled repurposed asylums and consisted of five floors each. The whole area belonged in a post-apocalyptic sci-fi zombie story. The middle one housed the evil manager. As we climbed the staircase and passed under a sign that read "Check-In," we noticed the door ajar. There was a TV blaring in Mandarin that sounded like animated voice brawling between two furious men. We walked in and saw an older man and Bruce. Both stopped, scrutinized us, and then Bruce gestured for us to enter. The older man sat down in front of the TV and ignored us.

"This is my uncle who owns Homely Haven," said Bruce, "but I can help you with rooms."

Ignoring his comment, I said. "Why did you pay for our hotel?"

"You want help, and I welcome you to my country," he simpered, looking much too pleased with himself.

"Well, let me pay you back," I responded, undermining his kind gesture by reaching for my wallet.

Bruce wiped all expression from his face and said, "No."

Taken aback by his stern answer, and not really wanting to argue in his home, I responded, "Okay, then can I buy you dinner sometime?"

"Yes," he said, his mouth opening so wide it seemed he would swallow his own face. Bruce was aching for friends. "Oh, your luggage is here this afternoon. The airport call and say they be here today." I had failed to tell him that our lost bags were being delivered to this address.

"Sorry, I forgot to mention that the airport would bring the bags here. I was tired and—"

"No problem, my friend. Good thing we have room for you or else I get all your free stuff. Two dinners will be good payment," he cawed. His uncle let out a smoker's cackle, but I couldn't tell if it was because of the television or his nephew's ridiculous guffaw.

I thanked him for understanding, and I asked about a room and prices. Then Liz blurted out, "How much is your best room, and does it have TV and air conditioning?"

"It is twenty-five dollars a night," said Bruce. "TV and AC included."

"Then we will be happy to take that one," said Liz. "Anything is better than that hotel." I was glaring at her, biting my lower lip, but she just shrugged her shoulders at me. Bruce pretended not to hear her brash comment.

"I'll pay for it," she said. "I'm here for four days, and then you won't see me again, anyway." *We aren't together*, I reminded myself. I turned from Liz back to Bruce. "What's the bed situation in that room?" I did not want to share a bed with her.

"Oh, it is two twin beds, but we can arrange a large bed if you would like?"

"No, that's perfect," I said. Liz paid for four days, and I explained to Bruce that I would need a cheaper room after that. He said it wasn't a problem.

There wasn't a numbering system or anything to identify the buildings—except for the one we were in which had the "Homely Haven" sign dangling from hanger wires at the front. All three buildings were shoddily clumped together. Bruce handed us keys to the room and directed us to the building closest to the main road. All of them seemed timeworn and haunted, but our building appeared more so since we had to live there for several days. On our climb, we passed several floors that were bustling with people speaking various languages, but then we got to our room. Isolation was a luxury here, apparently, since we had rented the entire floor for twenty-five dollars a day. Our floor came with an iron security door thick enough to keep a plague of zombies at bay. No other floors in the building had this feature, and I assumed it was in place to protect weary, paranoid foreigners from the tattered riff-raff outside.

After making it through the iron barrier, we entered a fully furnished living room area filled with repurposed wicker furniture. Liz turned around, shut the door behind us with an alarming clatter, and double checked that it was secure. She was paranoid. On the opposite side of the security door, across the lounge area, was another door that led to the bedroom. It required another key for entry. Despite the crumbling paint and general dilapidation, the place was an impressive full suite with a private shower and kitchen. We entered the bedroom, shut the door, and collapsed on separate beds. I grabbed a couple complimentary maps and brochures and began to peruse them.

"Now what do we do?" said Liz.

"Let's rest for a bit, and I'll see where we can go today without getting lost," I said.

The room was not American large. It fit two twin beds with about two feet of leg room between them. Shoving the mattresses together would have been better use of the space, but that was out of the question. A large gray Magnavox TV sat on a small stand at the foot of the beds. Liz slid off hers like a buttery pancake and crawled on all fours to turn it on. The chopstick legs holding the ancient box wobbled and creaked from the force of Liz's finger.

She kneeled in front of it. "Wow, I haven't seen one of these in ages," she said with wonder in her wow, as if unearthing an ancient artifact. "I think upgrades are in order. It's the twenty-first century."

"I know, right? But not with them charging eight to twenty-five dollars per room a day," I said, feeling like a snob for agreeing with her, and hating myself for it. Immediately, I was back on the defense. "I'm pretty sure TVs are as expensive here as anywhere else, though. We shouldn't judge."

Liz began to rummage through her backpack, and I felt the jet lag creep on me. I threw maps and brochures aside and grabbed the remote for a quick perusal of the channels. The shows were all in Mandarin, but everything on every channel was Americanized. The infomercials could have been American despite that it was the wrong language. I recalled my old Chinese language professor who mentioned that everything on TV was regulated by the Communist overlords. She didn't say *overlords*, but that's what I heard between the lines. I clicked through bizarre parodies of *The Price is Right* (What Price Has the Tao Determined to Be Correct), *Wheel of Fortune* (Spin the Karmic Wheel of Righteousness), *Magnum P.I.* (Amazing Beijing Private Investigator), *MacGyver* (Unparalleled

Han Genius in the Qing Courts), and *Guiding Light* (Unhappy Chen in a Happy World).

The most legit thing on the tube was the half dozen channels dedicated to old kung fu movies. I stopped briefly on a station with two vicious masters thrashing their rubbery legs about like rabid Gumby dolls. A Bruce Lee film was perpetually running on one channel or other.

"Let's hit some museums," I said, finally tired of the martial arts operas.

Liz rolled her eyes and said, "Come on. I want to see the real city. It's not like I'm ever coming back here again."

She made a good point, plus she had leverage, and I didn't want to piss her off too much. After all, it was her room, and I had no desire to sleep in the street with the rats.

"Fine. Fuck the museums. Let's go explore."

Liz jumped onto my bed and squealed, "Thank you, thank you, thank you," wedging herself into me before I could say anything. Then she dropped her lips on mine. She kissed me hard, her mouth hot and penetrative. Our first lip-lock since the breakup six months earlier. I let it happen, of course…like everything else.

Four

The Almost Kidnapping

There was a clatter outside our bedroom suite. We were curled up facing one another, but Liz didn't stir. I rubbed fog from my eyes and glanced at the intricate web of cracks all over the walls and ceiling, as well as missing chunks of paint. They'd fallen off at some point but were never retouched. I hoped there was no asbestos, but surely there was enough of it hibernating in the walls that it would be resurrected as a horrible malignant growth in our geriatric years. This place was run down but not as much as the last hotel. Our faces were an inch apart, so close that our lips could easily get tangled again. The clatter was louder, causing a buzzing reverb in my eardrum. Liz was gazing at me, as wide-eyed as humanly possible, still dazed from sleep. She let out an agonizing sigh as she rolled onto her stomach. Strands of back muscles tightened as she extended her limbs, flexed her calves and butt cheeks, and expanded her chest. Her curled toes popped from the pressure and her stretch was so profound that her ass swallowed most of her panty. She picked it loose with a sweep of her hand. This is what it was like to wake next to her every morning, but sans underwear.

I didn't recall stripping down to my boxers, nor her peeling off any clothes. We must have done it reflexively, half asleep, the way couples who have been together long enough will wake in the early hours in mid grind, unable to stop the reckless sex that's possessed them. Her eyes were normally a dull blue when she first woke, and they would lighten up as she gained momentum for the day ahead. I feared she could tell this was all on my mind, or that she'd spot the nostalgia on my face. The banging and rattling of iron continued.

I yelled, "Okay, be right there." I slipped into my clothes and shoes and stepped out into the living area. Bruce was outside the door.

"Luggage is here," he screeched unnecessarily through the iron mesh. I opened the door and he stretched his lips open, revealing large, buttery, crooked teeth. Smiling seemed unnatural for his face, as if he'd been practicing mouth posturing for years yet hadn't quite mastered it.

Surprisingly, Liz stood fully clothed behind me, impressive considering she'd been practically naked a minute before. Usually, she was slow to dress. "That's great. Thank you so much," she said and then glimpsed the bags behind Bruce. "Oh, and you brought them up here, too. You're so nice."

She walked back into the room as I grabbed the bags. I set them inside the living area and then, as I turned around to thank him for his kindness, Liz appeared again and slipped twenty-five dollars into his hand. Before he could say anything, she shut him out by slamming the iron in his face.

"Now, we don't owe him anything," she said and put her hands on her hips like Wonder Woman.

Shocked, I couldn't speak until I heard his footsteps fade into the hall. "That was rude," I said, aggravated. "You should have invited him in. He helped us out yesterday. And you don't need to tip here. This is a hostel, not a hotel."

"It wasn't a tip. We owed him money."

"I had that handled."

Liz ignored me, dragged her bags to the nearest couch, and began sifting through the outfits in her luggage. She scrutinized everything as if someone else had packed it for her. I went to inspect the kitchen area and found a sink, stove, fridge, and a coating of dust and grease. No cookware. A four-inch long petrified noodle was glued to the countertop. Even the roaches had abandoned it. *Not cooking in here*, I told myself.

When I went back into the living area, Liz's clothes were in a pile next to her, including the ones she had been wearing. She was in underwear again, holding a summer dress out in front of her, staring at it longingly.

"Damn, how did you undress so fast? You been practicing?"

She threw me a sarcastic *guess you never appreciated my superpower* face and then went back to the dress.

"There's a room you can change in," I said, ashamed at myself for enjoying the show.

"Nothing you haven't seen before," she said with sass in her voice, and began to slip into the new outfit. During our time together, I took for granted how undeniably seductive she was, but not in an ostentatious way or anything. She was subtle, mostly, and could switch to predatory mode at the drop of a hat. It was sexy. The dress was a shady blue with white and yellow daisies scattered in no particular pattern around the fabric. It wrapped itself around her voluptuous hourglass figure as if it'd been tailor-made especially for her.

"Do you like it? It's brand new. I bought it before we left, and it's blue. Midnight blue," she emphasized the color and spread its fringe as far as possible. It was my favorite color.

"It's the color of life, of water, of renewal," I said to her in our apartment one day after downing five beers. I became all existential when buzzed.

"Now add a touch of midnight, and that's my soul."

"That's depressing," she said. "Don't be a moody Judy."

"I have spiritual anemia." I squinted as if there were pain in my gut and, if I smoked, I'd have sucked the life out of a stick for dramatic effect.

"You're such a sourpuss," said Liz as she pitied me with her big blue eyes and then hugged the philosophical buzz out of me.

When I asked her to tell me her favorite color, she responded, "I don't have a favorite."

Her words sounded exactly like something a kindergartener would say to her teacher. She couldn't decide on any one color. It bothered me that Liz was so naïve. Her privileged upbringing had not prepared her for the hostility she faced in adulthood. She had been exceptionally unprepared for the brutality of our breakup. Denial was her strength, and delusion is a girl's best friend when she's in love.

"Do you like it or not?" she repeated, stretching the midnight dress out to me.

The color and her words redirected my gaze away from her bare feet and long legs, and up to her face where her eyes radiated against the outfit. It bothered me that she seemed happier without me. When we were together, she loved me till her heart ached. What if I never found someone like that again? The fluorescent light added a dull gray hue to her natural auburn, and I briefly recalled how the sunlight tended to lighten her hair to reddish blonde. The hidden layered strands of orange, remnants of a distant Scottish ancestor, were more than obliging to change with the seasons. Her hair was like a mirage, much like everything else in her life. I turned away as soon as the feeling of ownership crept up my chest. We weren't together, yet here we were.

"Yes. You look pretty," I said in a low voice. I was troubled with how attractive she had become since our separation, but I tried to shake the feeling off by justifying it as pining for the breakup sex we never had. We had simply ended. Dramatically, mind you. But, poof! Not a word between us for six months after that.

I grabbed the maps and brochures again to change the topic and was overwhelmed by the numerous temples open to the public.

"How about we go to a temple?" I said, picking the closest one to the hostel and pointing it out on paper.

"Don't care where," she said, ignoring me, and continued sorting through her stuff.

"Museum?" I said to check if she was listening.

"No."

I grabbed the subway schedule. The downtown railways were obviously modeled after the London Underground, but better. Getting around would be easy.

"Have you seen my sandals?" Liz said as she rummaged around the living area.

"Nope."

She walked into the bedroom and I followed her. Reflex, again. I could have stood where I was and said, "Let's go," but instead I watched her kneel to strap her sandals. When she stood, I swear she was about to attack my lips. But she just plopped down on the bed, crossed her legs, and planted her arms like tent poles behind her. She batted her eyes at me and tilted her head.

"Are we going to get lost?" she said, doubtful that I could get us to the temple.

"I can read a map, but what's wrong with getting lost?"

She straightened up and laced her hands onto her lap as if to challenge me. Sunlight briefly shined through a small window in the room and hit her skin. Her plain hands and untanned, un-pedicured feet, which were partially covered by the leather straps of her sandals, made her resemble a statue, a sculptor's finished product. She must have noticed my expectant stare because she raised her eyebrows in curiosity. I broke eye contact and bent down to point out the directions on the map. She smelled of flowers, and I was close enough that I could feel her toes graze my leg. Without warning, she dug them into me as if to say *I still want you, too.* The pressure sent a shiver up my leg. I cleared my throat to mute the sensation.

"How about the Tanzhe Temple? We can be there in under an hour. We won't get lost." She turned her head and pecked me on the lips, big cheese across her face. I straightened up and froze. *We aren't together*, I reminded myself. *Expect nothing.*

"The tan-what?"

"Tan-juh," I said pronouncing it slowly for her.

"Um, okay. What does it mean?" she said, moving on from the kiss as if it were nothing.

"The Temple of Pools and Trees," I read from the brochure. I tried to play off the smooch too, but she was doing better than me. "It says it has ancient trees and the Dragon Lake."

Looking pleased with my answer, Liz stood to gather her things. She brushed past me, her hair slapping me in the face.

After we secured all the doors, we headed downstairs, and as we passed the third floor she said, "I need to use the restroom before we go."

"Seriously?" I said, annoyed at her bad timing. "Why didn't you use it upstairs?"

But she ignored me and peeked into the dorm where a guy read on a tattered brown couch. Its long tufts of synthetic fabric coiled out of the pleather near another guy who was making fists at a computer—its worn-out speaker screeching bloody murder as it dialed into the internet. There was another person in the shabby kitchen area cooking something. No security doors anywhere. Only the rooms had doors, but even those were so paper-thin the owners may as well have hung curtains. You couldn't grunt in those rooms without everyone suspecting something godawful and lewd was transpiring behind your walls. We had entered the poor-ass folk floor, where I'd be living in a few days.

"I'll go here," Liz said and walked in like she owned it all.

She vanished beyond the kitchen, and I stepped into the living area so as not to feel like a creeper in the hallway. This floor alone likely represented half a dozen non-English speaking countries. Several women glanced in my direction to see what I would do. There was nowhere to sit, so I stood by the threshold and waited for Liz. A door opened and two more women stepped out of a room. I nodded and moved aside to let them through.

"Don't mind me," I said.

"You speak English," said one cute girl in a Midwestern accent, her eyes wide as she halted in front of me. "Are you rooming on this floor, too?"

"No. I'm on the fifth floor. My girlfriend is borrowing your restroom." *Damn it. Girlfriend?*

"I'm Heather." Then she motioned to the Asian girl. "This is Kana."

I shook both their hands and introduced myself.

"Have you explored the city?" said Heather.

"No, but we're about to head to the Tanzhe Temple," I said.

"No way. We're going there, too. Want to go together?"

Kana nodded and parted her lips to unleash a painful smile through rows of white semi-crooked teeth, but I suspected she wasn't happy to have me invited. Her English was probably limited since she hadn't uttered a word.

"I'm fine with that but let me double check."

"Of course," said Heather. "We'll wait."

I peered in the direction of the kitchen to see if Liz was on her way back. No sign of her. We all fidgeted from awkwardness, as strangers do when they regret saying something.

Heather spoke in a low voice to Kana, who pretended to acknowledge her. Kana responded inaudibly, maybe something to the effect of, *Please, repeat. Don't understand.* Then Heather whispered back.

Heather was the picture of a small-town girl—a perky brunette with long, straight hair matched to brilliant green eyes, small nose, fair teeth, dirty nails and freckles, dressed plainly in a white cotton blouse, jeans, running shoes, and a sunhat. Farmer's daughter, perhaps.

Post-whispering, Kana stood befuddled in a green t-shirt, white shorts, and brown hiking shoes, her boyish hair snipped short, making her Asian features more pronounced. Her face was serious, concealing all emotion.

I'm not very sociable, but I can bide time with the best of them.

"Where are you from?" I said, faking interest.

"I'm from Kansas," said Heather. "I'm here for one year to get teaching experience. I want to teach middle school."

"Why travel across the world to do that?"

"I needed change. A re-do. My fiancé dumped me."

She was the kind of girl who would confide her deepest secrets on the first date...no drinks needed. Heather was liable to say something like, *One time I put Nair in Sandy Buckner's shampoo after swim practice. I felt so bad. We could hear her weeping all the way down the hall. She killed herself after that. I felt responsible for so long.*

I wasn't so forthcoming. There was a toll of ten beers and three Cuervo shots for my secrets.

"I'm sorry," I said.

"Yeah, he was my sweetheart in high school. We were our first everything."

Too much information for me. I wanted out.

Luckily, Kana interrupted and began to over articulate her first words, "From—Ja—pan—and—I—am—here—to—learn—inter—nal—med—i—cine—re—flex—ol—o—gy—and—ma—ssage," and then she bowed slightly, lowering her eyes, and silently disappeared into the background of the conversation again. She didn't have any secrets, and I didn't want to hear them if she did.

"Where are you from?" said Heather. "I hear a small twang in your talk."

"Texas," I said proudly. "I'm here to conduct research on the culture."

"Oh, for school?"

"Yes. For my thesis."

Kana interrupted, "You are teacher?"

"Not quite. I'm studying for my graduate degree in anthropology."

Kana didn't follow what I said.

"Impressive," added Heather. "You look so young. And your girlfriend?"

"She's on vacation," I said. "But she's not—"

"Hello," said Liz, before I could finish my disclosure. She immediately sized up the new competition and politely extended her hand to Heather and Kana who reciprocated, though Kana seemed put off by the contact. After introductions and learning we were all headed to the same temple, she reluctantly said, "Great, let's go together."

We made our way to the subway station and, outside the entrance, we bought umbrellas for the inevitable spurts of rain that were forecast. It was eighty degrees and an aggressive humidity pervaded the air. While waiting for the train, Liz and I bought some packaged sushi to eat. The stall was run by a self-appointed sushi chef, who was more of a sushi dabbler, since he was not very good at his job. This bland and relatively cheap meal would become the staple of my diet for the rest of my stay, resulting in a fifteen-pound weight loss by the end of the month. The junk food for sale in the stores was too healthy by American standards, consisting of seaweed snacks and mung bean pastries, an array of flavored water and seaweed sodas, and countless brands of green tea drinks offered in cans, boxes, glasses, cups, pouches, and bottles, all with the customer's choice of hot or room temperature. There was no ice to be found, anywhere. And the seaweed. There was so much of it you'd think that's all they grew in this country.

The train ride was painless, and we made small talk all the way to the temple stop. There were signs leading to the holy site, and I triple checked on the map so we wouldn't get lost. The girls began to talk about girl things and casually followed behind me. As we approached the temple gates, there was a fat monk with a conical hat dressed in sweat-stained gray tattered robes standing some distance from the front gates. He saw us approaching and made a gesture for us to come on over. I accepted the invitation and when I got close enough, he removed the bamboo sunhat to reveal a shaved head and shockingly large balloonish protrusions at chest level, as well as a rounded body that had obviously borne children at some point. He was a she, and her androgyny was above par. The nun held up some Buddhist beads and then smiled, revealing jagged rows of onyx teardrops where pearly teeth should have been. Apparently, dentistry was considered a vanity in her sect. It was doubtful she was affiliated with any kind of holy order, of course, but I appreciated her effort, so I bought the beads since I intended to buy some anyway once inside the temple. They were handcrafted with Chinese signs and symbols representing the various mantras of Buddhist meditation.

The nun greedily shuffled off with my money in another direction while the girls stood at a distance. Liz was scowling.

"What's wrong?" I said as I approached them.

"Why did you do that?" she said, her nose turned up, hands clutched to her purse. Heather and Kana, sensing a lover's spat, began scrutinizing the construction in the area. A fancy KFC was going up across the street.

I rolled my eyes and moved past them through the gates and into the courtyard.

It was pristine. There were countless animals of all sizes jumping out of clumps of polished stone scattered about the temple grounds. Medusa herself couldn't have done a better job of catching those beasts off-guard. The figures told of an invisible foe as half a battle played out before us. Statues of dragons lunged out of the corners, their bony claws close enough to poke the arms of passersby. The temple walls were covered in bright red scales which often punctured or tore visitors' clothes, like a primordial animal skin fitted for war. Even the roof of the main temple was covered in winged serpents immortalized in flight and combat.

At the temple doors, two large foo dogs imposed their girth on visitors, their vacuous expressions the most frightening things of all. They were the appointed guardians of the original waters. There was also a bubbling pond nearby protesting the gusts of wind preluding the first day's rain. Countless storms had clearly raged against the impenetrable skin of the two sentinels. I reached up to the time-polished ivory to feel the slick surface of the massive eyes. Eyes so invasive and telepathic, aggressive and utterly profound, which bulged from sockets I could bury an arm in.

Liz touched my hand to see if I was okay, snapping me out of my trance. I followed her inside the temple but lagged and kept my sights on the dogs.

We stood mesmerized at the threshold of this other world. Then the other girls caught up and swept Liz away. Assuming I would follow, they walked on without me into the bustle of visitors. There was a pervasive hum enveloping us, making the space appear more crowded and solemn than it was. Everyone inside was praying in one form or another. Some swayed or rocked as they muttered to themselves, some kowtowed to statues. Shaved monks dressed in saffron robes asked bystanders for alms in hopes that they wouldn't have to venture out into the gloomy weather. There was a woman with her deformed child hunched at the feet of a golden Buddha. This was not a place of rest. All around us, prayer was in perpetual motion. Here, enlightenment made a person ache.

I walked around, taking pictures along the way, until I circled back to the entry. I exited to the courtyard where the dogs stood sentinel, and I saw Heather speaking with a man. Kana and Liz were not around, so I approached them.

Heather waved me over and said, "Liam, this is David."

The man leered at me. His eyes were hollow, abysmal orbs anchored by folds of saggy blood bags. Something kept him up at night. He extended a shaky hand, and I squeezed firmly, but his went limp. He was at least six feet tall, a comparable size to my five-foot-six, yet he was thin and brittle.

"Nice to meet you, young man," said David. His straight, and alarmingly oiled, graying hair forced a whiff of unwashed pillow head into my nostrils. Any day now, he would reach full dreadlock status. I coughed lightly to get his scent out of my sinuses as he spoke. "I was conversing with your friend Heather here about possibly being your tour guide. I'd love to show you around."

He had an accent, but I couldn't place it at first. Though the shape of his eyes and bridged nose told me he was half white and half Asian.

"Are you vacationing here, David?" I said, making eye contact as much as possible, but he wouldn't reciprocate.

"No, I live here," he said, staring off into nothing. "I'm retired."

Heather spotted Liz and Kana nearby and signaled to them.

"What did you do for work before retirement?" I said.

"I was a scientist for the German government," he responded. "Top secret work."

Bullshit.

Kana and Liz approached us and asked what was going on. David turned to them, and his face lit up when he saw Liz. He introduced himself but Liz froze, standing stone still as if realizing that David was the only male Gorgon in existence.

She then turned to me and said, "Can I talk to you over here?" Out of the group's earshot, she continued, "Who the hell is the creepy guy?"

For once, I was happy with her judgment.

"Heather was talking to him when I found her," I said.

"Let's get rid of him. He looks like a fucking pedophile."

"Yes. Let's," I agreed. "Tell the girls you want to use the restroom and make them follow. Then I'll lose him."

Liz approved my plan, and we went back to the group.

"I need to use the ladies' room," said Liz, widening her eyes while signaling to Kana and Heather.

Kana, bewildered, didn't pick up on the cue and simply pointed at a corner of the temple and said, "The restroom is in there." She seemed pleased that she could help.

Heather understood and offered to go with Liz. They trotted off, leaving me with David and Kana.

He was hypnotized by the girls walking off, his eyes so bulgy it seemed that they'd pop out of his skull.

"They shouldn't go by themselves," he said.

"Why not?" I said.

He did not respond and instead began to breathe erratically and froth from fear. David was crazy.

Kana, after finally realizing how precarious the situation had become, stepped behind me and grabbed my shoulder and arm to shield herself. David began to wring his hands frantically and sway in place. She pressed closer into me, and we began to back away. Without telegraphing, he broke into a sprint toward the restrooms.

"Oh, shit," I said. "Wait here."

I tore away from Kana and followed him. A sharp pain shot up my foot as I twisted it on a dip in the path, but I ignored it. When I caught up, Heather and Liz were clutching each other and saying something to David, who began grabbing at Liz's and Heather's wrists. As they swatted at his hands, I used my momentum to shove him away. His lanky body crunched against the gravel path that led to the bathroom doors.

"Run," I shouted at Heather and Liz, adrenaline coursing through me. Their eyes were wide in disbelief, and their jaws clenched tightly. They were in shock, so I took them both by the hand and dragged them back to Kana, who obediently stood in place, confused and rigid as a pole. We exited through the gates, clutching each other's hands like spooked school children, and hailed a taxi for Homely Haven.

Our labored, unsynchronized breathing was the only thing that filled the cab. When we arrived, we didn't say a word. We entered our building, and Heather and Kana headed straight for their rooms on the third floor. Liz and I went up to ours on the fifth.

She dropped onto the couch, put her hands to her face, and let some nervous sobs out as she spoke.

"I can't believe what just happened," she said, shaking her head. "Do you think he wanted to kidnap us?"

"Who knows."

I kicked off my shoes and socks to see why my foot was aching. There was bruising down the side of my ankle. Possibly a slight sprain. Then I tried to sit down and wrap my arm around her, but she brushed me off, hit me on my thigh, and said, "Jerk! Why did you run? You should have given that guy a beating."

I wrapped my arms around her anyway.

"Did he do anything to you?" I said.

"He squeezed my hand and said, *You're in danger*, over and over."

I squeezed her hand as well. "I'm sorry. No more temples. I promise."

The bruising had reached the top of my foot.

"Does it hurt?"

"A little, but it's not serious."

"Thank you for saving me. Us, I mean."

"Of course," I said.

Liz exhaled a broken sigh, her lips swollen and lacquered from crying. She gazed into me before resting her lips on mine, and we kissed for some time, like we used to when we had been together. It was familiar and comforting, yet displaced, but we were safe, and I tightened our embrace to reassure her. She abruptly broke away, our lips making a loud popping sound as she stood.

"I need a shower," she said as she entered the adjacent bathroom and left the door ajar. She wasn't putting on a show, or teasing, or tempting me. She was simply tired from the chaos and had forgotten that she had not been naked in front of me for months. Standing in the nude with her clothes scattered about, she raised her arms to tie up her hair in front of the blotchy mirror hanging over the sink. Every curve harmonized with her newly tanned, freckled skin which unraveled along perfectly measured limbs. I missed her.

Then she stepped out of sight, but I knew what was next. She would reach for the faucet handle and run the water, extend her left leg into the stream and point her toes, then wiggle them to gauge the temperature, like she usually did. A sigh flooded the room. The sounds echoed and ascended along grimy tiled walls. Liz was content with the hot water in Homely Haven. The curtain liner was drawn closed and the scraping of the rings made the hair on my neck stand. We had a history of showers together. The echoes shifted from a high splash to a low hum as her supple body intercepted the water's flow. I anticipated her singing, something she loved doing while bathing.

I entered the bathroom. The liner was so thin I could see the blurred outline of her body in motion behind the vinyl, as if I were staring at an artist's canvas painting itself. She washed her arms, chest, and flat stomach. Then she lifted her leg and placed one foot on the wall in front of her, and I was awestruck by how gracefully her silhouette danced behind the white liner. She scrubbed around her thighs, between her legs, down to her calves, and hummed a light melody that was difficult to distinguish because of the reverberation in the room. A familiar tune began to shape in my mind as she continued to hum. Her voice was low and paced, and she drew out every note. I couldn't quite place the song, yet I hummed along anyway. As she reached down to scrub some more, I opened the liner. Unmoved by my nakedness, she continued scrubbing her shins and knees with her pink loofah. Her toes splayed as she washed between them, causing her calf muscle to define itself. The water pricked at my arms, and Liz stood straight again and scattered the lather on her breasts. Her voice clung to the rising vapor as she shifted from words to humming and back to words. The song was ours, from our time together, but the name evaded me faster than her voice bouncing off the walls and vanishing into the air.

    Liz didn't protest when I hopped in with her. She faced me and stepped in as close as she could. Her toes covered mine, and she pressed down to keep me in place. The feel of her stomach against my own made me shiver in anticipation. Her chest rested on mine. I wrapped my arms around her hips, and we kissed. It was like our first time all over again.

Five

Love is a Cheerleader Running

After our very first movie, after my birthday underwear cookout, after deciding to make it work, I walked out to the university parking lot to find Liz leaning against my car. Her classes finished before mine, and she should have been long gone.

"Flat tire," she said, "and the spare is no good. I'm waiting for a tow truck."

"You want a ride home?" I didn't want to leave her alone in the parking lot.

"My dad's coming to get me in a bit. Want to hang out with me?"

"Okay," I said, "but do I have to meet your dad?"

She squinted and shook her head as if I'd said something stupid, "Of course you do. He wants to know who his princess is with all the time."

"Jesus," I said nervously.

"Oh my god, relax. He's going to call me when he's near, and then you can abandon me in this empty lot before he arrives." She frowned and wiped a fake tear from her face as she spoke. It was dusk, and her blue eyes filled with the impending shade of night. "I'm parked right there," she said, pointing to the row of vehicles in front of us.

We waited in her car, and I shared some leftover jerky from lunch. We munched for a while until she said, "How do you know it's love?"

"What?"

"Like, when two people are in love. How do you know?"

Liz had no clue. She'd never had a boyfriend until me. I didn't know how to answer without sounding idiotic. I'd been in love before, but if there's one thing love is good at, it's making whoever's involved seem daft.

"Love is the slowest death," I said, trying to sound poetic as I chewed meat. "Why do you want to know anyway?"

She ignored my question just as I'd ignored hers. "I don't want love to be that."

"But it usually is," I said.

"Tell me what happened to you, from the beginning."

"I don't want to talk about it." I paused then chewed more.

"Please. At least tell me how you moved on in the end," she said. "At least tell me that."

"I wrote it all out. Exorcised it from my head."

"But how can you forget if you wrote it down?"

I furrowed my brow. "Something like that is unforgettable." I kept chewing. "But having it on paper gives me distance. I stashed that experience away in my journals."

She batted her eyelashes at me in anticipation.

"Please, tell me the story."

~ * ~

Love is a cheerleader running, and I am following her through a field. It's a downpour, and I'm locked hands with a blonde, green-eyed girl from school. She's eighteen like me, slender and acrobatic. A gnarled tree with thin branches and malnourished leaves grows alone in this field. The grass is dead and flat from countless people using the land as a walkway, so it's easy to make a dash for it. Shelly and I climb the tree for shelter. It stops raining, but we don't move.

We sit atop the branches, holding on to what we can, and anticipate the storm as it rolls in. We're naïve and foolish, perched like two sparrows. The limbs bow from our weight, and our eyes bulge in hopes that nothing breaks, but we're surprised at how sturdy the tree is despite its frail appearance. The sky's rumbling shakes the slim trunk, and reverberations shoot up through the branches and into our bodies. The tree is helpless; at the mercy of the earth. The smaller, juvenile limbs feel hollow, and the leaves are like feathers fluttering in unison. It's a miracle how they all work to hold us together.

More rumbling.

"The sky is growling at us." Shelly snickers as the branches vibrate and tickle her hand. She stops inspecting the gray sky and says, "What are you thinking?"

"That there's a giant dog in the sky about to bark down at us," I say without hesitation.

She goes wide-eyed and snorts at my silly response and then covers her mouth with one hand to hide her embarrassment. The green in her eyes is highlighted by random specks of yellow. I want to ask her about it, but then the static in the air thickens, and she gets serious.

"It's going to be bad, isn't it?"

"I hope it is," I say.

Shelly closes her eyes, inhales profoundly, and says, "I love the smell of rain."

I don't love the smell of rain. Humidity attacks my lungs.

"I love the sound of rain," I say back. "It's like the ocean is collapsing on us."

She closes her eyes, lost in herself. Her nostrils begin to flare as she meditates. For a couple minutes, there is a lull between us, until she says, "I love that image. Do you think we're safe?"

My eyes shoot to the horizon toward the charcoaled clouds. "I haven't seen any lightning, yet," I answer. "It's just thunder." My words are comforting, and she doesn't object to our staying. "If we see any lightning, then we find shelter somewhere else," I reassure her, trying not to reveal my uncertainty.

I want to stay in the tree with her forever. Alone. Close. Together. Her eyes open, and she places a hand on top of mine. Adrenaline shoots through me, sending shivers up my spine, through my arms and down to my hands and fingers where our skin connects.

It drizzles. Then a violent downpour. The water begins to pound the earth, making the field resonate with a roar of white noise, as if the Earth has spitefully raised her volume. We look at each other, our teeth bared in expression of our adolescent insecurity. Shelly bites her lower lip periodically out of nervousness. We blink at sporadic intervals to fight the drops blinding us. After a few minutes, the shower thins out, and it becomes a popping trickle against the leaves. The raindrops lightly graze our faces. I wonder if she knows my nervous tics as well as I do hers. Reflexively, I shift on the branch, since it's making my gluteus cramp.

"Don't be scared," she says, misreading my movement as fear. "I'll protect you," and she jokingly flexes her bicep. A thunderclap stops us from laughing.

We are soaked but don't care if it goes on forever. The raindrops begin to feel prickly as we lose our body heat. It's a strange gale, with its whimsical stopping and starting. Shelly's lip begins to tremble, so I scoot closer to her and wrap my arm around her shoulder. We are hip to hip. Gradually, the infant drops that arouse our arms begin to splash repeatedly until our skin is bombarded by heavy pinches. Another downpour. The water continues to descend along the maze of leaves, and lands in our hair and faces. Her blonde hair is murky and flat. A gust of wind alters the trajectory of the rain and she squints at how much it stings. We endure it together. Some water ricochets off the bark and strikes my eye. I rub it in a hurry, hoping I'm not wiping away the most beautiful dream.

Her face is serious as I'm consumed by her green orbs.

"You're gorgeous," she says to me.

Shelly reads my mind, and we instantly, hopelessly, fall into a kiss, our embrace anchoring us like gravity. We are thrust into our first love. It sinks us with the force of a tidal wave. The torrent charges everything with its energy, and we remain locked. Balancing one another on the branches, we hold on tighter. The heavens resonate, reminding us that what is happening is powerful.

~ * ~

Liz studied the sorrow on my face. "How long did you love her?"

"Never stopped," I responded, but instantly regretted saying that.

"That's a long time," she said. "Was she your first?"

"First kiss? No." I said. "First love, yes."

"I know that," she said. "I meant your first sex."

I paused and, in a flash, I recalled the day with Shelly. It happened in the woods, like in the movies.

"Yeah, she was my first."

"Is it weird for me to ask how it happened? How you got to that point?"

"The point of sex?"

"Yes."

"I don't know. Why do you ask?"

"Because I've never had that, and I don't understand how you get there with a person, to share yourself like that."

There was no denying it: sex was forever, more forever than love. What bothered me most was knowing that Shelly belonged to someone else now.

"It's her touch I miss after all this time."

"That's it? Don't you miss loving her?"

"Liz, love is chaos. I don't miss that."

"That's sad," she said. "It can't have been all that bad."

"It was bad."

"I can't believe that," she said and stopped.

"Believe what?" I said.

"That a memory of a touch is the only thing that remains."
I couldn't argue the truth, however.

~ * ~

Shelly calls me one afternoon to see if we can meet at our normal make out spot, a wooded area between her house and mine.

"Can you get out for a few hours?" she says urgently.

"Yeah, but what's going on?"

"I have something for you, but don't tell anyone we're meeting."

I sprint there, and she is already waiting for me when I arrive. She's nervous in her white sun dress with orange diamonds divided into diagonal rows. It extends down to the top of her knee caps and I can see her legs glistening from perspiration. Her running shoes are frayed from years of cheering, her feet in socks so low she may as well be barefoot. It's humid, and I'm drenched by the time I arrive. Shelly's fine, blonde hair is up in a ponytail and, underneath, I glance the beginnings of dark roots. In ten years, she'll be a stunning brunette. I get close and plant my lips on hers, our usual hello, and the smacking sound bounces off the trees. We glance around at the woods that seem to be telling us off for sneaking around. The brightness of the day charges the yellow speckles in her eyes, shifting the predominant green to a much lighter jade. I keep forgetting to ask her about them…the forgettable speckles.

She says, "Your eyes are reddish in the sun. They're not brown," as if seeing my eye color for the first time.

"Is that bad?"

"No," she says, "but I haven't seen them in this light before." She continues musing over them. "Wow, there's some green splattered around in there, like the Aurora Borealis." And then out of nowhere, "You are going to make pretty babies one day."

Before I can say *let's make one*, something cracks in the woods, and we both turn toward it. Nature's sounds are mysterious, without a source. She tries to catch my eyes again, but I don't make contact because I'm slightly embarrassed that she can see so far into me. We're about the same height so she cups my ears and reins me in, kissing me harder than anyone has before. My lips begin to tingle from the pressure, and a sharp pinch makes me turn away and say, "Ouch."

Shelly glares at me as I cup my lower lip. "Are you hurt?"

"You bit me," I say, but I'm not complaining. I want more.

Her face changes to serious concern, "Oh, my god. I made you bleed."

There is rosy spotting on my hand. Shelly moves in and her mouth cushions my injury. She begins to suck gently at the puncture. It's an apology. The sensation makes my jaw tingle, and my lip feels ballooned, but she kisses me softly and rhythmically, moving from kiss to lower lip and back to kiss. My eyes are closed, and a swirl of colors manifest. Not colors that exist, but some otherworldly colors that my mind uses to paint her kiss for me. Her flowery scent fills my lungs.

She stops and says, "Your blood tastes good."

"I've never had anyone taste me before," I say as I dab at my mouth with the top of my hand to check for blood again. It's clean.

She unveils more teeth than I have ever seen, and then exhales with, "I love you, Liam."

Her eyes dart back and forth to gauge my reaction. She sees something wonderful, and sudden tears make her heavenly countenance appear disastrous. I kiss her back but only taste her saltiness. A light breeze makes its presence known, grazing us both on the cheeks, and I feel cool patches blooming on my jaw as my skin dries. I can't tell if I'm crying as well, but it feels like we are the last living creatures on earth. There is harmony, as if the world is conspiring to keep us together, to preserve what we have at this moment.

Unexpectedly, she rips away from me and sprints off deeper into the woods. I follow her, dodging trees, and nearly gouging myself on several branches. The cheerleader training makes her agile, but I try to keep up. Shelly disappears at a drop-off. I catch up and stop at the edge. I see a creek below about twenty feet down. I'm atop a retaining wall of dirt, and she is by the water waiting for me. I can see thick gnarled roots poking out of the crumbling layers of earth a few feet below me, like snakes frozen in time. I begin to use them to climb down to the water's edge.

Shelly sits cross legged and faces the creek, throwing pebbles into it. I stop to listen to the current make its away around the fallen branches and large stones protruding from the water. I'm standing some distance behind her and can see her shoulders through the thin dress fabric. She leans back on her arms and extends her legs, then turns her head to see where I am.

"Come here," she says. "You're missing it. It's so peaceful here."

We're sitting shoulder to shoulder, and we inhale at the same time. Water, dirt, and wood fill our lungs. She's taken her shoes and socks off, and the little sunlight breaking through the canopy of trees overhead hits her feet and makes them look jaundiced.

"My toes are freezing," she says and begins to wiggle them.

"But it's broiling hot." She ignores my words.

"I want to marry you," she says to the water.

I don't respond, but she knows I'd marry her without question.

"What do you think will happen to us?"

"After we die?"

She chuckled, "No, dork. You and me. Do you think we'll make it? Is this forever?"

The current is flowing away from us. I skip a rock, and it pops six times before it's sucked under by the creek.

"Let's get hitched after you graduate," I say. "Doesn't get more forever than that."

"Yes," Shelly says without hesitation. Her hoarse cheerleader voice has a calming effect on me.

I'm beaming from her reaction, and she's smiling back, glowing a bright pink from joy, because it's the first time I've set a relative date. Her color settles and freckles begin to emerge around her green eyes. It's like watching stars pop into the sky at dusk.

"I want a boy one day," she says, "and I want him to have my blonde hair and eyes, but with your curls."

"Curly hair is a curse," I say. "Let's give him your straight hair. Everything else is perfect."

We joke together and then listen to the water hum. It's the music to our love story. Shelly grabs my hand, urging me onto her, and we sink into the earth. I fear that my weight is too much, so I start to slide off, but her arms stiffen around mine to keep me in place. Our noses touch and her eyes soften when they meet mine. They dart around my face, exploring, reaching for something unknown. I say, "I'm in love with you," and her face tells me she's found everything she's ever wanted.

Her body is tense, her face serene, and her legs are parallel to mine – making it difficult for me to balance on top of her. Both my arms are extended in a push-up position above her shoulders. My arms begin to shake from fatigue. We've never been like this. She doesn't say anything yet understands me so completely I feel I'm being turned inside out. Wisps of her breath enter me, and I can't stand to exhale. I want all of her, me, this, to stay exactly where it all is. I inspect her face as she studies mine. Her hands move up to frame my jawline so that my head doesn't move far from hers. I start to slide off again, but her body softens. Her legs are shaking, and the sundress has rolled up by her bellybutton. Sweat glistens on her stomach and is running down her hips. A thin layer of white cotton panty catches it. My face must have shown surprise because she giggles at me. Her dazzling green eyes resist the sparse sunlight stretching itself out across them. We are in the grips of something powerful. I feel her stomach muscles relax, and her legs begin to open for me. My weight shifts from my arms to where our hips meet, and we are balanced, pressed into one another. We have never wanted more than what's happening.

"Make love to me," she says.

~ * ~

Liz pondered my story for a bit, and then said, "Your face changes when you talk about her. You're so happy when you say her name."

"It was a long time ago," I said, embarrassed of my transparency. "Doesn't it bother you to hear me talk about her?"

"No. She's part of your past and who you are now. I can't hate that any more than I can hate you. Have you ever tried contacting her?"

"Yeah. A couple years after everything went down, we emailed and talked, but it ended badly again."

"What happened?"

"We flirted on the phone, but I think the distance and time made it easier to ignore what had happened between us. I went to Florida to visit a mutual friend of ours from high school. He had a house party in full swing when I arrived, and Shelly was there waiting for me. I knew she lived nearby but wasn't expecting her there. I would've done the same thing if it meant I could see her again though. It all came back, everything that happened, and she started to cry in the middle of the party. She ran outside so I followed her. As soon as I caught up with her, she turned around, and I swear a thousand years had passed. We were both wanting what we had before our wrecked relationship, but it wasn't the same. We were adults tasting the bitterness between us. Our absence, our ending, was all there bound up in our lips. We kissed until it was too much. She couldn't stop sobbing, and I couldn't breathe. She ran off without a word, and I haven't heard from her since."

"Why did it end?" said Liz. "In high school, I mean."

I wanted to say we were too young, that we were ill prepared for the changes at the height of adolescence. That we had fallen in love ten years too soon. After Shelly, I understood how love could overwhelm a person to death. I knew why people killed themselves over it.

Yet, what I told Liz was less profound. "It was puppy love and was going to end no matter what."

Liz wasn't satisfied with that answer.

"Not true. Tell me why it ended," she insisted.

"Love turns good people into liars."

"It doesn't have to be like that," said Liz. "Can't you make it whatever you want?"

"No," I said, beginning to get irritated by her questions. "You lose everything. We didn't know how to stop and were worse off in the end."

I paused, hoping this was enough for her.

"Tell me," she said. "I'll never ask about it again. Promise."

~ * ~

I'm already drunk, and my friend Jonathan hands me the bottle of rum. Shelly doesn't let me drink with him because we pick fights and do the dumbest things, like throwing rocks at people on Ferris wheels, or chugging six beers in two minutes and rolling down hills. Shelly was fairly pissed at me for a week after pegging one of her cheery friends on the head. She didn't die or anything. They were small rocks. But J's my best friend, so I lie, and say we won't drink while he's at my house for the weekend. She knows we don't drink there since my parents are celibate hermits who frown upon abusive drinking and drugs. My response pleases her. She's going away with her family for a couple days, and after planting her dry lips on my cheekbone, she says she will miss me. We lie to each other now, when it's convenient, when the truth isn't real enough for us. It's a teenager thing. I take another swig of the Bacardi. We aren't really staying at my place. We're at Jonathan's and, luckily, his dad works out of town, so it's us and his older sister in the house. She's in her room humping twenty-four-seven with her boyfriend, so we never see her.

We hear about a party at a schoolmate's house, so we steal J's sister's car and swerve all the way there. We don't enter right away and instead sit on the curb near the house to shoot shit for a bit. The guitars vibrate the car windows and loose bumpers out on the street. The cars parked around us are jalopies owned by friends and acquaintances, or a rogue teacher or two. NOFX is playing. My eardrums tickle from the bass.

"I love this song," I say, without knowing exactly which song is playing, and try to mumble through part of the last few lines. Then it's over, and I stop paying attention.

"Hold my keys," says Jonathan. "I don't have pockets."

I grab them and stick them in my jeans. Another swig and pass. "Shelly has a secret admirer," I say.

"Who is it?" says Jonathan. He drinks and coughs from the burn.

"Some footballer from another guy," I say.

"Another guy?" laughs Jonathan.

I correct myself, "Another school. Fucking alcohol. I saw an email Shelly sent him. She said *I love you* to the prick, and he said it back."

"That's why you're getting smashed?" says J.

"I guess so," I say.

"She probably didn't mean it in the same way, man. That girl loves you."

"But she's not supposed to say it to anyone else," I holler. "Those are my words."

"Nobody owns those words, man."

Jonathan's felt his heart wrenched many times. The door of the house bursts open and a throng of people empty out into the front lawn and driveway. We stand up and run into some people we know, and decide to make our way in, but then one of the guys tells us the party is breaking up, and we may as well take off. We decide to avoid the dregs of the waning party and get in his sis's car parked a house down and across the street. Jonathan asks me for his keys, and I realize I don't have them. They've fallen out of my pocket.

"I'll find them," I reassure him. "I had them when we were sitting on the curb."

"You better, dude, or we're drunk walking five miles home."

I go back up to the party house and a lot of people are out in the street, on the curb, on the hood of a couple dozen cars. No one gives a damn about cops, and the block is buzzing like it's 7:45am on a school morning, fifteen minutes before first bell. The music has been turned down, and I can hear everyone chatting. *We missed a good one*, I think to myself. I kneel between an SUV and minivan. The keys are there, inches from a sewer grate. *Close call.* As I reach for them, I hear Shelly's voice.

"I can't believe you came," she says.

Then, some guy's voice. "I'm not leaving you yet."

I stand up and Shelly and some guy are holding hands on the lawn at the side of the party house. *Away for the weekend, huh? Bitch.* I can see them through the SUV window, but they have no clue I'm there spying on them like a creeper...the long line of cars so closely parked they're like a great metal wall separating the street from the house. He's taller so she stands on her tiptoes, as if she's trying to be kissed. She doesn't resist at all and lets him trap her. He leans in, and her lips are his.

"Let's go somewhere," says the guy.

"Okay," says Shelly, submitting to his lame advances.

The keys are in my hand, and I numbly walk off toward where Jonathan's parked. I can't stand to watch them face-fuck anymore. A wave of nausea hits me, and I puke before I get in the car.

~ * ~

Liz sensed I wasn't happy telling this part of the story.

"She made out with another guy at the party," I said, tensing my jaw muscles. "Probably screwed him, too."

"There's a chance she didn't," said Liz.

"Anyway, maybe she was drunk and had an excuse, but I never told her what I saw. I couldn't bring myself to hear what she had to say."

"What happened next?" said Liz.

"I started treating her badly at school and kept waiting for her to tell me what she had done. A week passed, then another week, and nothing. She never confessed. She was probably going to let me kiss her forever on her cheater lips."

I felt the betrayal knotting up in my throat.

"But you loved her," said Liz. "You should have said something."

"I know. I was dumb. I was eighteen."

What I didn't tell Liz was that I'd felt like death after the betrayal, that everything Shelly and I'd shared stunk like some cesspool. Everything we had was turned ugly as hell.

"She hurt me," is all I could muster.

The old feelings made my stomach tighten. Shelly was still with me. I had never let go.

Liz urged the conversation forward, "What did you do after that?"

"Something really stupid."

~ * ~

Jonathan shows up at my house with a horde of football players, cheerleaders, and camping gear, all crowded into a station wagon and a pickup truck. He barges in like a quarterback in a locker room, still charged from the ride here. I can smell rum on his stale breath. He wants to continue the phone conversation from earlier.

"Come with us, man. Let's go." Jonathan knows everything that's happened and is on a mission to force me to move on. Seeing me hesitate, he says, "If it bothers you that much, dump her ass, and jump on the next train to Bootyville."

"It's not that simple. I still love her," I say. J doesn't acknowledge the L-word. It's his only taboo, his garlic, cross, and wooden stake...scary, threatening, deathly.

I don't want to go camping. I want to sulk in my misery all weekend. My parents are gone, and I have the place to myself. Plus, Shelly and I have been fighting over nothing, and I'm depressed. She still hasn't told me about the guy she kissed, and the guilt is clearly eating at her because every time another girl walks in my line of sight, she becomes raging jealous and calls me out on it. It usually doesn't bother her that my eyes wander, because she is secure in knowing they always wander back. Not anymore, I guess. I lash back at her because I feel entitled to some leeway, considering I haven't kissed anyone except her in forever. She doesn't have sex with me anymore. We are like porn stars in the beginning, banging in school bathroom stalls, forgotten classrooms or unlocked storage closets, behind the theater stage during lunchtime, her porch at odd hours, my bed, the portable toilets at fairs. Of course, the woods are our favorite.

I miss the pregnancy scares when she's five days late, and the relief when it finally starts, and we say *It was stress*, but by then, we've planned whether we'll abandon the baby at some hospital or raise it together as broke ass teens. We usually take the high road and raise it together. When we don't, we can't speak for days. The guilt clubs at our hearts. I miss howling *shit shit shit* at the vomiting from days earlier which turns out to be a stomach bug that's going around at school. I miss the bouts of devoutness that compel us to beg the heavens for reprieve. And I miss the vengeful sex that ensues once her cycle ends. *Fuck you, Mother Nature. We win.*

We do nothing now, like some burnt-out, middle-aged, married couple who'd rather watch TV sex than bother taking their own clothes off. Vicarious sex is the lifeline of dead relationships.

I snap out of my mental tantrum, walk over to the window, and see several girls in tattered shorts and bikini tops jumping up and down on Jonathan's white truck. The neighbors won't like the ruckus. A brunette is sitting down by the tailgate. She's opposite the jumping girls who are using the roof of the cab to hold on and balance with their hands while their gymnast legs bounce the flatbed, putting on a hydraulic show for the neighborhood. My neighbors probably think I'm a slutty punk. The brunette's upper body springs up and down in the flatbed, cigarette dangling from her lips, her head bobbing back and forth to some distant achy grunge guitars emanating from the cab. She smirks at the sun, challenging it through her shades.

"Is that Dawn?"

"That's right, buddy," he says to me, his leer full of chipped jock teeth, and drops his heavy throwing hand on my shoulder, all while leading me toward my room. "I'll help you pack. I told her you were coming, so don't disappoint her."

I pause but can't find a reason not to go anymore. Shelly is out of town on some religious retreat, so she says, and with that prick from the other night, for all I know. No doubt he is one of those sly religious types that feigns virginity before he pounces on the girl's hymen and then bolts. *Surprise! I got to Shelly first, asshole.*

"Okay," I say. "Let's go. Give me a few minutes."

"Yes, sir," shouts J as he punches the sky in victory.

It's a two-hour ride out into the country and, at first, I think we're going to camp in the middle of nowhere, in the thick of the woods, until J says we're going to The Site. The place is legendary. Its location is like a ritual torch passed down between the senior classes. It's the Senior Site—the SS—the land of no parents, no rules, and debauchery.

I decide to ride in the bed of the truck with the hydraulic girls. Mainly, so I can watch Dawn. Jonathan is driving and, occasionally, he commits to a sharp swerve to remind us we are in party mode. The sun feels good on my skin, but I'm squinting because I forgot my sunglasses. I'm sitting against the cab of the truck, and Dawn's got her knees up to her chest, arms wrapped around them, leaning against the tailgate. In a flash of paranoia, I imagine the gate snapping open, and she flies out onto the pavement, scraping her way down the road to certain death. Thinking like this makes me restless, and I keep shifting my weight from the discomfort. There are four other girls in the bed with us. Two of them are sitting on one side whispering into each other's ears discussing the latest gossip about who is sexing who, and the other two are lying in the middle singing drunk songs as loudly as possible. Luckily, the roar of the wind drowns out the disharmony.

Dawn is staring out into the scenery, her brown hair revolting against the sixty miles per hour wind. Every so often, she moves it out of her face, but the wind is relentless. We are on a stretch of poorly maintained highway, and the untanned skin on Dawn's juicy thighs jiggles rapidly in arousing communion with the uneven road. She has high, rounded Native American cheekbones that also jiggle. She's a slender, hazel-eyed, girl-next-door kind of beauty. Her lips are thin, and she is quiet, and she's a bit introverted, but when she speaks, she uses a melodious voice that makes you pay attention. It's the kind of voice guys fall in lust with, the kind that could seduce a guy into debt on a phone sex line or lure a man off an edge on a crisis line. We rarely speak at the football games or in class, but the times we do it's obvious she likes me. Dawn isn't a cheerleader, but her best friend is one, so we are in the same social circles.

Our first chance meeting happens behind the school building, near a patch of unkempt grass and vines that block an old utility door. Students smoke, drink Wild Turkey (the choice booze in my high school) and hang out here to avoid the scrutiny of teachers. She offers me a cigarette and I accept without hesitation, so she'll think I'm cool. I offer her Turkey, and she swigs. It's my first stick ever, but she doesn't know that. The first inhalation feels like a typhoon in my lungs. I cough and make it apparent I don't know what I'm doing.

I sip the whiskey and pass it to her again. No food in my stomach means an instant buzz.

My lungs are still throbbing. "It'll be a cold day in hell before I have another one of these," I say to her and finish the cigarette anyway.

Dawn laughs at my response and downs half my mini-bottle. We share some stories. She makes smoking look like the sexiest thing ever with her commercial pose (foot on old crate, hands on hips, sunglasses perfectly balanced at the end of her nose, brown pleather jacket and chain wallet, ruffled hair, body designed for early procreation). All she needs is a sporty camel, and she's set. Somehow, she manages to smoke with no hands, all while my shaky fingers and lungs wrestle the cigarette. She's the reason why guys like me kill themselves with the damned things.

"You're Shelly's boy, right?" she says.

"I am," I answer, disregarding the reality that the whole damn school knows I'm taken.

"That's too bad," she says and flicks her cigarette away.

Shelly is my first love, but Dawn is my first lust. Nobody knows I have the secret hots for her except Jonathan, but I don't act on it because I love Shelly.

Dawn maintains her posture near the tailgate, hands down the most uncomfortable part of the truck because of the gratuitous metal that juts out for no apparent reason. Whoever designed this vehicle is a sadist. She faces me as the other girls begin a cheer routine, their voices taking on a much higher volume than normal, and their hands performing a complex patty-cake. Their clapping snips through the roar of the wind in my ears like a frantic barber with a new pair of scissors. I close my eyes momentarily and imagine a kaleidoscope of tiny scissors fluttering about my ear, like colorful butterflies, snipping songs of joy…anything to take my mind off the cursed cheering. I bare my teeth at the thought and at Dawn, but I can't tell what her eyes are doing in her sunglasses. I assume she's staring at me since, besides her, I'm the only person not moving. She still has her arms wrapped around her legs, knees bent toward the sky to form an upside-down *v*, and I can't stop my eyes from following the lines of her thighs down to where the zipper of her jean shorts splits her legs. My teenage thoughts overtake me, and I think, *she could swallow me whole.* The weight of the allure keeps my eyes down for too long. Dawn's mouth parts wryly, but she's just teasing me. She's caught me checking her out and loves it. Still, I'm embarrassed and abruptly turn away. The cheerleaders continue to carelessly yap rhymes into the air.

Dawn's sunglasses come off, and nobody notices that we're ensnared in a quiet seduction. Her eyes phase from light brown to radiant honey whenever the sunlight strikes them. A cloud passes overhead, and they morph to a dull hazel. There's so much turbulence that every imaginable bit of metal digs into all of us. She slides her hands and arms from around her knees and down to her calves, then to her shins and feet, and removes her flip-flops before tossing them in my direction. Her toes move like slow motion sea anemones. I can see her nails are sprinkled with the chipped remains of glittery purple paint.

She bites her lower lip and drops her legs into a butterfly position. Every move is an invitation, and I can feel my stomach tighten, because it's been forever since a girl made me feel this way…since before Shelly. Our spell breaks when one of the girls sits next to her and starts a conversation. Dawn's trying to pay attention to the cheerleader, but I can see her eyes sporadically pop in my direction to see if I'm still looking. Eventually, I turn away because a tinge of guilt is beginning to knot in my chest. We could not have continued our game in the truck with four other girls. It strikes me that there are no more houses in the distance. It's open fields. Emptiness everywhere. The scene makes me uneasy, but we're getting close to the SS.

By the time we arrive, the sun is rushing westward, and the trees stand high like domineering umbrellas. It's darker under the canopy, and our site is beginning to be washed with the colors of the dusk that will soon descend upon us. Besides sleeping bags, lanterns, flashlights, water, and canned food, there are all the party favors to unload. I help several footballers empty out the station wagon of beer, liquor, ice, cola, and the boom box. Everyone decides to sleep in the open since it's perfect out. The site is not accessible by the vehicles and the walk is uneven, a rocky fifty yards downhill to the edge of a creek with no name. After everyone dumps their gear, there is a mass dash for the river…booze in hand. I hang back and decide to settle away from the group in an area where the trees don't umbrella as much against the sky. I want to see as much of the stars as I can. After setting up my satellite camp, I take two fiery shots of a small bottle of Wild Turkey that I find in the makeshift communal foodbank set up in the middle of the camp. I grab a beer and walk to the river where everyone is splashing and cursing. They're playing chicken, except for Dawn, who is climbing up a twenty-foot chunk of rock that begins at the opposite embankment. She's halfway up, and I decide to follow her.

I wade through the cool water, and I'm splashed on all sides. One of the girls is tossed off the shoulders of a footballer, and her body slams me on the back. The beer in my hand goes under water. *Damn it*, I think, as I imagine some microbe or deathly parasitic worm making its way into my precious alcohol. I can feel her weight shift the water current around me, and a huge bubble pierces the surface as she breathes out on her way up for air. She emerges with a loud gasp, head leaning forward, hands up in the air, and then rubs her eyes. Without warning, she tosses her head back, the bulk of her brown hair slapping me under my chin and mouth.

"Ouch," I say.

"Oops, sorry," she says, "didn't see you there." I nod at her and keep wading through the water. My face stings.

I make it to the other side, set my beer down by the water's edge for a second, and hoist myself up on a flat stone. I grab my drink and begin the ascent. Surprisingly, each rock is stacked to form a staircase, nature's ultimate invitation to climb. Scaling them barefoot isn't a problem. I see Dawn sitting at the top, basking in the late afternoon sun and observing the ruckus below.

She hollers down at me, "Are you following me, mister?"

I stop and shout up at her, "Yes ma'am, I am."

"And you brought beer," she says. "What a gentleman."

Her voice trickles down the rocks into my ears like a sonic waterfall. I keep climbing and manage to reach the top in a minute. She takes the booze, and I sit next to her. Our legs dangle over the edge while we halfheartedly criticize the game of chicken that's still playing out below us. If we fall, it's a two-story drop into the creek. Nothing life threatening, unless we hit the rock edges on the way down. Some movement catches our peripheral line of sight, and we turn our heads toward the woods where two people are making out. The girl is topless and pressed up against some guy. He's already thrusting midair like a feral dog, his six-foot frame eclipsing her five-foot body like a fleshy bodysuit.

"Oh, my god," says Dawn as she covers her mouth to suppress giggles, "what horn balls." Neither of us knows them.

We sit on the rock as if on top of the world, absorbing the splashing sounds, and nature around us. It's picturesque. Unreal. A random bird chirps by and dives toward a cloud of dragonflies glimmering on the water's surface. Then a hawk makes its presence known over the trees and vanishes almost immediately…so do all the other smaller birds.

"How are things with Shelly?" asks Dawn.

Her question irks me because, for right now, I'm trying to forget Shelly.

"How are things with your dude?" I say defensively.

"Shut up. You know there's nobody. Every guy is wrong for me."

"Sorry," I say. "I don't mean to be a dick."

"I know," she says kindly.

Usually, Shelly and I thrive under the radar of vicious teeny talk, but I know better than to challenge the power of gossip. Word gets around and, even if there's no word, teens magically become expert behavioral analysts, scrutinizing every gesture like some cryptic language. They can make surprisingly accurate assumptions based on a hug, a bite of the lip, an inch of distance. I'm convinced every eighteen-year-old experiences a period of telepathy to one degree or another.

"I guess you know?" I say, uncertain of how much to divulge.

"It's so obvious when you two fight," she says. "Everyone knows."

"Not worth talking about," I say, and we continue viewing the chaos of guys and girls in the water.

Dawn grabs my hand and squeezes hard. The contact sends a current of electricity up my arm and down my spine.

"It'll work itself out in the end," she says and downs the last of my beer.

For a split second, our eyes meet, but then hers shift down to my lips. She's signaling. I don't want to talk about Shelly anymore, and the alcohol overwhelms me with a sense of desperation or courage, hard to tell which. I'm dying to do something, anything, so I lean in to kiss Dawn. My lips are bigger and thicker, and they easily obscure hers. She doesn't recoil or hold back, but instead opens her mouth to let me in. I can feel her pressing into me and, despite that the jocks and cheerleaders have spotted us, we continue to kiss over their splashing, chirping, and howling.

Blasts of woo-hoos from the footballers and eerie oohs from the cheerleaders bounce off the rocks and quarrel with the air, lingering like disembodied voices. Dawn and I fidget as we're lip-locked and our teeth accidentally knock into each other.

"Ouch," she says, disconnecting from me and covering her face from the painful embarrassment.

"Sorry," I say.

I can see a partial smile through her hands as she says, softly, "Totally worth it. I've wanted to do that for a while."

"What, knock our nice teeth together?" I say jokingly.

"No, you goof," she says, dropping her hands and nudging me.

I grasp the rocks for stability, bulge my eyes out for effect, and feign falling, "I'm falling," I screech.

Unamused, Dawn rolls her eyes, grabs hold of my arm and saves me.

"Stop it," she says and slaps my shoulder. "I meant that I've wondered how you taste."

Her cheeks flush red, and mine do too. Strawberry lip balm lingers in my mouth. Then it hits me. I'm terrified of what will happen afterward, when Shelly hears about Dawn and me. My only defense is that now we are even, a kiss for a kiss…assuming that's all she did that night. The terror doesn't last long because there is movement down below and we see that the rest of the group is climbing up to us. Electric guitars rise from the boom box, and the sounds that reverberate off the rocks cause the echoes to crash all around us. Someone has turned up the music. The band Oasis blasts through the air. I think to myself, *British music is the best. The Beatles, case in point.*

Dawn stands and lifts me up as well. "They're going to be here in a minute," she says with concern in her voice. "Let's jump together."

"I can't," I say, considering the two-story drop, "I don't like heights."

"But you made it up here fine," she says.

"I know, but I wasn't thinking about the drop and was motivated."

Her voice climbs a few notes, "What was your motivation?"

The shade of honey in her eyes stands out and sweetens her face.

"Getting to you," I say.

And then something inside of me ruptures, dragging me further than I've ever been from the girl I love. *Shelly, please tell me I dreamed your lips on his.*

For now, being with Dawn keeps me together. Everything she says sounds like a descending arpeggio, "Good answer, mister. How about you jump with me, and I'll let you kiss me as much as you want."

"Yes," I say excitedly.

I no longer care about what will happen at school next week as I imagine Shelly kissing that guy. Thinking about what drunk, horny teenagers do when they "go somewhere" causes a burst of resentment to cramp in my chest, and I squeeze Dawn's hand. We leap together and hit the water hard. Everything turns to a roaring slow motion as we struggle to find our equilibrium. Water thuds our ears, and our heavy bodies fold up into cradle positions. We are suspended, barely holding hands, yet entangled in the vacuous depths. We let go and burst through the surface for air. Our schoolmates are hooting and whistling down at us from the top of the rocks. They know we're running from them, from everything. Jonathan grabs one of the girls and begins to peck at her in a gross parody of our kiss. His mouth opens as she squirms and bellows an Ew! that echoes down. He's a lizard with his freakish, unhinged tongue.

Everyone howls except the tongued girl who is scrunching her face so much she's unrecognizable, and then, without warning, Dawn straddles me and digs her face into mine. There's an unspoken desperation between us. We're castaways, but at least we are together. There's no hesitation, even as we're showered by lewd comments.

The sun is long gone now, and the stragglers are making their way out of the water to gather around the makeshift fire pit that some of us have thrown together from stones and dead trees around the site. Some sit in camping chairs and others on the trunks of fallen trees on the ground. It's a chilly evening, and most of us are still in our bathing suits. We all shiver until the flames reach out to warm us. Wrapped in our own towels, Dawn and I sit next to each other on a stump but at a safe distance to avoid being heckled by the group. One of the cheerleaders takes a swig from a rum bottle and passes it around the circle. Whiskey is making its way around in the opposite direction.

Then Jonathan says, "So who wants to play *I dare you to OR take something off?*"

Everyone says *No* in unison, and he stands in protest. After sulking, he folds his arms like an angry bouncer and grunts, "Seriously? We're alone in the woods, people. Alone."

No response from the group.

"Why the hell are we out here?" he says dramatically, throwing his hands up in the air and plopping back down onto his blue and orange Broncos lawn chair. He takes a long dramatic swig from a bottle.

One of the cheerleaders says, "I'll play, but I'm putting more clothes on."

She runs to her bag for a few shirts, a couple pants, some socks, shoes, and a hat. The rest of the girls follow suit. The guys casually rise and throw on more shorts and shirts to level the playing field.

Once the game is in full swing, the fire dies down. Dawn presses up to my left side to hide her chest from everyone else. My left arm drapes across her shoulders. Nobody is messing around now, because we've all lost enough clothes to bring the game to a tense standstill. I can feel the smoothness of her right breast pressing into my left rib, and her breath lightly brushes my left shoulder whenever she shifts. Her shivers make me want to hold her tighter. Several of the guys are completely naked and cupping their groins in a pathetic effort to hide themselves, their restless silhouettes phasing in and out of existence as the fire stirs in the fitful wind. None of the girls are naked, but a good number of them are topless. Their panties are all that separates them from devastating embarrassment or sexual recklessness.

The air is heavy and hormonal, and I dread my turn as one of the guys says, "Liam, I dare you to lick Dawn right there." I turn toward her all boggle-eyed. He's pointing at her chest. All I have left is my underwear. I've lost all my other clothes.

Dawn can back out of the game any time without losing too much face, but I don't want to be a chump in front of the virile jocks. I've already lost some shorts and flip-flops to avoid feeling-up a couple of the strange reluctant girls, and to stop them from daring me to do gross things in the woods. Two of my shirts have been lost to the night to avoid chugging half a bottle of rum, and my socks have been thrown into the fire so I can stay on dry land and not have to dive into the frigid water. My hat saves me from having to tongue one of the guys. Of course, the dares become more sexual as the alcohol takes hold. Dawn holds her position, expressionless, staring into my eyes to see what I'll choose. She's forcing me to choose between my underwear and this lewd act with her. We've spiraled out of control. All of this will get back to Shelly next week.

Dawn can see what I've decided by the way my eyes drop to her chest. She backs away from me and says, "It's okay. Do it."

She unfolds her arms as I bend down low enough to run my tongue from her bellybutton all the way up to her breasts. I catch a nipple with the rough midsection of my tongue and a stifled moan escapes her. Her skin is chilled from the sporadic lashings of the wind, and the contrasting warmth of my tongue makes her stomach tense. Her eyes close tightly as if she's being burned and she grunts, but it's all pleasure. Everyone's whispering as I'm doing this. Once my tongue reaches her cleavage, Dawn snaps back and leers at the group, all of whom are nonplussed, half of them statues with mouths agape. Then she shoves me away and folds her arms again. She's smiling, and so am I.

The game continues, the torch passes to another, and the lewdness ensues until one of the girls dares Jonathan to let her take control of his hand and use it to explore another jock's body.

"I'm out," he says. "Game over."

"Pu-ssy, pu-ssy, pu-ssy," chant several girls in unison,

"That's the problem," says J. "I like pussy too much."

The group scatters, only pausing to slip back into clothes, and we begin to arrange the sleeping areas. Party mode: off. Almost everyone pairs off. Sex mode: on. Dawn disappears into a tent with a cheerleader. The whispering and giggling distract me, and I'm not content with my spot. I split from camp when everyone turns in and make my way uphill to J's truck. I spread my sleeping bag in the back so I can get a better view of the stars. Shelly crosses my mind. I'm conflicted about what's happened today, or whether I should feel bad. Time drags here. The dilation is strong enough to bend a person in half. The swarm of stars above keeps me entranced, making me wish the world would stop.

Then I hear footsteps coming up the hill from camp. The paced crunching of brittle rocks under flip-flops crescendos, and I sit up to see who is approaching.

"I can't see anything," says Dawn, her soft harmonious voice disembodied in the shadows. Her face appears after her words taper off.

"Hi, there," I say.

"Why are you up here all alone, mister?"

"Why aren't you asleep?" I ask, purposely avoiding her question in case she thinks stargazing is lame.

"It's a zoo down there with all the weird ape grunting."

"Ha," I say, "Get up here."

I pat my sleeping bag, and she climbs in with me. We lie next to each other.

"Wow," she says as she paces her exhalation into a melodic sigh. Her words harmonize with the sounds of the woods, and the light breeze that sweeps over us carries her fruity lip balm into my lungs. "Those stars."

"I know," I whisper.

She confesses, "Maybe I was wrong."

"About what?" I say and turn toward her.

We are an inch apart.

"Some things don't work out in the end," she avows under the dizzying uprising of stars above us.

Her hand caresses my face, and then she leans in, her mouth bracing mine. We linger in this position for a minute, submitting to the saltiness of our lips. Our hearts pound in our chests like crazed prisoners on the verge of escape. Without warning, the weight of her face forces my head back until she topples onto me. Our mouths are still locked together. All is lost. My love for Shelly is about to become a bitter memory, a fracture in my past, as I let Dawn take anything she wants from me.

~ * ~

"Do you think it could be different if you ever fell in love again?" said Liz, bringing me back to the present.

"I don't want to find out," I said. "When Shelly left, it nearly killed me. I was lost for a long time." I paused. "I don't think I'm meant to fall in love. Fairytale endings are not in my cards."

"Yes, they are. Everyone deserves love."

"It's not that I don't deserve it, but that it's not meant to be for me."

Liz hugged me, squeezing so hard I felt the thump of her heart next to my ear. It was a blissful reminder of lying under the stars with Dawn.

I wanted to tell Liz that some stories aren't epic, they merely fizzle away at the end. Shelly was everything I imagined love could be, but I was not prepared for it to end the way it did. A profound love had possessed us, but she made me an outcast with her betrayal. Dawn then shared in that betrayal.

"How does it end?" said Liz.

"Painfully."

~ * ~

"It hurts," says Shelly, as she sits and hugs her legs. Teardrops stream down her face. "How could you?"

Standing over her, I'm pale, nauseous, and shaking. "I'm sorry," I say.

Misery fogs everything in sight. I can't bear to sit down for fear I won't be able to get up again. My damn rubbery legs won't let me run away. I want to be far from her and our ending.

"Why her?" she says. *Why him?* I think.

I have no answer.

She sobs quietly to herself and, periodically, her chest convulses to take in more air. I want to reach down and lift her and wrap myself around her, but I can't find the strength to act. I want to tell her I know about her kissing that other guy, but instead, I submit to my role as a treacherous cheat who is selfishly crushing an unsuspecting cheerleader's heart. Adding what I know to what I have done isn't going to help us be together. No matter what we say, the end is here.

"I don't know," I say. "She was there, and I don't know." I run my hands through my hair. "Who told you?"

She ignores my question, and her face emerges from her hands, "You're a bastard. I hate you. Why the hell did you ever happen to me?"

She lowers her head into her hands again to cry. We're breaking to pieces from two separate guilts. Every word is an incomprehensible divide. As our love fades, I fade with it.

My chest begins to spasm, and I can't breathe through the tears that drown me. "Make it stop," I say, trembling all over. I bury my head in my hands and desperately wish I could go back to the SS and the river under the stars, back to the party house with Jonathan, back to our first time at the creek, back to the storm of our first kiss, back to before there is no possibility of ending. Then, without saying a word, without acknowledging me again, Shelly stands and walks away.

~ * ~

I hated to share my anguish with Liz. It was mine, and I wasn't ready to disown it.

She scooted up to me, gave me another hug and said, "I don't know what to say. I can't imagine."

But it was a repulsive hug. I didn't want it. Liz had forced my story out, and now all I wanted was to hold Shelly once again.

"It was a long time ago," I said, wiping my face with my sleeve.

Liz placed her hand on my shoulder and gave me a sad puppy face before she whispered, "Let's not talk about it anymore."

She didn't know what she had done to me by resurrecting the past. From then on, I was no longer haunted by the specter and guilt of my adolescent love. I was stalked by it. Liz's role was the opposite of Shelly's. When I met Liz that day at my university, I knew what love wasn't.

Six

The Blizzard and the Virgin

"I want to tell y— someth— ," she yelled through the phone.

"Liz, I can't hear you." Nothing from her end. "It's snowing pretty badly here. I'll call you back," I said, unsure if the message got through. I hung up and helped Jonathan maneuver through the flurry of snow hitting the windshield. We were on a road trip.

My old high school buddy and I were driving his SUV through the North Carolina wilderness. I had gone to visit him in December, six months after Liz and I began celibate dating. Dating her was easy because she confessed she had no experience with men, and planned to remain inexperienced until marriage. And since I didn't plan to marry her, we were a dead end in the bedroom. For the most part, she was decent company and easy on the eyes, and we got used to one another. Jonathan stopped at a rest area so we could sleep. We couldn't drive further in the snow, anyway. The next day I was supposed to be on a plane back to Texas, so we'd have to finish the trek to the airport then.

I waited a while until the blizzard passed and then called Liz. She picked up.

"Hello?"

I was whispering so as not to disturb J. "Hey, we're at a rest area. It's crazy up here. Fuck the cold. Last time I come here in the winter."

She groaned and said, "I'm dying to have you back."

"Tomorrow," I said without revealing the mild excitement I felt in seeing her again.

There was a long pause, like she had run out of things to say. "You there?" I said.

"I love you," she responded. Her words sliced through me, and I felt my stomach tighten. "I know you can't say it back, but I do, and it's okay if you don't."

The anticipation I felt for her turned to dread, and I didn't know what to say. We had talked about love, and about my past, and about all the deception and lies that came along with this destructive emotion. But she didn't understand because she hadn't been through it and wouldn't accept my reluctance for it.

"Liz, I—"

"Don't say anything. I just wanted to let you know how I feel," she said.

We sat on the phone for ages. I knew she was waiting for me to say something more. Perhaps not those three words, but something.

It began to snow again, the flurries larger than usual, and I could feel the iambic thumping in my chest through the thick ski coat I wore to battle the winter. My skin went clammy, and I couldn't suck in enough air to feel comfortable. The pale-yellow glow of the rest area shined into the SUV, adding a depressing hue to the surroundings. Occasionally, a series of flurries landed on the windshield and synchronized with my heartbeat. The roar of a brave semi plodding through the snow on the highway shook the SUV. I needed a distraction, but the flurries returned to another turbulent downpour, snapping me back to our conversation.

"Liz, it's snowing again so the signal may go out."

"Okay," she said. Her voice had dropped a couple levels from excited to a slow, husky whisper. "Call me when—"

The connection went dead, and there was a delay before I said, "Hello?" She was gone. Call dropped. She'd been robbed of this moment, but I'd been saved.

~ * ~

I was back in my apartment unpacking when she knocked. Liz lived ten minutes from me in her own place, alone. I had a roommate who was gone. I let her in, and she made herself comfortable on my bed. The mattress was old, a hand-me-down from an uncle who insisted it was perfect for a struggling university student. More like a medieval torture device, the four middle springs were permanently warped, causing a sizeable slump, and unwanted pressure against the middle-back of whoever lay on it.

"Why didn't you let me pick you up from the airport?" she said.

I lied. "My uncle usually does it. You know how family is. I couldn't say no."

Actually, I wasn't ready to see her, because I still didn't know what to say. I needed words that would weigh as heavily as *I love you* but wouldn't be as absolute or potentially crippling.

But she didn't give me a chance and wanted to dive into it.

"It's what I said, isn't it? I can't help how I feel."

My back was turned to her as I kept busy with organizing my clothes.

"Can you please sit next to me and talk?" she said.

I stopped folding clothes, clenched my jaw in tense anticipation of the conversation we were about to have, and went to sit. She had no makeup on. Normally, she applied eyeliner to bring out her eyes. Her eyelashes were blonde, and the absence of paint diminished the vibrancy of her face. Her blue eyes were lackluster in the overcasting shades of my room. She obviously hadn't slept.

"I care about you, Liz," I began, generically, hoping these words were enough for this moment.

This is about the weakest response a man can make to a woman who has confessed her love. Something like, *I love you more…times a million, times infinity, baby*, is more appropriate. Saying *I love you* back was damn flaccid at this point, an afterthought. Timing is everything, and I was not in sync.

Liz's eyes were darting back and forth and up and down my face. She wanted a way in.

"What are you afraid of?" she said as she grabbed my hand and ignored my insincerity, disregarding everything I had told her about my past.

"I've never been in this situation."

"We don't need more of a reason than we have for us to be together," she said, "and, we don't need to reason this out. I know how I feel, so let's not make this a huge deal."

She clearly expected more but was too focused on my anxiety to press the issue.

"But it is a huge deal," I said as I stood and began to pace in front of her. "Don't you think a person should reciprocate? I'm not feeling in love, Liz."

She was following my movements from one side of the room to the other.

"You could grow to love me," she said. "Even if you don't feel it now, that doesn't mean you won't later."

I stopped moving and stood over her, trying to lock eyes.

"But I think it does mean that," I said.

She rejected my answer, and her eyes darted everywhere else but into mine.

"I think you're wrong," she said, shaking her head. "Give it a chance. Nothing's going to change between us because I told you that I love you. I promise."

Liz was composed about the whole thing. She was the one taking all the risk, yet, I was the one in shambles.

"But you're expecting that I will say it in the future because you've said it. Aren't you?"

She paused at my words.

"I think you need time to see how perfect we are for each other."

I sat next to her again.

"Liz," I cupped my hands on both sides of her face as gingerly as I could, "you can't expect me to—"

She put her hand against my lips to stop my sentence. "I'm ready," she assured me. "This isn't about you anymore."

She moved her hand and kissed me. Our embraces often felt mistimed to me because of her inexperience. It's as if we were kissing through a glass wall. She would try to find her place on my lips but couldn't figure out the sweet spot, the place where her lips and mine fit precisely.

I backed away from her. "Ready for what?" I said with my brow furrowed.

"I'm ready to do it," she said. "I want you to be my first. I love you, and you are the one I want."

"Liz, no," I raised my voice and tried to stand back up, but she held my hand tightly, and sat me down again with surprising force.

"Stop getting up and talk to me," she said sternly, never letting go of my hand.

"I can't do that to you," I said. "You don't know what you're asking. Everything will change."

I used my free hand to massage my eyes. I was tired, and Liz knew that, yet she pressed on. She wanted an opening, anything that could potentially lead to those three words.

"You haven't considered this before?" she said with expectant eyes. "Has it never crossed your mind? Don't you want to have sex with me?"

I sensed the spark of panic in her questions. She had no idea she'd found my kryptonite. I didn't say anything for a while so I could choose my words carefully.

"Yes, of course, but thinking and doing aren't the same. We could never return here, to this place, to how we are now. We could never take it back. And what about marriage, and saving yourself for a husband, and all that stuff you told me?"

"I don't care," she said. "People change. I've changed. Messing around and daily dry humps aren't enough anymore. I don't care if you don't love me, now. It's you I want, and there is nothing you can say to change that."

"I think there is someone out there who is worthy of this," I said in my last shot to fend her off.

"You are worth it," she said. "I'm ready, and if you don't do this with me, then some other guy will. I'll have to take a chance with someone else, and what if I choose wrong, and they use me or worse?" she said.

"What could be worse?" I said.

"What if they tell me they love me, and they are lying the whole time? And what if I fall in love, and he's an asshole, and uses me, and dumps me afterward? This happens to my girlfriends all the time. They meet someone nice, they bone, he splits. At least with you, I know what I'm getting into. I trust you."

This was her worst fear, that the next guy would be worse than me.

"If you don't do this with me, someone else will," she reiterated, "and they may not be like you."

"That won't happen," Liz. You deserve more."

"But I may not get more. This is it. I know it. You're a good guy and are so sweet to me."

I wasn't that sweet, but she had no other comparison. She held my hand with both of hers now, squeezing periodically, urging me to give in.

"We have a chance," she said in opposition to my denial, "and, I'm in love with you."

There was no clear way out of this. Her determination eclipsed my hesitation. I squeezed her hands to let her know I understood, and I softened my face in acceptance of her resolve. Her face softened as well, and a smile exposed her two front teeth. Deep inside myself, however, I suffered from a far-off guilt. Her words were true, but only for some future event that would never happen. She deserved more and would get more. This future guy who would take her for granted and use her didn't exist beyond me. For now, though, she had won, and there was nothing I could say to show her that she was foreshadowing her own damned future by being with me. I was the asshole.

Liz leaned in to establish her place on my lips. Fail. As much as she wanted it to happen, we didn't fit. Nothing about us fit except our friendship. Instead, she refocused and began to strip off my shirt and pants. My clothes resisted her. They wouldn't budge because the zipper was stuck, denying her access, but she was persistent and began to tug on it until it was evident her efforts were futile.

"Wow," she said, "help, please?" and folded her arms to demonstrate she wasn't giving up, and that she meant business.

"What's wrong?" I said sarcastically. "Don't virgins practice this stuff on jeans and bananas?" It was my own weak way of accepting what was happening.

Her jaw dropped in a playful way at my snide comment. Liz then pushed my chest and made me sprawl backward onto the bed. She growled and then tried to pounce on me like a cat, but I held her off gently.

"Are you positive about this?"

"Absolutely," she grinned big as she kneeled between my legs.

She slowly peeled her shirt off, moving the curvature of her hips in a hypnotic sway, like a snake dancing its way out of a woven basket. Liz tried to dramatize the short striptease and threw her shirt across my room. Her face muscles were flexed in a way I'd never seen on her. She was predatory. Then she slithered her way up my body, and I could feel the nervous clamminess of her flesh sticking to mine like rubber. She went up my legs to my thighs, and then up my stomach to my chest, until her face was in front of mine. I felt her weight sink into me as she bumped her lips on mine. Then she clumsily grabbed both my wrists and forced them above my head.

"There's no going back, Liz," I said. "Last chance to change your mind."

I could taste her sex breath as she exhaled into my mouth. Her chest expanded and contracted shallowly from the adrenaline in her veins, all in anticipation of the biggest night of her life. Her sweet scent and anxiousness made my throat tingle.

"No chance that's happening," she snapped back and sank her face into mine.

For the first time, we fit perfectly, she was dead on…that is, until Liz prematurely shifted her lips to my neck, oblivious to what she'd found. A shiver ran through my body, causing me to tense.

Liz stopped kissing me when she felt my body jerk.

"What's wrong?" Her hands kept clutching mine so as not to lose her dominant position.

"Nothing," I said. "I felt something."

But before she could respond, and before I could doubt myself more and change my mind about the whole thing, I rolled her over and pinned her hands above her head like she had done to mine. Liz squeaked and stopped squirming when she felt my hips press into her. We locked eyes one more time.

Doubt reared its ugly head, "Liz, I don't—"

"Don't finish that sentence," she said, knowing that if I did, we would be done.

Her face became serious, and I felt her hands relax in mine. I let go, and she wrapped her arms around my back and squeezed. Our bodies were so close it hurt.

I was lost in the depths but not with Liz. This first time did not belong to her: it was Shelly's face that I saw, and we were in love again. I tasted her strawberry lips during our stormy kiss. I felt the heat of her body in the woods and could taste her sweat as I kissed her stomach for the first time. I felt Liz's thighs tremble beneath me, but it wasn't her...it was Shelly's legs that I felt shaking me to the core. And though it was Liz's words in my ears, all I could hear was Shelly's voice. *I love you.*

~ * ~

Liz slid off the edge of my bed, leaving me wrapped in the sheets. We were nude and soaked.

"I'm going to hop in the shower," she said as she turned her back to me.

She'd never walked away from me in the nude. Liz had gotten what she wanted, and her body expressed victory by striding confidently across my room. She entered my bathroom and left the door cracked. The water began to flow and, after a minute, a cloud of steam drifted into my room. I sat at the edge of my bed listening to the water splatter, and then Liz began to sing. Her ghostly alto filled the walls of the bathroom, and the melody rose with the vapor, filling my ears. She sang the saddest love song: The Carpenter's *Superstar*. Liz's version haunted me, like when I'd first heard Sonic Youth cover the tune. Each word crawled up the walls of the bathroom and hung in the air momentarily before vanishing.

I couldn't stand to lie there alone anymore, so I entered the bathroom, closed the door, and peeked through the curtain. Her back muscles were tensing sporadically as she moved her shoulders in and out of the stream. The fog was thick and making me sweat again.

She turned around, not surprised at all to see me, and said, "Water's nice. You want to come in?"

"You're doing fine in there on your own," I said, a little embarrassed at how intrusive it all seemed.

"You could scrub me down," she said and fluttered her eyes, inviting me in again.

I didn't budge.

"Keep singing," I said in a pathetic attempt to distract her from my presence. She didn't object and continued the song as she ran soap all over her arms.

She stopped abruptly after a bit, as if she'd discovered me standing there all over again.

"Get in here, already," she growled as she yanked my arm.

"I'll get in when you're done," I resisted.

"Or this could be another first with me," she yanked at my arm again. "I want you to be my first everything."

Liz kept her eyes fixed on me, digging into mine the entire time to see if I would acquiesce. I felt another shiver run up my spine, pressing me to take a step into the water.

I turned red, and then her face softened, though her grip tightened.

"Haven't you showered with a girl before?"

I cleared my throat and said, "No."

"So you're a shower virgin?" she said and released me so she could clap her hands like she'd won the lottery.

Before I could turn to go back to the bedroom, she pulled me into the shower. The water made my eyes burn and the pressure forced them closed just as I felt her lips connect with mine.

She broke off, our mouths making a smacking sound, and said, "You're mine."

"Yes," I said, "I'm yours," but I was lying.

It didn't matter what I felt because this is what she wanted more than anything. I rested my head against hers, forehead to forehead, and let her in.

"Keep singing," I said, and she did.

Seven

There is no Going Back

"You don't want kids? Ever?"
Liz was facing me and sitting at the opposite end of the two-person raft we had rented. Our legs were intertwined to maximize the scant room we had between us. We were floating idly down the Guadalupe River near San Antonio, in the middle of summer, with a dozen of both our friends. She was in a green bikini and old cop glasses so dark, I couldn't tell what she was gazing at. I was in gray basketball shorts, a white wide-rimmed canvas hat, and layers of sunscreen. My face was indigenously painted for war: thick white sunscreen lines under each eye, a stripe running down my humped nose, and the same on each cheekbone. The beer was messing with my thoughts: *Damn, she's white, as white as a white girl can be. She's like a ghost, a ridiculously sexy ghost, with her haunting grainy alabaster flesh.*
"I'm serious," she said as she folded her arms.
"Pass me a beer."
"Not until you answer my question."
"No way," I said and burped. Liz handed me a can, and I cracked it open. "No kids. They're a curse. You make one mistake, and they're all fucked."
I downed half the beer to maximize my buzz.

"Oh, and they make you age like crazy," I continued.

Liz was not happy with my response, but she pressed on.

"What about marriage?"

I mocked her, "You know my answer," and began singing, in my best Frank Sinatra voice, the theme song to *Married...with Children*. She hated when I did that.

Liz made it a ritual to ask me about kids and marriage every couple months to see if I had changed my mind. By the time we passed the one-year mark, she was nervous I wouldn't change. She was right.

"Yeah, I'm starting to think the same thing," she said and turned her head to face in another direction.

"Bullshit. I know you want it all, the whole package."

She turned back toward me and pursed her lips in an agitated way. "You don't know shit."

"Calm down," I said. "You're the only girl I've ever known whose parents made it—who are still together."

"So, what?"

"So, I can see why you want that, too," I said. "Can't you see why I don't? You know my parents split, Liz, and I don't care if you think it's an excuse. It was horrible, and I never want to relive it."

I gulped more beer to stress how terrible an expectation she was imposing on me.

"There are many ways marriage and kids can go for people," she said.

"Statistics disagree with you. Either it works, or it doesn't, and usually it doesn't."

"Don't be an asshole."

I swigged from the last third of my beer.

"I'm talking odds," I said. "There are loads of kids who suffer because of bogus lifelong contracts, you know. Why can't two people be together without all the paperwork?"

Liz sighed. "It's not the same. You aren't taking a real chance with someone if you aren't willing to marry them."

"You only care about the paper that says you're officially married, like a decree. A person isn't real estate, Liz. You can't claim someone and expect them to remain unchanged because you signed papers."

"Stop trying to convince me that marriage is a dumb relic, or whatever," she said. "And stop being so angry at life."

I began feeling bad that I had opened my mouth, so I kept quiet. Regardless of our argument, Liz had been a devoted partner up to this point. It was me who had the problems, not her.

We stopped talking to ease the tension off the conversation. There were numerous rafts filled with people drinking and chatting, and listening to music, as well as several inner tubes of dozing drunks lazily spinning downstream with us. Several rafts lagged, and we could hear slurred echoes off the muddy banks. *Merrily, merrily, merrily, merrily, life is but a dream.*

But the temptation to have the last word was too much for me in my buzzed state: "No kids. No marriage. No papers. No way."

"Whatever," said Liz. "Dick."

A long time passed before we said anything else. The water was calm as we drifted with the current. There was an occasional breeze that swept across our faces as we floated along, while some of the trees and leaves fluttered and swayed, as if waving goodbye. I draped my feet over the side of the raft to feel the water slip through my toes. The motion made me feel as if stranded on the slowest spinning yo-yo in the world. It was difficult to gauge our speed since the water was a thick muddy brown, and we all moved at the same pace.

Then Liz surprised me. "I bought the seat next to yours."

"What?"

"I'm going to Beijing with you," she said casually. "I was going to surprise you later, but now—"

"You're flying overseas with me? But it's for research. I won't have time to sightsee. I have work to do there, Liz."

"It's done," she said. "I'm going for the first four days. You can't spare a few days for me?"

I was pissed. Beer pissed.

"Damn it," I said.

I wanted to travel alone. Now, I'd have to worry about Liz in another country. A flash of future events flooded me: Liz complaining about the seat, bitching about the food, moaning about the heat; Liz sassing every living Asian soul.

"I knew you weren't going to like that I was going," she said and folded her arms.

"If you knew that, why did you buy the ticket?" I said. "Get a refund. It's not for six more months."

"No," she said. "It's non-refundable, and I'm going because you should have asked me to go, and because I'm your girlfriend. I shouldn't have to sneak around your back and buy a damn plane ticket so I can go with you."

I counted backwards from ten and tried to focus. The booze was making me volatile. I needed more space from the conversation. Plus, there was nothing I could do from a raft in San Antonio.

"Let's deal with this when we get home," I said, not wanting to keep talking for fear of losing my cool in front of all our friends.

"Of course," she said with a winner's grin. She turned her head toward the shore, away from me.

The San Antonio incident was the beginning of the end for us, and then we had to resolve the issue of *our* trip overseas. I didn't want her to go, but she was unwilling to stay. We argued heatedly about it the entire drive home. She wouldn't budge. We had been living together for several months, and our relationship had evolved from platonic to romantic to complacent. We were co-conspirators of a mutual delusion. I shouldn't have been with her, and I wasn't the guy she should have been with. We didn't know it was all wrong, I suppose, at least not then. After we arrived home, we didn't speak like we said we would, neither of us willing to bring up the trip or compromise our resolve. Two days later, Liz returned to work, and I was left alone in the apartment. Who knows how this would have played out had I not been there that day? Her parents might have changed their minds and abandoned their agenda. Liz and I could have probably worked it all out. Who knows?

There was a knock on the door and, when I answered, her parents stood impatiently in the doorway.

"Oh," I said, startled to see them there. "Liz didn't say you were coming by. She's at work."

"We're here to see you," they said.

They had never shown up to see me. We weren't close and had kept a healthy distance between us, especially her father and me. No man wants to be friends with the guy who deflowered his princess. They knew of me and about me, but we never hung out without Liz. They entered and sat down at our uncomfortably cheap dining room table that was more decorative than functional.

Her father spoke first. "We aren't going to beat around the bush," he said. "We want you to propose to Liz. It's time to buy the cow, son." *Did he just compare his daughter to a cow?*

My jaw dropped open, yet no words came out.

Her mother proceeded in a smug tone, "It's time to commit or split," she said.

I almost laughed (nervously) at her rhyme, but she wasn't playing.

"Listen, Lee," said her father, "We like you." *They did not like me, and I hated being called Lee.* "Liz loves you. But we need to know where you stand in all this. Are you going all the way or are you passing through?"

They were in attack mode, and I was cornered.

"I'm sorry," I said, "but this is a conversation I should be having with your daughter."

"Yes, it is," said her mother, "and we want to know when you'll be having it."

The daggers in their eyes demanded an immediate response. Of course, I didn't have one, because I had never planned on having this conversation with Liz. I never saw us as forever. *But didn't she know that?* Her parents saw the defeat on my face, and her mother produced a small silver jewelry box from her purse.

"Here," she said as she slid it across the table to the edge of my fingertips, "open it up."

Inside was a one carat, sparkly diamond resting atop a white gold band. It was simple, elegant, and exactly what Liz would have wanted. I don't think she'd even dreamed this ring up yet, but there it was…taunting me with all its brilliance, urging me to take the leap. The difficult part would be explaining to her where I'd found the money to buy it. Suddenly, it occurred to me that Liz might have put them up to it.

Her father continued, "This is for you. Liz doesn't need to know we were here but propose and do it soon."

They stood, not saying another word, and walked out of the apartment. It was the last time I ever saw them. In a fit of rage, I threw the fancy box against the door, smashing it apart. The ring lay on the floor, waiting for Liz to get home.

~ * ~

"You told them you wanted to marry me?"

"Please, don't leave," she said as I packed my stuff. "I didn't tell them to come here and do this."

"I don't believe you," I said. "Why else would they try to bully me into proposing? That ring is exactly like something you would have picked out."

I kept stuffing things into my boxes. Liz was sobbing as she spoke.

"I didn't. I swear."

This was probably the one and only time Liz had lied to me. I was livid as I crammed unfolded, wrinkled clothes into my bag. "Why couldn't you leave things alone, Liz? Why do you insist on pushing this thing further and further? I never wanted it to get this far."

"Well it is this far," she said between sobs. "And nobody forced you to do this with me."

"You know what? You're right. Nobody forced me. And nobody can force me to do this anymore. I'm done, Liz. I'm not going any further with you."

I was nearly packed.

"I love you," she said. "Why don't you feel anything when I say that?"

Her breath was sporadic, and her chest seized as she gulped for air. Her face was flushed and wet.

I froze. Packing was done and my chest tightened from guilt. My hands were shaking, and I began to feel my throat tighten. I covered my face and hid.

"Liz, I—" I began as I dropped my hands. Her face began to brighten as if all her hopes were about to become reality. "I could never marry you. You're not the one, Liz."

The illusion was over. Her voice was soft when she spoke again. Her love, tragically, fell short of any possible reconciliation between us.

"You *are* the one," she sobbed.

I didn't love her, and if I did, then it was in a damning way. My love wasn't present. For me, love was about to happen in the future or had happened in the past, but it was somewhere and sometime beyond this. Certainly, happiness would happen for her, a future happiness without me in it, with some other man perhaps. She was a good person and good things would come.

"Don't leave me alone," she said.

It was a pitiful surrender.

"It's over, Liz," I said as I walked out of her apartment with my army duffel bag, a gift from my parents who had disowned me when I was eighteen, and a small stack of boxes.

Through a fit of sobs and gasps, she managed to exclaim down the hall, "But where will you go?" Her voice echoed, *GO, Go, go.*

"My own place," I yelled back.

"Wait," she said and ran to stop me.

My guilt felt heavier than gravity, so I dropped my stuff and waited. She deserved that much.

"Can I at least come see where you live? To see if you're okay?" she said, arms crossed, lips trembling like it was the dead of winter.

I couldn't see the blue in her eyes anymore, only webs of red veins, busted vessels, and the large teardrops that magnified them. And so, in my weakened state, I gave her the new address, more out of pity than any unconscious need to see her again.

~ * ~

A week passed before I saw Liz again. I relished the distance but was certain it was torturous for her. She stood at my door composed, a bit too serene, with her porcelain smirk, pretty teeth and said, "Surprise!"

"What are you doing here?"

I felt the pangs of guilt in my chest again.

She giggled to herself. "You gave me your address, silly."

"Yeah, but why didn't you call me before you came over?"

"I didn't think I had to," she said.

I frowned. "Well, you do."

She decided to ignore me and instead said, "Are you going to invite me in?"

I hesitated as she stood in front of me wide-eyed, anticipating my next move. My guilt was so damning.

"Damn it. Just come in," I said as I moved out of the way and let her into my halfway furnished apartment. She surveyed the room.

"You don't have another girl here, do you?" she asked nervously, half-jokingly, as she faced me again.

"No," I said, "but that's none of your business anymore. What do you want, Liz?"

"The trip to Beijing," she said. "We should talk about that."

"It's not a vacation so you shouldn't come," I said.

"So, you don't think we could be friends six months from now?"

"Us being friends is how we got to this point in the first place."

"Well, that's not an issue anymore," she said, adamantly, then adding, "and I'm going whether you like it or not. I'll be there next to you unless you change *your* flight and plans."

She got me there. I was too broke to change the itinerary, and so I conceded in hopes that sometime in the next six months she would abandon the idea.

"Okay, Liz. Whatever. Do what you need to do. Thanks for coming by to tell me all this in person. I'm done talking and have shit to do now. Next time, call."

I ushered her toward the door.

"Wait. Before I go, I have one more thing to talk to you about," she said.

"Just leave, okay?" I pleaded but she kept on talking anyway.

"I have a proposition for you that I think will make us both happy."

"Liz, stop."

"Wait, hear me out," she said excitedly. "I'm okay with you moving out and needing your space. I get it. I messed up." She paused to find her courage. "But I'm not ready to let this go. I think we're good together and can make it work."

I broke in, "Liz, we shouldn't have to *make* anything happen. If it hasn't happened by now, what makes you think—" but she interrupted me.

"Let's stay together, but you live here, and I'll live at my place. And I'll come by whenever you want me to. Or, I can stay over sometimes, or not. You can come to my place whenever. It'll be a nice vacation from each other."

"No," I said. Her proposal was a desperate one, birthed from the irrational panicked frenzy of a broken heart. I tried to stop her from going further into it. "I can't be with you, Liz."

Her breathing became erratic. "Yes, you can," she cried.

I raised my voice, "I don't want to be with you."

Unexpectedly, she pressed her face into me. Her lips were wet and salty when they touched mine. She trembled, begging for me to give back, but I didn't move so she broke off.

Examining my stern face for a sign, she said, "Please," and began to undress frantically. She kicked off her shoes and peeled off her shirt and stood barefoot in jeans and bra. Her eyes were digging into mine for a way back in. "Be with me," she said. "Make love to me. Now."

I stopped her before she could unbutton her pants.

"We can't anymore. Get dressed," I said.

She sobbed uncontrollably, defeated, as she slipped into her shirt and shoes again. Love had stripped her to the bone.

"Don't kill us," she said as she pressed the palm of her hands to her eyes. "Aren't we worth saving?"

"Stop," I said and went mute.

My silence caused her hands to drop, and she kept sobbing, waiting for me to say something, but I couldn't.

"I don't want to forget how we feel."

Of course, it was my fault she'd arrived at this point, tattered, a shadow of the woman I'd met at college. The guilt was intense but not enough to move me.

All I could muster was a bland, "Just leave."

"Not like this." She groveled, moments before she walked out. "Come back to me," her voice cracked. She lowered her head and cried loudly into her hands. Her body shook in one spasmodic wave before she rushed me, our lips an inch apart, and snarled as if possessed, "Do you want me to forget you forever?"

"Yes," I said bluntly, the finality in my voice undeniable.

"Goddamn you, Liam. What are you running from?"

I had nothing.

"Tell me."

She saw our death in my eyes and turned to leave. I let her go. There was no going back for us.

Eight

The Last Goodbye

The words haunted me: *there is no going back.* But part of me wanted to go back. I missed the comfort, the routine, the predictability of having Liz there to care for me. A conversation I'd had with a friend, before ending things with Liz, came back to me.

"Ask yourself this question when breaking it off," he told me. "Can you imagine her with anyone else but you?"

"I don't get what you mean," I said.

"I'm talking about sex," he said. "It's the only way you can gauge whether to stay or not. If the answer is no, if you can't bear to see her with another man, if it drives you crazy, then you're still holding on, and there may be something worth preserving. But if the answer is yes, and you can imagine her waking up next to someone else every morning, then you don't own that person anymore. They are gone from you, and there is no going back."

I kept playing the conversation in my head. A part of me felt guilty for doing nothing, for not putting up a fight for Liz. Long after we ended, on the other side of the world, in the great city of Beijing, I asked myself whether letting her walk away had been the wisest thing to do. I questioned everything we'd been through, from beginning to end. Yet, no matter how much I scrutinized our story, no matter what hypotheticals and alternate decisions I made, it ended the same every time; never together.

Liz was still asleep in the other bed. At some point, she had shifted over. It was the last time we would ever be in the same bedroom. In fact, today was the day of last times. It was her last day in Beijing, and I had to take her to the airport. It was a two-hour bus ride there and a two-hour bus ride back. Two days had passed since she had sung in our shower, and I knew it would be my last chance to clear the air.

"I love you, Liz," I said under my breath to see if by some off-chance the words finally meant something. They didn't. She didn't stir for a while, her light snoring filling the room.

After opening her eyes and batting them at me, she stretched her legs. Her bare feet peeked out of the sheets and then hid again.

"How long have you been awake?" she said as she extended her arms above her head and groaned.

"Not long," I lied.

She rubbed her eyes and then sat up. "I can't believe this is it. This time tomorrow, I'll be home. I can't wait to see everyone and tell them about the trip. It's been fun."

I had no idea who "everyone" was anymore. We no longer shared friends, or things, or a future, and there was relief in her voice, as if she'd scaled Mt. Everest and survived to tell about it.

"I know," I said, trying to bring her back into the present. "Can I say something?"

"About what?" she said.

"About everything."

I was apprehensive to initiate the shower conversation, to discuss what all had happened between us, and how we should deal with it, but then she very casually verbalized what I was feeling.

"It was nothing," she said, straight faced, as if she were reading a shopping list, or recounting the most boring story. "We both wanted to, and it was fun. Let's not dwell on it. Think of it as our last first something." There was a brief pause before she said, "It's funny, isn't it?"

"What's funny?"

"That it's exactly how they say. You know, time heals all wounds, rebound sex is reckless, and that you know you're over your ex when you can screw them and walk away as if it's nothing."

I couldn't tell if she was purposely being mean, or if she meant all she said, but this time I relinquished control. *Let her have this one*, I thought. For the rest of the morning, she packed and sang to herself.

When Liz was ready to depart, she said, "You don't have to go. I can get there on my own."

Her words stung. Not the words exactly, but how she said them, all blasé, as if I were expendable, unneeded, superfluous.

"No," I snapped back. "I want to see you off."

She didn't protest, and we didn't speak the entire two-hour bus ride to the airport. I followed her inside and needlessly hung around waiting for her to check in. She kept glancing back to see if I had left the airport yet, but it didn't feel right leaving before she had disappeared beyond the glass doors leading to the gates.

After she had her ticket in hand, I walked beside her until the security checkpoint. I was ambivalent because I sensed we wouldn't speak again after this. Despite that I was the one who had broken up with her six months earlier, this time felt like finality was on her side. It bothered me that I hadn't found the words to express how I felt, that I did in fact care for her, but that we had been foolish to try for love. I would never be the one to say the words she deserved, or to end things properly, amicably. After all, our first ending hadn't been ideal. This time, though, I felt the absoluteness, like she was the one ending it all.

Her eyes cut through me as she said, "You know, I've cried and cried until there was nothing left. I've been sadder than I've ever been in my entire life these past six months. Getting on that plane and coming here with you, and seeing you again, is closure for me. It stings, but nothing hurts more than that first time. After this, I'll erase you. I won't think about you or ever contact you."

"Why did you come here, Liz? I don't get it."

"Besides not wanting to lose twelve-hundred dollars? To see if I could face you without crying anymore. To see if what I felt for you was still real," she said.

"And?"

"You *never* happened, Liam, and you'll never know how happy I could have made you."

Without giving me a chance to utter another word, she turned around and left, disappearing into the bustling crowd of travelers.

Never is the most devastating word in the English language. It's absolute yet infinite; it's eternal yet void; it's crippling yet comforting. *Never* is the barricade of life journeys, the antithesis of love itself. But *never* is just one path, and Liz followed hers to the plane, back to her life without me, while I followed mine back into the city.

Part Two: Forever is Just Like Never

Nine

Twice in a Lifetime

It was lunchtime when I saw her on the same floor of my cheaper, air condition-less, bedbug infested room at the Homely Haven hostel. I was walking out as she was striding in. We brushed at the threshold, or rather she shouldered me out of her way like I didn't exist.

Her non-apology came as an unapprovingly sharp, "Excuse me."

I turned around to respond to her rudeness, but all I caught was her backside. Her wavy, raven hair extended past her neck and rhythmically bounced directly away from me, while her abnormally broad shoulders made me realize why mine ached. She obviously worked out. I figured I'd never see her again, so I let it go. I had no choice but to rush off anyway, since I had an appointment and had to catch my train.

Dozens of people scrambled into the subway car all at once. We stood, packed tightly like canned cockles, then smooshed as the cab reached capacity. Sections of concrete whooshed by as the train sped from station to station. My shoulder throbbed. The pain was a lingering reminder that alluring women still roamed the earth.

~ * ~

At 11pm, I made my way up to the roof of my building, the drinking hub of the hostel. My belly was stuffed with stale sushi I'd bought on my way back at a mini-market strategically stationed outside the waiting platform. These stores were everywhere and taunted weary travelers. I also bought two sixteen-ounce bottles of Beijing's permier beer, unimaginatively named Beijing Beer. As usual, there was an eclectic group of people from around the world chatting about their respective countries and their reasons for traveling. The climate felt surprisingly fresh, since the air wasn't as heavily laced with its usual measure of pollution. This was due to a series of storms that had rolled in days before and blown away the smog to some other unsuspecting Asian country. In the sky were clumps of stars, a rare sight in the blaring city of Beijing. The moon made an appearance as well and raged through the sky, trailed by long lines of muscly clouds marching to the pace of Earth's wobble.

The group was jabbering about the ethics of legalizing smokable drugs when she appeared again. She wore black cargo shorts, a sideways yellow hat, and a peach shirt with a daisy pattern that said *London* on it. She was 5'6, around my height, and slender in every part of her except her shoulders. I rubbed at the purple bruise hiding under my shirt. I suspected she was a gymnast but wasn't quite as bulky. She sported blue and white Vans, and her calves were sculpted to sizable muscle. Mystery girl was evidently strong, not at all petite.

Everyone in the room stopped briefly to scrutinize the new visitor stepping onto the roof. She stood at the doorway under the brightest light bulb, swept the floor with her eyes, and sat at the empty chair across from me. Her hair moved in the same bouncy vibrancy that had shoved me out of the way, but now it had a face. Her sharp features hinted at a highly intelligent, perceptive woman. My eyes fixated on her straight, pointed nose resting atop an exaggerated set of lips. The top lip was larger than the bottom one, making her appear pensive. She was the opposite of everything I desired in a woman: dark hair that fell in waves down by her shoulders like hanging vines, and uneventful medium-brown colored eyes.

Yet, it was impossible to ignore her flagrant British accent, and I hung on her every word.

"I'm Briana," she said, offering her hand to one of the guys.

I turned away again, so I wouldn't look like a lion who's spotted his lioness, but every few minutes she was in my sights, my mind frantically recording her features. She was into a conversation about music with an American, a guy from Idaho of all places, who was at the end of a Chinese language immersion program, and who sat next to me strumming his guitar against the breeze, adding a light melodic fragrance to our ears. I was jealous of his ambidexterity, playing an unknown tune with one hand while occasionally displaying his interest in the fascinating stranger through left handed cues. He was a talented showoff, and I envied him, because she'd picked him first.

I would tune back to the conversation about 1960's drug culture and then quickly glance to see how her lips articulated each syllable. She was so charismatic and focused on Idaho guy that, secretly, he must have felt giddy.

Then I heard her voice in my ear, "So how long do you guys normally sit up here and drink?"

She was speaking to me, and I couldn't believe this was the gentle voice of the rude girl who had bruised my shoulder.

"Depends," I said. "Till one o'clock, maybe, weather permitting." *Weather permitting? Just call me Mr. Mary Poppins.*

I was speaking for myself, for how long I'd be there, and I felt stupid for being so hasty in my response.

Someone else broke in, "I'll be here until the sun comes up."

Then Idaho guy added, "I'll be here a few more hours, at least."

"Oh, good," she said as she absorbed the rooftop enthusiasm, "I'll come back after my practice to see if you guys are still here. I'm done at 3am."

"What do you practice?" I heard someone say.

"I'm a dancer," she responded.

"A hip-hop dancer?" said Idaho guy.

She bared teeth as if we were dead wrong and said, "Something like that. I'm off now. See you in a bit." Her *something* sounded more like *somethink*.

She waved at us from the doorway and dashed down the stairwell. I figured I'd never see her again (yet again), since I planned on leaving by one so that I could be up at eight for my workout.

But I didn't leave at one. Instead, I found myself making up excuses for staying until three, in case she came back. After being treated to a couple beers, I lay down a beat with some drumsticks, a bucket, and the back of a chair. I rarely exposed this hidden talent of mine, except when fueled by the liquid courage of beer. My drumming was a relic talent from high school. The guys were impressed at my ability to make any surface hum with rhythm, and they paid me in free drinks to keep it going. For a while, there was an Irish guy present who led us through slurred drinking songs. Slowly, as the hours passed, the group's energy went from a high party buzz to a weary murmur. Some people left, some remained, and some new characters appeared. I did a few beer runs for the group in exchange for more free booze. After a couple frail attempts at singing, and three more beer runs to the gas station around the corner—as well as refusing a dozen cigarettes, several shots of a mystery liquor and unsavory seaweed chips—I asked for the time. It was past three, and I decided we had all been stood up by Briana.

I made a grunting noise as I stood and said, "Well, I'm turning in."

I reached down for my two unopened cans of lukewarm beer. A couple other people piggybacked on my cue and stood to leave with me.

"You guys aren't leaving, are you?" her voice cut in.

We hadn't seen her enter because of the poor light on the roof this early in the morning. The rooftop felt bleak since the bustle of the city had died down significantly, especially with the taxis and motorcycles parked till the start of the workday rush. Two light bulbs lit our early morning: the one at the entrance, placed there so nobody would trip on the minefield of uneven concrete, and one hanging over us in the middle of the space in a clothesline fashion so nobody would be impaled by the scraggly nubs of rebar sticking out like rogue hairs on a bald head all over the roof. I plopped back down in my chair, and Briana sat across from me again. Thankfully, Idaho guy had disappeared an hour before. No more competition.

Her eyes were almond shaped, and she squinted slightly as she listened to what the group was discussing. Now, it was all about the ineptitude and corruption of the U.N. in war torn countries, the fumbling drunk version. She was refined, educated, and an aggressive poststructuralist to the core. Her boisterous mannerism and quickness to argue the contrary matched her heady articulation. She wasn't drunk, so the rest of us made for easy intellectual pickings.

I was quietly admiring her, hoping my eyes weren't lingering too long on her, when she turned to me, and said, "Mind if I borrow a beer?"

"Go for it," I said and handed her one of my sixteen-ounce cans.

Briana happily guzzled it and said, "I need to catch up." She noticed my eyes studying her, and I couldn't look away before she asked, "So what's your name?"

"Liam," I said with no follow-up and turned my head in the direction of the group conversation. I was nervous.

She kept drinking, and after a while she playfully reached for my other can. I smirked at her, and she winked. I pretended it was nothing and continued to stare ahead into the group.

Then Jimmy, the Columbo lookalike, walked in and we focused on him. There lingered an unspoken consensus within our group that he was crazy. He communicated through a splay of words, and we couldn't figure him out. This was never confirmed, but he'd probably dosed a lot of LSD in his youth. We concluded, through broken sentences, that he was from California but had lived with Mexican shamans in his 20s, and that he loved to seek out brothels in the shadiest avenues of the city. Due to his current unemployment, he attempted to sell his computer to every soul on the roof. Eventually, everyone quit the conversation because Jimmy was annoying. He continued to whisper to himself even though nobody was listening.

There was Joe, the computer programmer from New York who, on his seventh beer, confessed: "I'm never going back. I'll die here, run over by one of those toy mopeds they call motorcycles. Or, I'll jump from a building as dignified Americans do."

Joe joked about death like an old man approaching his last days, brushing off the Grim Reaper's grip as if it were a child's hand on his shoulder. He'd followed a girl here years ago and never left, even after she left him. After his foreshadowed suicide, we didn't engage with Joe. We merely nodded our heads in fragile admiration of his inevitable demise.

The group was rounded out by tragic lovers. There was Shawn from D.C., who kept quiet, since he was eighteen years old and didn't have much to say about a life he'd barely lived. When he did speak, he said semi-intelligent things to balance out every else's life experience. Shawn knew more about words than anyone on that roof, yet he still had not puzzled together that no amount of dictionary work would make a boy grow. That's what protein and exercise were for—two things he hadn't discovered. He was draped in curly chocolate hair, à la Justin Timberlake but not as dreamy, and darting light-blue eyes, as well as a bony jaw that his face refused to infuse with adulthood. He carried his 115 lbs. of self-imposed veganism on a teeny skeleton frame.

Shawn was quiet until Amhali, his love interest, showed up. Her South African accent made her name sound like Ah-mah-lee, but in

America she would have been called Emily. It was easy to see why Shawn was smitten with her. She was half-Japanese and half-Dutch, buoyant, good-natured, outgoing, curvy where it counted, with a face befitting a model. Her single oddity was the conspicuous alopecia. She didn't even try to hide it. Perhaps she believed it wasn't that bad, or didn't see it as a problem, or simply didn't care. Amhali wore her baldness like a gangster wears a chunky chain to church, and it was likely she would be bald by 30. She was twenty-two at the time, and Shawn saw her as the most beautiful woman in the world. The way he adored her—with his puppy love eyes—made all of us ashamed to lust after her. The kid was totally enamored. Amhali, however, saw Shawn as a playmate. Her lusty sights were set on more established, moneymaking men. Sometimes she eyed Shawn as an older sister would a younger brother and spoke to him as such when we were around. But I knew they had fooled around, and slept together at least once, making their situation twisted and a bit incestuous. Shawn reciprocated her public passive-aggressive rejection with awkward kisses on the cheek, by asking her to dinner, and with spastic hand contact. It didn't help the little brother image he had going on. Initially, we all suspected the sibling routine was an act. Once when the lovers didn't show, I'd heard people on the roof say there was something way more sinister occurring behind the scenes.

    This was, of course, part of the short list of things I observed and heard over time. Before Briana ever appeared on the roof, my suspicions were confirmed when I overheard a hurried conversation between the two. They were inside Shawn's room, and I had no choice but to pass by so I could fetch my clean laundry from the communal machine. They must have forgotten that the walls and doors of the hostel were paper-thin:

Shawn: "Don't go."
Amhali: "We shouldn't be doing this."
Shawn: "Stay with me."
Amhali: "I can't. Don't ask me to."

Shawn: "Please."

Amhali: "I have to go."

Shawn: "To him?"

I sneaked away with a lump of guilt in my gut and scratchy shame in my throat, like I'd discovered my parents having sex. Minutes later, from my own window, I saw Amhali bawling and speed walking in the direction of the taxis. For a moment, I thought maybe she was a hooker, but then surmised that there was nothing wrong for a man to expect her to go to him at midnight. It wouldn't end well for either of them. Shawn loved her, but he was her side gig. He was her mistress, her mister. It was heartrending to see them together after that, but I never told anyone else what I saw or overheard. By the time Briana came along, Shawn and Amhali were relatively content sitting next to each other. It had been a good week for them. A newcomer would have had to inspect closely to understand how unfulfilled the two were.

Idaho guy reappeared.

"Couldn't sleep," he said. "Heard you party animals all the way in my room."

He began to strum out of synch and out of tune, but nobody cared this early in the morning. Each stroke of his hand was akin to a bumbling pied piper, one who'd missed his magic flute lessons yet still wanted the rats to follow. Briana focused on him. *Lucky bastard, striking gold twice tonight.* I felt growly by this point, but thanks to him the conversation shifted to music and Briana mentioned she played the drums.

Someone then pointed at me and said, "He plays drums, and damn good, too."

Briana turned to me and said in her British accent, "Play something, please."

But I didn't like being put on the spot and instantly lost my courage. The thousand gigs I'd performed over a decade vanished from me. All confidence vaporized.

"No, I'd rather not," I responded in my southern drawl which had become more pronounced from drinking.

Her raised eyebrows revealed an interest in the way I spoke.

"Where are you from?"

"Texas," I said.

"Okay, Liam from Texas, I implore you to play us a beat."

She bared her teeth to signal another "please." The weight of her expectation made me shift in my chair.

"You first," I said as I handed her my sticks.

She didn't hesitate, grabbed them from my hands and began to pound on the table. I could tell she was self-taught, and now I felt stupid for asking her to go first. Whatever I did on those sticks would make me the arrogant showoff.

After a minute, she handed me the sticks.

"Your turn."

"It's a drum battle," I heard someone say. But it wasn't. It was a massacre, and I frowned in disapproval at the comment. *I could fake being bad*, I considered, but everyone knew how I played. They'd call me out anyway.

I gripped the sticks and was apprehensive about the whole exhibition. I wanted to make a good impression on Briana. I didn't know her, yet she rattled my nerves. I began running a series of double-stroke rolls over the chair and table. I continued the roll onto my lap, on my thigh muscle and back to the table. It was a trick I used to impress audiences...in this case, Briana. I hoped she wouldn't think of me as an ass if I made my demo totally amazing. My hands delivered a flurry of strokes through a blur of twitching wrists. I could make any surface purr. After feeling that a lot of time had passed, I stopped. Briana sat very still, mouth agape at my demonstration.

"That was wicked," she said as I wiped some perspiration from my brow. The weight of the humidity descended on me all at once.

"Thanks," I said.

"Can you teach me?" she said and scooted her chair close to mine.

"Now?" I responded. "I was about to turn in."

My nerves were shot, and I was sweaty. A bed and a shower sounded heavenly, but I wanted to be with her.

"Teach me one thing before you go," she said, stopping my hands before I could put the sticks up. Her persistence was too much for me.

"Do you have two coins?" I said.

She fumbled in her pocket and produced two Chiang Kai-sheks about the size of an American quarter.

"Are you charging me for this lesson?" she laughed.

She dropped them in my hand, and I said, "Don't worry about the coins. Show me how *you* hold the sticks."

Briana hesitated.

"Aren't you supposed to show me how to do it properly?"

I didn't say anything and waited for her to do as I said. She got the hint.

"Is this right?" she said.

She was holding them incorrectly, so I began to position her fingers around the sticks, then I angled her wrists properly, pushed down her shoulders, and told her to straighten up. I reached around and pressed my fingers into the middle of her back. A solid layer of dancer muscle flexed and then relaxed under my fingertips. Her hands held the sticks in a perfect ninety-degree position, one inch from the surface of the table. I told her not to move and then gently placed the coins on top of both wrists.

"This is how I was taught. Hold this position without dropping the coins. It's called the matched grip. If your wrists turn the wrong way, the coins will fall off. The goal is to practice sticking without dropping the coins."

I let her hands go.

She concentrated but failed to move without disturbing the coins. Of course, she kept dropping them.

"This isn't something you'll get in one lesson," I said trying to reassure her. But she didn't accept my answer.

"Want to bet?" she said and continued to try.

After a while she managed some simple sticking without dropping any of the coins, a feat demonstrating her triumph over my challenge.

"See," she said in defiance. "I did it. What's next?"

"Keep practicing."

"But I'm bored now," she said. "Show me something else."

"Okay," I said, giving in, and began to show her some intricate patterns.

We did this for a long time, back and forth.

"Now, teach it back to me," I said to her.

Her brow, furrowed from deep concentration, softened as her eyes shot up at me.

"You're good."

She handed me the sticks and reached for my hands so she could teach me, but then a few prickly raindrops fell on our faces. My eyes followed hers up toward the early sky. Rain clouds had moved in and swallowed up the stars and moon. It was nearly five, close to sunrise, and the clouds jammed together, like they'd wrecked above us. A low rumble seized the city.

Someone from the group quickly stood and pronounced, "That's my cue. I'm going for shelter."

Others followed.

"What do you think?" I said to Briana, hoping she wouldn't decide to flee and cut our time short. I'd finally hit my second wind and wasn't nervous around her.

"It's typhoon season. I bet it will storm all day," she said as she held out her hand to catch an orphan drop. I did the same without thinking about it.

She stepped up to the edge of the building to get a fuller view of the bedazzling downtown. I followed. A net of humidity combined with the drizzle to form a creeping fog floating about the sidewalks. A childhood memory crept up my spine. I'd tried to breathe water while swimming in the ocean once to see if I could train myself to be Aquaman. I'd failed miserably, nearly collapsing a lung, all because someone at school had told me that fog was floating water. It seemed logical: if water could float, then it could be inhaled like air, too. For years, when I saw fog or mist, I believed if I inhaled too deeply, enough droplets would pool in my lungs and drown me where I stood. I forced the idea from my mind. The climate rejuvenated the air around us. There was no thunder anymore, the earlier rumble a faint memory, and no lightning, only wet air. We sat back down as the horizon began to hint of light. The squall had passed over us, and we were near the point when the sun peeks out to cast the night away.

The roofers left one by one, except for Jimmy. He stayed with us the whole time and barely uttered a word while he heard us talk about music, life, and traveling. He sipped his beer as if hypnotized, entranced by the city. I began to crash and tried to subtly end things and head to my room, but she kept me in place.

"No, show me more."

I was flattered.

"I'm about to collapse."

"Where's your room?"

"Three-o-one," I said.

"I was on that floor yesterday."

"I know. You bumped into me."

"I did?" She didn't recall. "Perhaps you bumped into me."

"You walked through me like I was nothing," I said.

I instantly regretted mentioning it.

"Interesting," she responded in a confused tone. "That happened?"

"Never mind," I said. "Not a big deal."

I broke into a fancy stick solo to divert the conversation back to something pleasant, like an encore before the big departure. After a while, I placed the sticks in her hands and positioned myself beside her. Then I wrapped my hands around hers and began to motion a double-stroke roll. Our hands bounced together on the table's surface.

"That feels weird," she said. "I can feel your forearm muscles twitching."

I let her go and she played on her own for some time. Jimmy was fixed on her.

She was handling the sticks, focusing on what I had showed her. Her hair bounced at her shoulders to the newfound rhythm. She was fully present, totally immersed, and gracefully tuning herself to the mechanics of the drumming arts. It was mesmerizing to witness beauty so absorbed. The first rays of the sun washed over our faces, and I imagined the rooftop of this ratty hostel was home, and that I wasn't leaving to the U.S. any time soon. I had never perceived highway bypasses as more than stacked slabs of concrete but here, atop of this building, there was an eerie opposition between the future and the old. She didn't pay mind to the dawn, as if a sunrise were something that should be taken for granted. For me, it was something I hadn't enjoyed in some time. I was suddenly awash with dread, fearing we'd lose ourselves, and that there was no significant point beyond this one. The feeling subsided a bit as first light illuminated Briana's face, and I could see that she had light-brown chocolate eyes, instead of the medium dirty brown I had observed earlier. Her hair retained its threatening raven hue, as if she'd been caught in a downpour of darkness.

It was 6am when we finally packed up. Like an idiot, the last thing I said to her was, "In case I never see you again, have a nice life." My bravery was ever dwindling.

She took my hand and thanked me for the drum lesson. Assuming the worst, I attempted to memorize everything about her.

"You never know," she responded, and dashed off, bouncy hair and all, as fast as she had appeared.

I sat dazed atop the hostel roof, hypnotized by the rising buzz of the city bustle and entranced by the early morning rays puncturing the night. I was annoyed at myself for buckling under pressure, for lacking the courage to get her number, or ask her out, or anything at all.

Then Jimmy blurted out, "You know she'll use you."

"What do you mean?" I said, not amused by his sweeping statement.

"That's what she did tonight. She used you for music lessons, and you fell for it. You got hustled by a parasite, man."

Jimmy spoke more clearly than he had the entire evening, and I thought maybe I'd adapted to his cryptic speak. There was also a chance the encounter with Briana had left me delirious.

"That kind of girl will use you up and leave you empty. I've seen a thousand of them. Don't waste your time. Now, if you want company, come to the Tai House with me. I'll find you a very nice girl. Here's my info. Call me after five," he said and slipped me a sticky note with his number on it.

I reckoned he carried a booklet of those in case he had to give out his details at a moment's notice. *That's something a crazy person would do*, I thought. *First his computer, and now, he's trying to sell girls?* I was astounded by his tasteless gesture. His cynicism was making me uncomfortable, but I didn't know him well enough to get mad. I'd never visited any brothels and I wasn't going to start then. I left Jimmy on the roof without saying a word. I would never see him again.

~ * ~

I was resting in my bed before going out. It was 8:15am, and I had an hour to catch the train. Briana crossed my thoughts, and I began to imagine an impossible love story with her, one where we lived happily ever after. But we were both thousands of miles from our countries, surrounded by dizzying potential, and I was certain the last thing from her mind was to see me again. Shelly popped into my mind. Long, lost Shelly. My first love. She had been a near impossibility in my life but had happened anyway. Liz had happened too, and I had been the impossibility in her life. I hadn't believed in love in a long time, not since I was eighteen. I refused to believe love was a possibility after Shelly, and less so after Liz. The universe, on the other hand, didn't need me to believe in anything—love being the inexhaustible fuel of fate and all.

Ten

Room 301

    My body was punishing me for missing sleep. I dragged through my morning and afternoon routine of exercising, visiting new temples, speaking to monks, and venturing into new parts of the city before I finally decided to go home. It was 3pm, and a brewing typhoon held the city hostage, just as Briana had predicted. The weather could turn on the city at any moment. My journey home was spent underground speed-walking or running through the labyrinthine tunnels leading from the subway station to about two blocks from the hostel. As I stepped out onto the street, the sky collapsed over the city in a cloudburst, like a tidal wave breaking to pieces. One block into my sprint, I nearly collided with a motorcyclist who ran a stop. Here, drivers tended to ignore pedestrian lights. In the States, it's the green or white unmoving stick-figure that signals pedestrians to cross at their leisure; but in Beijing, the figure is fully animated and, when the countdown reaches zero, a stealthy cartoon sprinter lights up to indicate that whoever is about to step onto the crosswalk should be running for their lives.

    I was drenched when I stepped into my room, so I changed into dry shorts and lay down to hear the rain pellets knock at my awkwardly small window strategically placed six feet up and without a ledge, possibly to prevent suicidal lodgers from splattering down onto the busy road. It seems there were enough maniacs checking in, that the builders thought to install windows like this. The oppressive humidity dominating this part of year was horrific. Pollution was a killer, and the long stretches of gloom were enough to end a person. The click-clack rhythm on the window made me sleepy.

~ * ~

The day was gone, the rain had subsided, and the early evening lull made me feel like I was back home in Austin, until I was startled awake by a knock at my door. I answered it wearing mesh basketball shorts. It was Kana, the Japanese girl who had escaped with Liz, Heather, and me from the psycho at the temple. Her room was a convenient two doors down from mine. She turned pink at the cheeks as her eyes scanned me from head to legs, but I was too groggy to cover up. I had become accustomed to her bringing me pastries, dinners, or some other exotic snack several times a week so I wasn't surprised to see her. It was her way of thanking me for coming to their rescue. We had an arrangement where I would teach her English and she would practice reflexology on me. I liked Kana. She was quiet and never objected to anything I wanted to do. That evening she brought sliced fruit to share with me.

My room was large enough for a twin-size bunk bed and an intrusive six-foot dresser, but I kept my clothes in my suitcase, an old habit of mine, in case I had to disappear fast. The top bunk was unoccupied since I'd paid to have the room all to myself, an extra two dollars a day luxury. The hunks of furniture occupied two-thirds of the space, along with a meager three-foot wide tile strip that ran about eight feet lengthwise from the left end of the room to the opposite wall-framing of the anti-suicide window. It was an unappealing layout, and Kana was the first woman who had been brave enough to spend any time in there alone with me. I motioned for her to come inside, and she walked in with her fruit, in the only direction she could, shuffled forward a couple feet, and sat on my bottom bunk. There were no chairs, and I assumed Kana, who seemed traditional, felt more awkward refusing my invitation than to sit on the bed next to a hairy, bare chested foreigner.

She owed me a reflexology and massage session to make up for the lesson I had given her days before. After I popped a couple pineapple chunks and strawberries, I plopped down on the bed facing up. She was a woman of few words, which I appreciated, and she began to feel around my calf and thigh for tension. We had done this several times before, so I closed my eyes and relaxed.

"That is sore?" she asked softly while kneading around.

"No," I responded. "But it's sensitive." She continued to press with her bony fingers.

After scouting my lower legs, she rolled my knee-length basketball shorts up to my thighs and then searched for knots. I was dozing off when I felt her hand inch up too far. The sensation forced me to sit up abruptly. Luckily, I was short, and the bunk was high, so I didn't hit my head. I snatched her hand as her fingertips landed high on the inside of my left thigh. Too close. She let out a gasp from my tight grip.

"You don't want?" she frowned, concerned about my reaction.

"Kana," I said. "What are you doing?" I held her hand in place, still on my thigh.

"I like you," she whispered, eyes downward. She exhaled a slow, meditative breath. I'd never seen her this flustered, as I was used to her stoic demeanor. Her plain confession had changed the dynamic, however. She was hopeful the rejection would pass, and I would change my mind and welcome her into my bed. Clearly, I'd been leading this confused woman on without realizing it. I was stupid for hanging out with her.

I stepped off the bed and stood, and she stood to face me.

"I can't, Kana. We are friends."

I put my hands on her shoulders and squeezed to reassure her she hadn't done anything wrong.

"Yes, we are friends," she agreed.

Her lips parted to form a painful expression, begging for me to change my mind. In her eyes, drowned a tortured soul in a river of crippling melancholy. Inside of them was housed an unconfessed loneliness, unexpressed to anyone else before me. I sensed she wanted to be part of someone, or something, but Kana had never met anyone that wanted her. Tragically, I think she wanted me to be that person. Unfortunately, her introversion made her elusive to others. She was an enigma. Around her, silence felt like the unbending of voice and thought. It was pitiful that nobody had ever loved or appreciated her, but she was expecting too much from me. Her hopes overreached into the desert of my unavailability.

She leaned in to kiss me, but I turned away.

"This isn't what friends do," I blurted out.

Her eyes welled up from embarrassment or heartbreak, or both, and I ruminated on whether I was passing up an opportunity with this gentle Japanese woman.

Then fate stepped in with a knock on my door. Kana recovered, wiped her eyes, and cracked it open. I stopped breathing when I saw Briana's face. Kana froze in place, not knowing what to do. I reached over her shoulder to open the door more so that Briana could see me, but there was a pause between us all as Briana considered my half naked body, my shorts, the fruit, my bed, and Kana. Confused, both women eyed each other.

It was all so incriminating, but I didn't want to miss the chance to see Briana again.

"Hi," I said with a wide grin to dispel the awkwardness between us. "What are you doing here? I mean, how did you find me?"

"Um, is this a bad time?" Briana said in her perfectly articulate British.

"No, not at all," I said, turning to my suitcase for a shirt.

I was losing her. Her voice disconnected from the situation as she stepped back. Kana stood at the doorway between Briana and me, waiting for us to finish our conversation.

"Well, you're busy, so I'll come back another time," she said and turned to leave.

"Okay," I said as I manically slipped my white t-shirt on. I stuck my head out in the hall. "Yes, please, come back later. We'll be done soon." *We'll be done soon?*—the sleaziest words ever spoken. "Come back in an hour," I beseeched her, feeling like an idiot as I heard myself talk. She would disappear forever this time.

Damn it, that's the end of that, I thought. But as Kana was about to shut the door, Briana blocked it with an open hand. A thud rang across the floor, and I was reminded of how strong she was. The jolt made Kana bump her head on the door, but we didn't pay attention to her.

Briana continued as if nothing had happened.

"Have you eaten?"

"No," I said stunned that she had come back.

"Okay, I'll return in an hour, and we can go for a beer and dinner."

"Uh, what are you going to do now?" I said, trying to keep her at the door. I had completely forgotten Kana who by then was numb from rejection.

"I'm going down the street to find something to drink. Do you want me to bring you something?"

I hesitated as Kana came back into view again. I was doing her wrong, but I couldn't stop myself from answering, "Yes, but seriously, come back."

"Okay," said Briana as her sinewy hand slowly released the door.

She turned to leave again, and all I saw were muscular shoulders and bouncy hair. Her British accent made any embarrassing situation seem like a polite exchange.

The next hour with Kana would be torturous, and she made no signs that she wanted to leave. No doubt, she was hoping Briana was gone for good. When we were alone again, she closed the door and sat back down on my bed. I had an hour to get rid of her, but she was determined to be alone with me for the rest of my damn life. Maybe, by riding out the awkwardness and rejection, she believed she would be the last woman standing. I lay back down on my bed because it was so uncomfortable to sit, but I didn't have the heart to ask Kana to leave. Outside, I maintained my polite demeanor, but inside I ached for Briana to return.

"You want to finish?" she said, thinking we could pick up where we left off.

"No, Kana. I think we're done."

She paused to find her words.

"And the girl? You know her?"

"I met her yesterday," I responded, somewhat riled that I had to explain myself.

Kana had more questions but couldn't figure out how to ask them, so we waited while she figured it out. Briana was the only thing on my mind, and I was nervous about what to do if she decided to return. I sat up and grabbed a change of clothes. Kana offered me some fresh fruit from the market as I began to take my shirt off again. She was embarrassed and turned away to give me privacy while I slipped out of my shorts and put on a pale blue polo shirt and khaki cargo pants. Still, that wasn't hint enough for her to leave. Kana sat on my bed with her head turned away until it was obvious I'd finished dressing.

Unexpectedly, Kana spoke louder than I'd ever heard her speak, but her inflection and volume were all wrong for the English language.

"You like her?"

Her tone begged for resolution.

I stopped rolling my socks on, and said, "Yes," as articulately as possible.

"But you like me?"

Man, was she obtuse.

"I do, Kana, but it's different."

"I don't understand," she said, lowering her voice to her normal whisper.

How could I explain to a woman who didn't speak my language that I was attracted to someone else, and that a platonic exchange was the best she could hope for? The situation was Liz all over again, except this time the language barrier prevented me from stopping it altogether. I imagined I was the first guy Kana had ever wanted, a foreigner of all people, and that the entire time I had known her she had been mustering the courage to make her move. Here I was rejecting her, a reasonable companion eager to do anything with me, so I could make space in my room for a strange British girl I hardly knew.

Had I known these were the last moments I would ever share with Kana, I might have made another choice, but a while later I heard a light knock. Kana shot a terrified glance at me, as if to say: *Please, don't open it. Please, no, don't.* I stood to open the door. Briana held two large beer cans and walked in without a word. She commanded the room as she had done on the roof. I sat back down on the twin sized bed, and Briana wedged herself between Kana and me.

Briana hissed, "Excuse me."

Defeated, Kana scooted to the end of the bed near the door.

"Sorry, my room isn't very luxurious," I said to Briana.

"No worries," she said as she took in the space. "I'm fond of this room."

Before I could ask what she meant, she targeted the fruit Kana had brought. "Oh, fruit. Is this from the market?" she said and grabbed some without asking whose it was.

"Yeah," I said, "but it's not—"

"It's so good," interrupted Briana as she popped various bits from the tray into her mouth.

Kana was pitifully staring into the wall. She had no interest in joining our talk, not that she could have anyway. I knew her face. She was devastated. Briana turned her back to Kana and shut her out of our conversation. This kind of body language was unmistakable, universal. I made an excuse in my mind about British mannerism, but I was in denial about the whole dejected mess. I was selfishly and destructively attracted to Briana.

In the end, Kana was forgotten. She slipped out of the room at some point, unnoticed. I never bothered to say goodbye, and we never spoke again. When I wanted to explain things days later, when I made the thirty-foot walk to her room and knocked at her door, an adolescent Russian guy answered. Kana had moved out.

~ * ~

I followed Briana's strands of hair down to her shoulders and understood why it bounced. Her wavy locks acted as springs with each step, rebounding off the curving landscape of her back. Under the fluorescent light of the room, her hair was jet-black. She didn't bother with makeup but there was no need since her skin was lightly tanned by the Beijing sun. She sported a loose, oversized cutoff t-shirt leaving her shoulders and pierced bellybutton exposed, as well as the same cargo shorts from the rooftop. Kicking off her tattered flip-flops, she plopped cross-legged in the middle of my bed, and faced me.

"Finally," she said, smirking at the empty spot where Kana had sat. I let her comment go, since I felt guilty enough. "What's her story? Is she an old girlfriend or something?"

"Kana?" I responded. "No. We're friends. I mean, we hang out sometimes."

"Oh, so you two aren't together?" she said.

"Not at all," I said, embarrassed that she had suggested it.

"Okay, because it was a bit awkward when you answered the door in your knickers."

I corrected her. "I wasn't in any knickers. I was in my shorts."

"It was odd. Plus, she had sexy fruit and everything."

She was teasing me.

I said, "We're friends. That's it. She's sweet but after what you did, I'm not surprised she vanished."

"What did I do?" she snickered.

She knew what she had done.

"Never mind. Let's talk about something else."

I was still in shock that we were alone and found myself rambling on about the temples, until she made a bored face. Then, in a panic, I said the dumbest thing:

"Is your accent from Australia?"

She squawked and said, "What? No, I'm British."

It slipped my mind that she had been wearing a shirt that said "London" less than twelve hours earlier. She nearly dismissed the comment but was amused by my mistake.

"It's okay. People in America think it's the rest of the world who has the accent. That's what happens when a bunch of poor farmers settle a country and then don't bother to educate their children for hundreds of years."

It was a well-deserved jab.

There was a pause as I admired the shape of her eyes. They were a skinny almond shape but couldn't figure out how to place her.

"What is it?" she said. "See anything you fancy?"

"Are you white?" I rudely blurted out. I was embarrassed at my very confederate question.

She crossed her arms and furrowed her brow.

"What is it with you Americans and your racial profiling? You don't see the rest of the world going on about people's color, do you?"

I was bright red.

"I'm sorry for staring so much," I said.

"I'm half white, half Asian. Is that what you want to know? Wait, is this your pickup line? Because it's pathetic if it is. You've got me alone in your room, so quit the theatrics."

"N-no," I fumbled. "No pickup lines."

I didn't know where to take the conversation next and was relieved when she suggested, "Want to view a film?"

"You mean go to a theater now? It's ten o'clock," I said, glancing at the 1980's public school style clock hanging above my suitcase (the hostel's only functional amenity besides iron doors in the expensive rooms).

Her eyes hardened at my response. She glared at me and folded her arms.

"Is it your bedtime? Am I keeping you up, grandfather? I can go, if you'd like," she remarked.

"Stop that," I said with slight panic in my voice.

She was enjoying my awkward discomfort. Then her eyes softened. "We don't have to go out for a film. I've got several ripped onto my notebook."

"Okay," I said, relieved. "What do you want to watch?"

"I'll be back. Don't go anywhere," she said.

"No chance," I responded.

She had to go upstairs and get her laptop so we could choose our film. When she returned, I felt jittery. We both sat cross-legged in the middle of my bunk, our heads almost hitting the bed above us. The awkward space didn't bother her as she called out random titles.

Whenever she paused, I tried to keep the conversation moving so she wouldn't threaten to leave again. Joking or not, she'd put the scare in me. Plus, it was obvious she was easily bored.

"Hey, how often do you have dance practice?" I said in hopes she didn't have to go any time soon and would stay with me.

"I go every day and usually arrive by eleven, sometimes twelve. We practice until three in the morning seven days a week," she said.

"Why so late? Those are odd hours."

"The dancers work at their day jobs and have to practice at night, or when they can."

It meant she would have to leave in an hour and a half to make it. I felt a pang in my gut at the thought of her absence.

"Do you have to go after the movie?"

"Not if you don't want me to," she responded with a devious undertone.

"Don't go," I said without hesitation. "Stay with me."

She was pleased with my plea and continued, "We practice at a studio, and they run classes until about eleven, but the owner opens it up to breakers after business hours. It's free, and we are too poor to do anything about it anyway."

"Breakers?" I said.

"Breaking, b-boying, b-girling. Ya know? Like the street dancing from the eighties but with acrobatics and flips and power moves."

Her eyes were animated, but I had no idea what she was talking about. At least I knew why she was so muscular.

"You should come see me battle sometime."

"What's a battle?"

"Have you never heard of this before?" she said with disbelief in her voice. "It's when two dancers face off in a cypher and judges decide on a winner."

"Cypher?"

"It's the circle where the dancers battle," she said, rolling her eyes.

I decided not to ask more questions so as not to push my luck. I didn't know if she realized it, but her words implied a near-future together...at least at this battle.

"I'd love to see that," I said.

"Alright," she said, "so which film do you fancy?" She poked her screen to show me three movies: *Superbad, Mr. and Mrs. Smith,* and *Howl's Moving Castle.*

"I love Studio Ghibli," I said. "They make incredible anime."

Her face lit up when I said that.

"Ever seen *Howl's*?"

"Of course, I've seen it several times," I said. "But I don't mind seeing it again."

"Do you watch hentai?"

"What's that?" I said.

"Never mind," she said. "What haven't you seen then?"

I said, "*Superbad*," and she hit play.

As she spoke about how funny this movie was, I kept watching her mouth move. I didn't want her to stop because her accent had me entranced. She was gorgeous, and I wanted to kiss her, but then Kana crept back into my mind. I didn't want to be the Kana in Briana's story. I was friend-zoning myself into inaction.

The previews began and she said, "There are some adverts. Do you mind?"

"No, it's fine. Let it play," I said and began to talk over them. "So, how'd you know my room number?"

"I knocked on all the doors in this building until I found it," she winked.

It would have been impressive had she been telling the truth. It was tough to catch the subtle sarcasm in her accent. Everything she said sounded sarcastic and theatrical, and made it difficult to gauge our conversation sometimes. I almost told her to stop with the fake but lovely accent, and to speak roughly with edges, like an American, so I could understand her. But her speak was damn charming, and I didn't want her to stop talking. I understood why the early Elizabethan courts had purposely put on this kind of speak: to separate themselves from the ruffians and paupers, the pre-Americans, and to make speaking an art.

"Is this your way of hitting on me?" I said. "Because it's pathetic if it is."

She expelled a soft snort and covered her mouth.

"Okay, hold on. I'm pausing the film."

She set the computer on the bed and said, "I didn't actually knock on any doors. This was my old room before you stole it. The other day I was on this floor to see if anyone was in it. I wanted it back."

"O-kay," I said in a slow, suspicious tone. It was strange how all the minute details were adding up.

"You told me your room number, you silly American. Or were you too pissed to recall?"

"I guess I did, and I suppose I was, but I didn't steal anything. I'm paying rent," I said. "Anyway, how do I know this was your room, huh? I don't believe you."

"I'll prove it to you."

She jumped out of bed and went to the six-foot dresser. Then she used the frame of the bunk to boost herself up. Her calf muscles flexed as she tiptoed for reach, making the sinews in her feet protrude. Briana possessed a beguiling symmetry.

She extended her arm and caught something, "It's still here." Then she jumped down with an old tea tin in hand and rattled it. There was vanilla incense inside. "This floor used to smell off from a broken toilet, so I kept this hidden up here."

"And why are you hiding incense?" I said.

"The owners don't like fire in the rooms. It's a liability issue, so the hostel doesn't burn down. They'll kick you out if they see you own anything flammable." She threw the incense at me with a mischievous grin. "Told you. I win."

"Okay, fine, you win," I said, amused by her competitiveness. "It *was* your room. So why did you move out if you loved it so much?"

She climbed into the bed and sat next to me again. "I left Beijing to travel Japan for a bit and then came back here," she said. "This is a fun city."

"Well, what are the chances I ended up in your old room?" I said. "I almost moved to another hostel but this one grew on me."

I paused. Liz flashed through my mind, then the psychopath David who'd tried to do whatever the hell he was going to do, then Heather and Kana. Poor, lonely Kana. But mainly, it was Liz who haunted me. Fixtures of my past were encased within the walls of the room we'd shared two floors above us, and here I was two floors down living out my future.

"We were one random decision away from never meeting," I said.

Briana grazed my hand and said, "I'm glad you stayed."

A shudder coursed through me, and Liz and our last memories were quickly lost to the abyss.

The computer was overheating, and so we confiscated a cheap wooden chair from the hallway and set the laptop in front of my bed. Then we lay down next to each other, our legs hanging off the side of the mattress, and propped our heads against my very thin pillows. Periodically, I would chuckle at something in the movie, but I kept thinking about our chance meeting and how she had sought me out. I fantasized about being more than chance strangers. But I wasn't foolish; nobody expects more than casual when traveling abroad. We had our lives to get back to, and the last thing anyone wanted to do was become attached because of a whirlwind romance.

I tried concentrating on the movie, but my eyes kept making their way down the features of her face. Our lying down made it difficult to see her completely, so I sat up. She readjusted and casually rested her head on my lap. It was a bold move on her part since we were hardly acquainted, but I didn't complain. She was where I wanted her to be…with me. I was no longer fearful. I wanted her and, surely, she wanted me.

About halfway through the movie, I cracked open the beer she'd brought. "Thanks for the booze," I said.

Briana sat up when I spoke and said, "I'll drink mine in a bit. I'm going to the loo."

She hit pause, slipped on her flip-flops, and left the room.

It was quiet and, without her there, the room felt vacant. Then, an overwhelming feeling of unwarranted dread swept over me. A voice in my head said, *kiss her*.

When she returned, she picked up her beer, sat next to me and, as if reading my mind, said, "What are you waiting for?"

"What? I—" I fumbled.

There is nothing more terrifying than a first kiss, even if you know it's a sure thing.

"Press play," she said.

But I ignored her and leaned in to catch her lips instead, grabbing her head with both my hands to press her closer to me. Had a fortune teller been present, she could have laid out the trajectory for my entire life with this girl. All the weight of the world was lifted from me, and our lips were entangled for ages. I was lost in the ebb and flow of our kiss. Her mouth pressed harder into me, as if she weren't close enough, and I was unable to detach from her any more than a disoriented swimmer can escape the rending nature of oceans. She was like the relentless stirring of water in a merciless storm. Without warning, she broke away, leaving me gasping, robbed of breath. Briana sat bewildered, speechless, still facing me, and then without a word she stood and began to undress. She stripped and threw her clothes to the floor, exposing the full curvature of her body. Strength was etched into her every limb from years of dance. I had never met a woman with such a tidal design.

Eleven

Kairos

    We hardly slept and, as the sun broke through the anti-suicide window, we lay next to each other, our faces practically touching.
    "Do you know what *bella* means?" I said.
    "No, but it sounds like a good thing."
    "It means beautiful in Spanish," I said and ran my hand down the line of her jaw.
    She approved by wrapping her legs around mine and scooting into me. We were naked, and the stickiness of our sweat bound our legs together. Every time we shifted, there was the odd sensation of our skin peeling off. We were as stuck as possible.
    "Do you know what *kairos* means?"
    "Is this another lesson, teacher?" she grinned.
    "Funny," I said. "It's an ancient Greek word I learned in school."
    "Don't keep me in suspense," she said. "What does it mean?"
    "It means disjointed time, or time-in-between-time."
    She interrupted me, "Like when people say that time flew by?"
    "Kind of. But more than that, it's more about falling in love or finding God. Special time," I said.
    "Oh, so it's about things that don't exist in the real world?" she teased.

"Let me explain," I said and gently ran my finger over her lips, but she swatted me away.

"You learned this at uni?"

"Yeah."

"It's not very useful. What do you call our time then?"

"Our time is ordered. It's *chronos*."

"You sound like a text book. Do you make it a habit to have profound discussions after sex? Because, you should know, this is not a turn on."

"No. I wanted to share something with you," I said, somewhat annoyed she wasn't taking me seriously.

She saw my frustration and twirled her hands in the air as she said, "Do continue, dear professor," in exaggerated Queen's English.

"We lose ourselves in kairos time."

"Wow, you are a nerd," she interrupted, "but I get it." Then she yawned, stretched her legs through mine, and stroked my face. "I think it's too early for philosophy, darling."

"Obviously," I said and then yawned back, embarrassed at my own rant.

I wanted to tell her that our meeting felt like kairos, that what we had was disjointed and out of time, and I wanted to know if she felt the same or if it was in my head.

I leaned in for a kiss, and she inhaled sharply, holding her breath until after our lips popped apart.

"What?" I said.

"Morning breath," she said as she covered her mouth, in case I decided to kiss her again.

I turned away and offered to buy her breakfast.

~ * ~

We left the hostel and lost ourselves in the endless tenement alleys for about an hour before we stumbled upon an old woman stirring a large iron cauldron. I had no idea what she was cooking, but Briana insisted this was the place we were eating. It wasn't anyplace, however. It was merely an elderly woman who'd set up a fire and a few wobbly chairs and tables on the sidewalk. I was certain none of her cookery could pass any health and sanitation inspection. Briana held a playful grin as two large soup bowls full of an odorous dark liquid were set in front of us. We sat across from each other. She wore the same cargo shorts again, same skater shoes, a tank top, as well as an earth-green baseball cap hanging sideways over her eye. She used the cap to set her hair back, and it brought out her almond shaped eyes. The sun hit the side of her cheekbone slightly, and a few rays of light grazed up her left eye, causing the almond shape to complement the almond color. I barely caught a flash of the swirl of light browns that dissipated as the sun continued its rise across her face. Her eyes dimmed as the sun faded.

The food smelled pungent.

"My turn to teach you something," she said as she scooped a black egg from the soup. "Have you ever tried *pi-dan*?

"Is that what this is? The smell is captivating," I said sarcastically, hesitating with my spoon. "How do you say it?

"Pee-don," she said, and nibbled the egg. "Try some, and then I'll tell you what it means."

I bit a chunk off to show her I wasn't a coward, but then my throat tightened. I coughed and spit the egg chunk into a napkin then slid the soup away.

"Oh my god, it tastes exactly how it smells, like moldy gym socks."

She snorted slightly, a habit of hers when she found something funny. "Don't be a wuss. Pi-dan means hundred-year-old egg."

"It tastes like it's a hundred years old," I said, trying to cut a smaller piece to eat.

"It's an acquired taste," she said and gobbled hers down.

I tried my best to eat, but I kept talking to mask my reluctance for swallowing the dirty soup. After a feeble dry cough, I playfully asked what she wanted to be when she grew up.

"I want to be a dancer and open a school."

"You're so dedicated to your art. I admire that. I played music professionally for some time but gave it up. I had so many people tell me that I couldn't do anything with it, I believed it. That's how I ended up in grad school. People usually can't live off dreams."

"That's a cynical approach, but understandable coming from a failed musician," she remarked snidely.

"Ouch," I said.

She was already halfway through her egg soup. After a few greedy slurps, she stopped and softened her tone.

"I mean, you could have done the music thing if you wanted to. You're an incredible drummer." She went back to her soup. "Some people should live off dreams, or else what's the point?"

"Is dance all you want?" I said.

She was on the dregs of her soup.

"I want a castle in Europe somewhere. One of those old abandoned ones that nobody would think of making new again. I want to fix it up and live in it."

"I've never met anyone with such a crazy dream," I said.

"What, you don't think I could do it?" she said.

"Oh, I'm not saying you can't, but it seems a bit of a long shot."

"That's why it's a dream," she said.

She cupped the bowl with her hands, picked it up, and tilted it toward her to get the remaining bits. Then she wiped her face with a napkin and said, "How about you?"

I was embarrassed about my very pragmatic dreams, but I told her anyway.

"I want to finish grad school and then write books. That's it."

"You can do that," she said.

"I guess my dreams aren't a castle in Europe."

She ignored my comment, peered down at my full bowl of soup, and without asking, she slid it over to her side, and began to eat my portion of the putrid egg slop. I didn't complain, and she didn't comment.

"That's not really a hundred-year-old egg, is it?" I said.

"No," she cringed and coughed. "It's not that old."

I'm sorry," I said, imagining the thick fluid dripping into her lungs.

"It's a preserved egg."

I couldn't believe how fast she devoured the rest of the abysmal liquid. At the bottom of the bowl emerged my putrid egg with its jagged flesh dangling at the side from my two front teeth. Its shiny, mineralized, oval skin was mesmerizing, like onyx, yet terrible for consumption. Amazingly, Briana gobbled it down like it was steak. I imagined the egg in its original state...untouched, raw, luminescent, anxious to be opened and released from its confines. *Dreams are like this*, I thought. The hundred-year-old egg is altered, transformed, and preserved in its final marbled state. The older it gets, the tougher its meat, the more impossible it becomes to recover its pureness. At its absolute end, it stands putrid yet intact, a testament to its resilience against time.

~ * ~

After our date at the soup lady's cauldron, everything changed: she knew when I wanted her to kiss me; she grabbed me when I wanted her to touch me; she made me reconsider when I was being obstinate; she contemplated my eyes when I wouldn't divulge my secrets. Our moments fell into a rhythm and time stopped. We were consumed in the *kairos* sense, but almost out of time in *chronos*. Without thinking it through, we had abandoned everything else we should have been doing in Beijing and, instead, we woke together, ate together, and explored together. Neither of us planned it this way, but we couldn't be apart.

We planned a mock battle at the subway station. Briana casually mentioned that she had done some martial arts in the past and wanted to work out with me. We dressed and made our way underground until we found a deserted platform, which was easy to do, since the trains had stopped running at ten. It was ten-thirty so there weren't many passersby, but occasionally we heard the clicking of heels or the squeaking of sneakers walking hurriedly toward an exit. We began with some touch-sparring, but she kept testing the limits. Every few strikes, she would hit harder. Then, without warning, she committed a solid roundhouse kick to the side of my skull, causing my jaw to wobble. For a second, I was certain I'd heard the strike echo through the subway tunnels. My face was on fire.

"Time-out," I said as I distanced myself to feel where the instep of her foot had landed. I was shocked she'd hit me with such force. "Damn, it's going numb. Weren't we supposed to be sparring lightly?"

Her face revealed some concern, "At first, but it got intense."

There was a double echo in my head, and the reverberation in the subway tunnel made it all the worse. I rubbed my jaw, moved it around, and tried to click it.

"You've trained before."

Briana lowered her voice, "I mean, I've trained off and on for some years now with my best mate in London who happens to be a sensei."

"That explains it," I said wincing. "You made yourself sound like you didn't know anything."

"No, you assumed it," she rebutted with a defensive tone.

There was no apology in her eyes. "You misled me," I said.

Briana stopped talking, and her eyes darted back and forth between mine.

I stopped complaining and said, "What is it?"

Her face softened.

"Your lip is bleeding."

I felt my mouth for blood and noted the smear on my index finger.

"I'm sorry I hurt you, darling," she finally said.

Then she cupped my face with her hands, closed her eyes, and squished her lips into mine – soaking up the red droplets with her mouth. The embrace was violent as she nearly knocked me off balance. Her fingertips pressed into my face, holding me still so she could lean into me. We were ensnared in the vortex of our disjointed love.

Twelve

Chronos

The sky broke overhead, and a torrent of rain hit us halfway back to the hostel. We sought shelter, to no avail, under some construction platforms running the length of a block. It was a labyrinth of pipes and wood, and we chased one another back and forth—dodging, hiding, hollering, unleashing punishing kisses on each other—until we were spent. Drenched, we sat on the sidewalk to hear the rain pound on the aluminum roofs of the shops. Without meaning to, some part of our skin always touched. The aggressive humidity of the Beijing season made us sticky, and anytime our skin peeled away, we reflexively leaned into each other. Briana had a camera and began to capture the few motorcyclists in colorful plastic rain gear weaving through the street to avoid puddles. They were like strands of rainbow gliding through the street with their kiddy yellows, candy reds, and fluorescent greens flapping behind them. There were also handfuls of pedestrians in umbrellas scurrying to their jobs. As it poured down, we sneered at a woman whose umbrella was crushed, and then bent inside out, by a wild thrashing of wind. It was as if a violent phantasm had descended on her. The big vehicles had yet to invade the streets, and the emptiness lingered long enough to make it feel like a ghost town, a contrast to the usual early morning hive momentum.

My clothes felt heavy, anchoring me to the cement, and I wished the rain would never end, that we could sit here for eternity. This was our last day together. We had stayed up, so we didn't have to surrender ourselves to the abyss of sleep. Our time was gentle, involved, intense, yet hauling us ever forward. Being with her, I felt thin enough to break, and our silence made these final moments feel delicate, brittle even, like the way dried rose petals will crumble when touched. As the hours began to feel like minutes, we held each other, paralyzed, terrified of letting go, uncertain if we would ever be this way again.

"We have to go back," I said. "My flight's tonight."

Briana didn't respond, so I pleaded, "You have to come back to me."

"Of course, I'll come back to you," she reassured me. "I can't forget you."

"It's not me I'm worried about. Don't forget *us*, this feeling, what we have," I said.

"You talk as if you'll never see me again," she said and pecked me on the lips. "I'm following you back. I promise. I'll meet you at The Colonies in three weeks." Her accent made every word she spoke seem unreal.

She often referred to the U.S. as The Colonies, and it would usually amuse me, but not today.

"It's not that," I sighed, trying not to taint our remaining time together, "but if my plane crashes, you should know I would have been yours forever."

Then she kissed me, but it was different. Her lips mourned for us.

~ * ~

I rested my head on her lap the entire two-hour bus ride to the airport. As her fingers dragged through my hair, I wished for some horrific cataclysm that would force me to stay a bit longer. But everything went smoothly, and we arrived early. There were no lines.

I was issued my flight pass without hassle, giving us enough time to explore the café upstairs. We shared a dinner and sipped two beers, just as we had on our first date. Then, the intercom blared that it was boarding time, and she kissed me as if it were the key to making the world stop. Briana broke away, grabbed a pen, held my arm on the table and wrote *Property of Briana P. Please Return If Found*, and she carefully jotted her email address. I wanted to hear her say she loved me, like I loved her. The anticipation made my soul ache. As we walked to the terminal, tears ran down my cheek. I wanted her to see me as strong, but I was crushed by the weight of my love for her. Again, I told her to come back to me.

"You are my gravity," she said as her eyes welled up. "I can't help but fall into you." Though her words made me happy, she never said the three words.

Then it slipped out: "I love you, Briana," and I kissed her until my lips throbbed. I was the weak one, obviously.

With those words, I tore myself from her and headed for the one-way glass doors. *Stop me and tell me you love me. Call me back*, I begged her telepathically. But nothing happened. We left it at that. I kept walking, since I couldn't bear to turn around and see her again. I would have crumbled into a pile of ash if I had. As I walked further into the terminal, I could feel the distance tearing me apart. Though my legs walked forward, seemingly on their own, my heart moved backwards.

I sat on the plane, fearing fourteen hours of solitude, terrorized by the possibility that we would never see each other again, that we would be banished to the past…to the land of ghosts and memories. I feared things would never be this good again. *I'd give anything to be with her forever*, I told myself. But *forever* is just like *never*.

Part Three: The Real Forever

Thirteen

Losing Ourselves

We sat across from each other at the table in my cramped one-bedroom apartment in Austin. Briana had been here for three months, and we faced the reality of our recklessness. Her visa waiver was about to expire, and she would be forced to leave the country without possibility of return for six months to a year. Our honeymooning was over.

"You can't leave for Canada and come back?" I said.

"They won't let me enter again. The Colonies are strict about re-entry. And what about money? I can't work here without a permit," she said, and I didn't make enough as a substitute teacher to sponsor her. I felt embarrassed to mention it, but she knew we didn't earn enough to make it work.

Love stories aren't supposed to be like this, I told myself, *but logistics trump love every time.*

Then she said, "Why don't you come back to England with me for three months?"

"I can't leave," I said. "I'm in the middle of my semester, and they'll kick me out of grad school if I disappear. I'd lose my job and financial aid, and it will all have been a waste of time, plus I'd be throwing away over a hundred grand I've put into my degree."

Briana was not impressed with my list of excuses, and her usual luster was gone from her face. *Love* was our problem—well, my problem, at least. She still hadn't uttered the three words to me. Loving her was the slowest poison.

The last three months had been ecstatic. She may not have said she loved me, but everything we did said otherwise. We were never apart. Romeo and Juliet had this same problem, yet they killed themselves in the end. Clearly, love was the villain in every love story I'd ever read. For the star-crossed lovers, it wasn't familial pressures or rivalries, or social expectation, or friendship, or God's wrath that ended them. The love for their families, love for their friends, and ultimately the venomous love for each other doomed them to the point that they would never escape Verona alive. Love is the oldest, most destructive force on the planet…from the first caveman who was clubbed to death because of his promiscuous life partner, to Helen of Troy who caused the Trojan war resulting in the end of the age of heroes. So far, what we had was all about learning conditions, and I was beginning to understand that there was no such thing as unconditional love. The world was more than happy to impose its restrictions on us.

"I don't have a choice then. I'll have to go back to England," she said.

Then I said something that would change our lives forever.

"Marry me."

These were the two words binding people for life in body, mind, and spirit, through loss and absolution. *'Til death do us part*, all lovers vow, enchanted by the idea that only death can void those words. But when things go wrong, divorce isn't enough to erase promises. It's just enough to break them all. Divorce is a pause, a reprieve from the destructive nature of vows turned legal. Though the words themselves are forever.

"What? Are you serious?" She was stunned as she got up and walked around the table to face me where I stood. "We've known each other for a few months, and you want to marry?"

We were nose-to-nose, closely examining one another's eyes for any sign of doubt.

"It's meant to be," I said. "It can work."

Briana held a blank expression on her face. She was thinking. Then she snapped back and said, "I want to be with you."

"Is that a yes?"

Her gigantic smile said it all. I lifted her up and then kissed her on the way down.

I was broke, so the next day Briana spent the rest of her cash on the cheapest wedding bands we could find at the mall: two rings made of white gold. Then we had our initials engraved inside the bands. Hers said *L4B* and mine said *B4L*

Nobody knew we were to be wed, except a close uncle of mine who wished us heartfelt luck. A week passed before the license was approved, and then we headed to the courthouse and made it official. We stood in our best clothes, pitiful for a memorable occasion, and handed the judge the paperwork so he could begin the ceremony. We got through it, but before we exchanged rings, he called for us to approach his bench.

"Can I see the rings?" he said, and I handed them to him, not knowing why he'd stopped the matrimonial rite. He held them both up as if assessing the true value of the metal. "These are white gold?"

"Yes, sir," I said.

I thought he was going to ask, *Are you sure?*

About what? The white gold, or about getting married?

But he handed them back with a straight face and had me slip the ring on Briana's finger. Then she did the same for me and the judge declared, "I now pronounce you husband and wife. Now kiss your bride."

It was a quick, bland peck since we were in front of the judge.

"You chose the purest substance on earth to represent your everlasting bond," he proclaimed as we were leaving. We stopped in our tracks at the threshold of the courthouse wondering if we had overlooked a part of the ritual. "I wish you happiness forever. Take care of one another. Treasure what you have, and never lose sight of what brought you together. If it's love, then keep loving. And never forget that these rites are sacred. No matter what happens, you are bound together for life in the eyes of God."

We were twenty-three, perfect marrying age, and with those words we went into the world together.

On our drive home, Briana was bothered. "Why did he say that at the end? You didn't find it odd?"

"I have no idea," I responded, still on a high from what we'd done. "But I guess you're stuck with me forever." I squeezed her hand and brought it to my lips to reassure her, like a good husband would do.

I wish I would have known this was as happy as we'd ever be. We were newlywed and had figured out how to keep Briana in the country without worry of deportation. After dealing with more paperwork, it was a waiting game. I had convinced my uncle to sponsor her, in case the pittance I earned yearly was an issue. I was so stubbornly focused on keeping her with me that I failed to think through the repercussions of our actions. There would be at least three to six months that Briana couldn't work, and survival on my meager stipend was impossible. My savings were gone from the trip overseas, and my graduate studies made it unfeasible for me to take another job. Being in love taught me a brutal life lesson: Money makes the world go 'round.

~ * ~

"I can't believe you," I said as I gripped my hair.
"What choice do I have?" said Briana.
She was much too composed.

"You are *not* taking your clothes off for money," I commanded across the apartment. "No."

"I don't have to do it for long. When my papers come in, I can get a normal job," she said.

I was pacing around the small living area, and she was standing in the kitchen trying to calm me down.

"You're my wife," I said. "You don't do this when you're married."

"You'd be surprised," she said.

I stopped in my tracks. "Hold on. Have you done this before?" I desperately wished I was wrong.

Briana was biting her lip. I'd never seen her this nervous before. "Yes," she said.

My voice cracked from the adrenaline and rising anger.

"I can't believe I'm hearing this." Again, I paced. "Were you a prostitute or something?"

Her face tightened with anger. "I'm not a whore," she shouted. "I've never done anything like that."

"You know," I shouted back, "some of this information would have been useful months ago."

"I couldn't tell you. I was afraid you'd see me differently," she said as her lower lip began to tremble, her entire face fighting the emotions back.

I lowered my voice. As angry as I was, I couldn't bear to see her so upset.

"Briana, if you do this, there's no turning back for us. You won't be mine anymore."

She walked up to me and placed her lips on mine.

"Of course, I'm yours. You're my gravity, remember?"

~ * ~

The next few months were torturous for me, filled with anguish and a runaway imagination. I had never set foot in a strip club, and never did. I imagined entering some forgotten underground themed cave and seeing my soulmate on a stage, naked, gross men throwing money at her. Then she would make her way down for a round of lap dances, their hairy arms and stained hands slithering up and down her shiny stomach and thighs. A quick twerk from her and they would bulge. Each time they touched her skin, they laid claim to her. She was theirs for five minutes, for a twenty-dollar bill. And then I would kill them. I would snap their necks. That was fantasy. Really, I would sit at home and suffer. The days she had to dance felt like I was waiting in the hospital for someone to die. Myself, perhaps. When she was gone, the fear of losing her plagued me until we were together again. My hands began to shake all the time. Nausea washed over me after every meal. I was being consumed by a cancer and couldn't listen to music anymore. All melodies were hell in my ears. Even after I confessed my nightmares, she never said she loved me. There weren't any attempts to reassure me that the abomination we were living would someday pass. When I told her that her absence made me feel suicidal, she lightly grazed my jaw with her hand and said, "Gravity, darling."

One evening, I was feeling as if she'd fucked every guy in the club and then came home to serve me sloppy dozens. I let her have her way and didn't move an inch. She used me like a shower is used to cleanse a broken rape victim, as if having me inside her somehow neutralized all those other assholes. We were in bed, and I couldn't shake the feeling that something had gone wrong with her, something before me. We had to talk about it, but she wasn't ever going to bring it up because that's how she was, the kind of person who maintained distance from emotional depth. Those waters were ice cold to her. The three words were like a devil in the fire for us. All I needed was a sincere *I love you*, and I swear all would've been right with the world. Nevertheless, I held her hand under the covers, always playing the pathetic fool, forever hopeful I would be the one who saved her from the Beelzebubs at the club.

After she arrived back from work, we would have blackout sex and screw until our bodies were twitching. Then we'd pass out. The heart-wrenched screwing empowered us for the time being. Eventually, we became desensitized from the friction, and every movement was like the death throes of a wounded snake. One night, after the empty sex, I couldn't sleep but kept feeling Briana's left leg twitching. Her skin was clammy and sticky from sweat.

We were shoulder to shoulder when I said: "Do you believe in God?"

"Trying to sleep, darling," she whispered in a fading British tone.

"I'm serious."

"Why didn't you ask me this earlier?"

She was peeved that I'd interrupted her flight to Neverland, but I didn't care.

"Answer the question, and we can go to bed."

"No," she said and let out a long yawn and sigh. "There is no old, bearded man in the sky dressed in white robes glowering over us and punishing bad guys after they die."

"That's the devil," I said. "The devil does the punishing not God."

"I don't believe in him, either," she said and began to nudge the pillow with her head to find a more comfortable area. Once she was still again, she continued, "Don't tell me you believe that nonsense. That's a deal breaker, you know."

I shoved her hand and nudged her ribs with my elbow.

"You mean the d-word?"

We never said the d-word—*divorce*. It was forbidden in our household. Mention of it fouled our way of life more so.

"Ouch, no. I didn't say div—," but she stopped. "I can't stand people who believe in fairytales."

"Don't be so calloused," I snapped back. "Belief in God and marriage both require a leap of faith, you know, and since you married me, *you*, my dear, are the latest chiseled groove of this two-sided coin. So, yeah, you could say I do believe in something."

"Fine, but you know where all the believers ended up. Married or not," she mocked, "they're all dead. See? God and marriage kill."

"Oh, okay, really funny," I said sarcastically. "Nothing can stump you. But if you do believe in us, then you're a lot closer to faith than you think."

Briana inhaled deeply, as if contemplating the secrets of the universe. "I don't believe in things I can't experience," she said.

I had her.

"You're here with me. You're experiencing me. Isn't love when two people can't help but experience each other?"

"You and I could still exist without the word *love*."

"You don't believe in love, or us?" I said.

"I'm here with you. Isn't that enough?"

"And how about unconditional love?" I said ignoring her evasive tactics. "The love between child and mother?"

"If love had to exist, I'm certain it would be full of conditions. And you made my point. Babies only care about learning the conditions of their environment, mothers included. It's the most conditional type of relationship—the one between mother and child."

"That's one way to see it," I said, "but the word *love* exists to shape out those parts that go beyond our material experience. It's about transcending conditions."

"How poetic of you to say that," she cut in. "So, you *do* believe in God?"

She was evading again.

"No," I said, my strained voice cracking from frustration. "I believe in love. And I believe it, because it's happening with you." She went dead silent. "Why can't you say it to me?" I felt as if I were talking to myself. "Tell me you love me."

The darkness weighed on us like a slab of concrete.

"No," she said, "it wouldn't be real."

"Why can't you say it to me?" I repeated.

My chest was tight, my eyes heavy. It felt as if we were at the airport in Beijing about to part ways again, but forever this time—the real forever.

"Why can't you be happy that I'm here with you? Why can't that be enough?" she said again.

Then I felt it. Somewhere inside her was a festering wound, and I was being punished for the terrible things the men of her past had done to her.

"I need to know why you can't say it," I said, with obvious desperation in my voice.

I hoped she would have pity and tell me what I wanted to know, but there was nothing for a while. Our outlines danced chaotically against bright headlights intermittently sweeping across our bedroom walls from the apartment parking lot.

The conversation felt like an underwater dream. It didn't help that we were lying there talking into the abyss, instead of face to face. But after she answered me, I sensed she didn't feel the same about us, as if I'd been part of all her life's hurt, like I was some great conspirator. Beyond this point, in the back of my mind, I was a vulture, scavenging for the dregs of her affection. It wasn't obvious to the eye, but we were tweaked from then on, a sidestep of ourselves. We waned from glow to glint.

"My whole life," she began, "has been a book being torn apart page by page, and I don't have more pages to spare."

"Briana, I'm not asking for more. I'm asking if you love me."

"I don't think we are supposed to be like that with one person."

"That's not true," I said. "I love you and only you."

"What makes you say that?"

"It was love at first sight," I said. "I couldn't stop noticing everything about you. And when I tried to walk away from everything, telling myself that there was no chance I had found someone, you showed up at my room and never left. That's got to mean something."

"Those things are arbitrary," she said flatly.

Her voice cracked toward the end of her sentence. I couldn't tell if she was crying, but it felt as if she should have been.

"You idealized some random details about me. Here's the truth: I was acting on impulse. You were a one-night stand to me. But the way you spoke to me," Briana's tone softened, "Liam, you held on so tightly and wouldn't let go when I tried."

"You chose to stay with me. I didn't force you. Why the hell did you bother to come to my room?"

"It wasn't love at first sight—I can tell you that. I don't know." She paused before continuing, "You can be so mysterious sometimes. Girls love a man in agony, you know, and your pain is so magnetic."

I kept hearing her words in my head, *You're my gravity*. Now I understood why she'd said that, why she gravitated to me. It hurt to hear her side of things. Now that the spell had ended, it was becoming clearer to me. I had made it all up in my head, all of it: falling in love with her, her falling in love with me, the *kairos*, our feelings, kisses, our sex. I couldn't bear to rip these pages out of my story, but she continued to do it for me.

"You know why I can't tell you?" she continued, "Because I don't know you. Because I haven't found you."

And here is where it stung the most, when she said she hadn't found me. Though she was the one I'd been searching for all this time, by a cruel stroke of irony, I wasn't her *one*. There was no universal conspiracy that'd magically brought us together. That was fairytale. I was a mere facsimile of her *one*, a close reminder of her past. But I loved her even if she didn't love me, and that was enough to keep going. She began to sob quietly—for who or what or when, I don't know. I wanted to reach out and touch her hand, but I knew she'd reject me.

"Briana," I said, anxious about how she would answer me. "Are you going to leave me?" I was willing to remain in a loveless marriage rather than let her go.

"Never," she said as she reached for my hand.

And this gave me all the hope I needed. All the false security was squeezed back into me. *Never* was as good as *love*. She could have said anything to me at that point if it meant she'd stay. I'd have snatched whatever word hung in the air and clung to it with my last breath.

Then she said something I never expected.

"You'll leave me one day, darling. I know it."

"Never," I said without hesitation.

I turned on my side to face her and struggled to say more. She shoved me back with the force of her lips squishing into mine, as if returning all my words to me.

~ * ~

It's impossible to accept that your lover wasn't always yours. Love is the worst torment. It's all the same: finding it, or not finding it with the wrong person. I'd arrived too late in Briana's story to stand a chance.

It was her journal that proved she didn't belong to me—since she already belonged to so many other men. And I don't mean the stripping. That was a purely physical thing driven by economic necessity and, though it hurt us, I don't believe she wanted to do it. If anything, the stripping was a band aid, or a mask used to cover up a painful scar. This other thing went deeper. Her journal was saturated with loathing and disappointment.

I could only guess what she wrote about me. Its rough cloth cover was littered with stickers from a couple dozen countries, symbols of the places she'd been. I read and read, but I was not in this book. I did not exist in her writing. I was not someone she wrote about. This hurt a lot. The journal was all about men she'd met before me, and the things they'd done together. There was a period in her journals, in 2006, two years or so before she met me, that mentioned her being in love. She could utter the word, her journal was proof of that, but she couldn't bring herself to say it to me. That hurt more than anything. It wasn't very detailed, but it was one of the only times that sex wasn't the focus of her writing. I felt a malaise when I read her words:

January 5, 2006 – Thursday

Met a guy named James at the club. He kept buying dances from me to keep our conversation going. Said he was a talent agent. He was older, like ten years, but could have passed for younger. He was fit. I met up with him at his hotel after my shift, and we bonked. I can hardly walk today. I probably won't see him again.

March 22, 2006 – Wednesday

Been seeing two guys at the same time. James the agent who tells me he's scouting for talent like mine but really isn't (I suspect he's a dealer), and another guy, a personal trainer named Eric who works at a small gym where I began to work out. Neither knows about the other, and they aren't serious about me, anyway. James is charismatic and screws like a porn star. Eric is a normal guy but sweet.

April 18, 2006 – Tuesday

I think I'm in love with James, but he broke it off with me quite suddenly. Screw him. I feel stupid. He found out I was sleeping with Eric as well and was livid. James showed up here at my apartment a while ago, and we fought. Then he fucked me on the balcony and left.

April 28, 2006 – Friday

Eric knows I'm in love with another man, but he won't accept it, and keeps showing up here after I told him I was done. He stayed over, and I kicked him out early in the morning after drunk rebound ex-sex. James hasn't spoken to me in a week. I left a voicemail telling him I was done with Eric but still not a word.

May 1, 2006 – Monday
I went to James's place. He was home. It was horrible. There was another girl there, and I broke down and told him I loved him. I think I recognized the other girl from the club. She didn't say a word the whole time but sat there in his lounge chair smoking and snorting coke. James kept serving me drinks and pills. I woke up this morning in bed with both of them. I feel numb.
May 10, 2006 – Wednesday
I told James I loved him again. He told me not to come by again, but all I do is cry when I'm alone, so I went back to his place one last time to see if we could talk. Nothing. He fucked me and threw me out.

It was sad. The pages went for months, pitifully building up to near catastrophic things that James made her do with him: other men, and countless women, not to mention the booze and drugs. By the end, she was not writing much. Their sexual exploits continued for a solid year until she packed up and left the city. In early 2007, there were dozens of entries regarding strange, random, one-night stands, a gross assembly line of regrets. Each man and woman was used to suture together the Briana I fell in love with. There was nothing in 2008 except future plans, mainly schemes to make it rich. Not one mention of our being married. Nothing about me. There was nothing about the present in her journal.

The journal was a loathsome remembrance, something a person kept after they'd had their chest torn open, and their heart diced up. There was nothing but denial and torment in its pages. It was a series of emotionally wrenching fallouts. Briana had met her *one*. In those pages were her memories of him, and all the men she'd met afterward—all the men she'd used to put herself back together. No wonder Briana couldn't say those three words to me. Love had been grotesque to her. The man she'd fallen for was the devil, but at least I had my answer to why she couldn't say *I love you*. She would never say it to me because it had been said to another man, her *one*. Those words had been used up on someone else. I'd fallen in love with a frayed woman who had no room to love me back. Yet, I couldn't let her go.

~ * ~

Briana showered at 6pm. At 6:20, her head wrapped in a towel, she pedicured and manicured herself with ruby polish. *She never painted her nails for me. Not once.* At 6:45, after walking into a cloud of perfume, she slipped into something lacy to go under her street clothes. She then packed her outfits into a satchel, and I drove her to the club for her shift at 8pm. Each time I dropped her off, we died. I wanted to take her out of that place. As the months passed, I grew dejected, and the quiet suffering that settled within me became routine. Whether she worked or not, my life was anchored by an unsubsiding despair. Regardless, I always hoped Briana, my wife, would come back to me—whatever was left over, at least.

On post-club mornings, she'd show me the stacks of one-dollar bills and twenties she'd earned. The ones were for her nude dances on stage, and the twenties for grinding on middle-aged pervs. I couldn't bring myself to touch the money because the stacks felt filthy, as if I'd get the clap if I touched them. I was conflicted: those bills bought her body each night and fed us each day. The stack was bigger this morning, and I asked how much she'd made.

"Twelve-hundred."

"How did you make so much?" I said. Her usual shift brought in three to four hundred a night.

Her face changed when she spoke, "I worked VIP."

"What's that?" I said, dreading the answer.

"It's when a client pays for a couple girls to be alone with them in the VIP lounge," she said matter-of-factly. I hated her tone when I would ask about the club, as if not knowing what went on in those seedy places meant I was an ignorant asshole.

My tone darkened.

"Alone? What the hell does that mean? Did you do something stupid to get that money?"

"No," she said, "but there's more privacy there."

But her guarded body language, her frigid demeanor, told me she was hiding something. Her voice was dull, unfeeling, as she spoke.

"What, so he paid you that much money to stand there and dance? You didn't touch him?"

My words flustered her.

"There was touching, okay? It's part of the job."

I couldn't hear anymore. I left the apartment in a fury to suffer on my own.

~ * ~

Briana called to tell me she was getting a ride home from one of the girls at the club, but she never arrived. I stayed up late calling and texting her, but no response. I passed out before sunrise. When she walked into our apartment at lunch time, I was numb.

She stopped at the door and saw me sitting at our small, square dining table.

"Before you say anything," she said, "I was drunk and passed out at Mandy's place."

"Who the hell is Mandy?"

"She's one of the girls," she said.

There was no further explanation. She just walked by me, dropped her bag, and showered.

I needed to leave for a few days, to detach and clear my head. She pleaded with me not to go, and that she wouldn't disappear again, but the sight of her made me nauseous.

"I'm done," I said as I brushed her off and exited. "I refuse to live this way."

It hurt to love her so unconditionally.

I was gone for three days, but I didn't tell Briana when I was returning, or that I had gone to stay with my uncle. She sent messages, but they were short and sweet: *Darling, come back—It's lonely here without you—You are my gravity, remember? Can I expect you home today?* I answered her messages, but mine were not so sweet: *Why should I? You'll disappear again. How lonely do you think I feel when you're gone? I'm not gravity, I'm the guy who loves you. I'm not coming home today, not until I'm wanted there.*

But I did go home. I was getting over it and wanted to surprise her. It was early morning when I entered the apartment, and it was on this day that I broke, my love for Briana reduced to a cancerous lump.

As I stepped into my apartment, my eyes would not register what they were seeing—piles of women's clothes strewn about, shoes, as well as a man's shirt.

Briana came out of the bedroom in the nude and was shocked to see me there. A blankness settled on her face.

"Why didn't you call?" she said as she tried to cover herself with whatever was nearby.

I couldn't speak. As she dressed, another nude girl came out of the room. I assumed it was Mandy, a fake blonde with a boy's haircut shaking from the morning chill in her crackhead body. Her ribs protruded from her sides. She had been pretty at one point but was now largely decrepit because of her lifestyle. Mandy was a rundown stripper, cursed with premature crease lines by her eyes, and wrinkles that ran like spider webs around her mouth. Saddest of all was the careless makeup smeared across her eyes and zit-riddled mug. As she picked up the clothes around Briana, I caught scent of stale smoke and old beer. They both smelled of sleaze. Mandy was bewildered at my standing there agape and tried to nudge Briana out of her trance. She knew things were about to go bad, so she gathered the last of her clothes, including the man's shirt, got dressed, and walked out without a word. Mandy was a fucked up mechanized sex display.

I was at a loss. My hands were shaking, breath racing. We stood facing each other, expressionless, staring into nothing, fearing whoever would react first. Her eyes didn't reveal a thing. Briana was an unspeaking water, ominously gathering her power, sustaining me on the brink of life and heartbreak.

My eyes welled up and gravity forced the gush down my cheeks. "Who was the guy?" I heard myself saying. Life was hell, a mangling of spirit and soul, a grinding down of my very essence.

"It was Mandy's boyfriend, but he left earlier."

There was no guilt in her words.

"Why didn't he take his shirt when he left?" I said.

"He had a spare outfit in his bag, I guess," she said. "I don't know. I think Mandy was wearing it."

"This was planned?" I said and broke into hysterics. "How could you do this! You just killed us!! Fuck!!!" I paused to shake the wetness from my face and wiped what was left over with my hands. "You're not a whore, huh?"

I felt disembodied. My skin was prickly, as if I'd jumped into a wintry lake. I was aching to wake up in my warm bed and find Briana peacefully, undeniably chaste, sleeping next to me.

"It just happened," she said, "but you're the one who left, Liam."

"Oh, right, it's my fault your clothes came off and you fucked two people in the three goddamn days I was gone? Un-fucking-believable."

The worst of it was that Briana was unmoved by it all. There was no panic in her, but there was a hint of ordinary concern. Her face was serious, concentrated, meticulously choosing what words entered our dialog. There was no sadness in her, no grievance for the death of us. I felt the claws of karmic vengeance puncture my soul, digging deeply into my gut, leaving me wounded forever. A mass decay consumed me, rooted in angst so profound that the very energetic center of my being ruptured. I scavenged for any sense of normality as my soul bled out, and for some reason I deliberated whether Juliet would have whored herself out to save Romeo, or if they would have run off somewhere had they no other way to survive. *Juliet is a whore, Romeo her pimp.*

"It just happened, huh," I said, struggling with words. My eyes must have been tired from crying, or I was delirious, because a demonic laughter hung in the air, like the way villains do when they think they have the upper hand. I didn't have an upper anything, however, since I was dead inside.

Again, I was disembodied. Images of the things that had gone on ran through my mind. I had no idea a person could choke on air, but that's exactly what happened. The weight of it pressed into my lungs so hard it felt as if knives were shredding my insides.

"Are you okay?"

"No, I'm not okay, damn it."

"I'm sorry," she said, "I made a mistake," and she finally burst into tears. There settled a deeply shameful, spiritually crushing devastation between us that day. It was an unsurmountable rift that would forever keep us apart.

"Did you sleep with him?" I said.

I could feel my face was swollen from being so upset. My nose was stuffed with mucous, and my heart was shattered.

"No, but I did with her," she said. "I'm sorry, darling. I was drunk and on pills, and I thought if I didn't sleep with him it was okay."

I lost it. She was lying.

"God damn it," I screamed. "You can't be serious. How could you think if you were so fucking high? Did you touch him?" I said, feeling a wave of gelid emptiness spread through me.

"I don't remember," she said. "I may have."

I shoved past her into the bedroom. Three people had slept there. I yanked the sheets off the bed, walked out, and threw them at Briana.

"Keep your disgusting sheets," I said. "Get out of my apartment. We're done."

It was difficult to understand her since she was breathing erratically as she ran to me, grabbed me by the arm to keep me from going back to the room, and said, "Don't do this. I didn't touch him."

"I don't believe you," I said and shoved her away.

Her touch felt like death. I walked back into the room to see if I had missed anything and spotted her camera lying on the floor by the bed. I picked it up, turned it on, and then began to sift through dozens of pictures of nearly every sexual act imaginable by three people.

After viewing a half-dozen cock pics, a heavy, primal howl rose out of my chest and burst through my vocal chords as I threw the camera against the wall, smashing the porno reel to bits. Briana stood in the doorway sobbing.

"I'm so sorry," she said in a broken, raspy voice. She hid her face. "I'm so, so sorry."

"I would give anything to have never met you," I said, totally crushed inside, "I wish you had never knocked on my room. You goddamn liar. If you were so fucked up, then how did you take those pictures? How did you do all those things if you were so wasted? You obviously planned all of this."

There were no answers to my questions because she had been caught. This was all premeditated. She wasn't trashed enough to have lost control. The posing was proof enough. Had I not walked in so early in the morning, she may have gotten away with it. She would have never told me, surely deleting all proof in the camera before I got to it. I didn't bother asking how many times she had done this to me, but I knew this wasn't her first. Nothing was ever her first time. Briana continued to sob into her hands and a muffled, "I'm sorry", escaped her. But I wasn't fooled anymore. Her dejection wasn't from our death or from hurting me. She was ashamed of being caught, of being exposed as a great deceiver.

"You have no idea what you've done. If you don't go, then I will," I said.

"I have nowhere to go," she said. "But please, don't leave. This is our home."

"Not anymore. You're not my wife. You're nothing."

I walked out of the bedroom, removed my wedding ring from my finger, and slammed it on the table.

"Here. Take your ring back. Sell it, trash it, I don't care."
She ran to the table and grabbed it.
"Don't," she implored. "Put it back on. Please."
She tried to grab my hand to replace the ring, but her touch was so repulsive, I reflexively yanked my hand away, and the ring fell to the floor. She stood tearfully, my unspeaking water.
"You're free, Briana. This is your out."
"But I don't want out."
I kicked the ring away and it bounced off her leg. Our unbreakable symbol of love landed by her feet. It was mere flashy metal at this point, its meaning lost to impulse and flesh. Briana stood frozen, trembling. I grabbed what I could and walked out, which wasn't much anyway, since I was so damn poor. The finality of her actions made the world bleak, and there was insuperable distance between us. I left every good part of myself on the floor of that apartment, at the naked feet of my lost love.

Fourteen

Never Let Go

    It was impossible to feel as real as I did when I'd first fallen in love with Briana. Since I'd left, things hadn't been good again. There was a time, in the beginning, when Briana was life. There was nothing now.
    Not seeing her every day was killing me, yet being in her presence would be worse. I doubted she'd stopped sexing those other people, and my leaving was the free pass she'd been waiting for this whole time. I wished we could pick up where we left off and pretend her cheating had been an amoral act of nature we could leave behind us.

~ * ~

    It's three-thirty in the morning, and I'm startled by the force of my own heavy gasping. It's as if I'm coming up for air after a long dive, but I'm in bed. My voice and body aren't mine—yet I manage to keep my eyes shut, and then quickly fall into a dream.
    I'm nine years old and want to live underwater, because a kid at school tells me it's possible. *Of course, you can breathe water*, he says. *You can't drown from fog, right? If you practice enough, you can live in the ocean like Aquaman.* Gullibility is my teacher. I wade into the shallow part of the beach where fledgling waves feel more like silky rose petals against my skin rather than the barbed liquid

found at the depths. I squat and dig my toes into the quicksand, ten tiny anchors, then submerge until the water line begins to tickle at my nose hairs, and I wait until a wave blankets my face. As I'm splashed, I begin to inhale and go under, expecting that as the stream of air enters my body some water will go with it, fooling my lungs into using aqua instead of air for its oxygen supply. My lungs seize. Then my legs, with a mind all their own, spring me upward for air. I cough up water for a couple minutes before stubbornly trying again. By my eighth try, it feels as if there's a broken bottle lodged inside my chest. I can't stop coughing. My hope of being a submersible warrior is lost to waves that can't help but roll back into the sea. I've had enough of this dream, but then Briana walks the shore. She's in faded black shorts, the same shorts she had on when we met, and her shirt is blue with a Union Jack print splashed all over it. She's waving me over, but the quicksand has me. My feet are shackled at the ankles by sand and by the spiteful water. I wave back and try to get her to come in, but she doesn't recognize me. I'm a kid, and she doesn't see me anymore, so she keeps walking until disappearing beyond some large rocks. She's gone, and I feel the broken bottle in my chest again. A wave slaps against my back with such force that my feet pop out of their sandy fetters. I'm free, but she's vanished. I'm awake, but she's away.

~ * ~

The things we believe as children, the things adults neglect to mention, are impossible, are what we dream about. I wish my parents would have told me: *One day you will meet a girl, and you will love her more than God loves his angels, but even that won't be enough to keep her.*

~ * ~

The Miami air invades my room around one in the morning. The breeze sneaks through my cracked window and carries the ocean with it. My eyes pop open, and I rub them. I can almost feel the sand grinding into my eyelid skin. The salty humidity is wretched. It scratches at everything. It's in the air, in clothes, in food, in sleep, on the hood of cars. There is no getting away from it. Fits of nostalgia overwhelm me at the sight of waves, or the smell of sand and salt, or anything that sounds like crashing water. My childhood is the culprit. Salt and sand, in fact, have a smell, but detecting their scent is an inborn sense possessed by those birthed near oceans. It's our superpower and our curse. The smallest waterfalls have a gravitational effect, and I can't help but place seashells of any shape or size up to my ear to hear the white noise. The sound in shells, of course, doesn't exist except as an aural illusion—a product of my resonating vascular system and ambient sounds caught between spiraled shell and flesh.

The Pacific feels different from the Atlantic. My return to the Pacific, after being absent from it for so long, was like winter stroking my insides with its icy claws. The Atlantic was like a lost friend's warm embrace. Once, while winter camping in Switzerland's mountains, I jumped into crystalline water and was surprised at how the shock of the cold made my body feel as if it were being wrapped in a fuzzy wool blanket. That lake had its own way of affecting a person. Some claimed it was the perfect amount of icy, while others complained that it felt as if they'd jumped into a pit of broken glass.

~ * ~

Dreams take me back to when I would test myself in Olympic pools as a kid; when the ocean wasn't there for me. I dive deep and, as I touch the floor of the pool eight feet down, my brain feels as if it's vibrating in my skull, begging the rest of me for a lungful of air. Then I flop around and frantically paddle with my feet before really knowing which way is up. My hands automatically grasp toward the surface, the life-preserving movements reflexive and primordial, but I barely make it back. It's heaven when the pressure of the chlorinated water bursts around me, and the air recklessly fills me with life. All I need is one dive to remind me of the sluggishness of the water world.

That world fights my every movement, all the way up to the inevitable life sustaining gasp. Ironically, it repulses my downward thrusts after diving in, as if expelling me from some ancient treasure, but then works to keep me at the bottom despite that there is no spectacular discovery to behold. Slowly, the water robs me of air, making me lightheaded. Diving is more dangerous as an adult. The body grows lethargic, joints degrade, fears grow larger, and lungs fail to hold life as tightly as the year before. The strength of the water persists, yet the spirit and mind wither.

~ * ~

I've been lucid dreaming, and the ghost of her comes to caress me awake. She tells me it's all been in my head, that it's not real. She tried, she said, to stir me, but I kept fighting to stay asleep. It wasn't really her. She was a dream. Real Briana hasn't caressed me in forever and teardrops roll heavily down my face. I want to speak to her, but there is nothing to be said. There is no going back. I can't help but think of *The Butterfly Effect*, that haunting film. Maybe if I write passionately enough, if I cry loud enough, if I bleed enough, these words will take me back to the days when we lived drenched and intoxicated by possibility.

~ * ~

Here are the things I wanted to say to you when I could find words again, when the trauma began thinning out of my life, when I was not being asphyxiated by heartbreak, and sleep began to be a healing event again rather than a reminder of your absence:

Dear Briana,

I was foolish to think we met for a reason. This can't be it, can it? Was everything that happened just to show us love's desolation? There was life in us, but you let go, or didn't know, or care. I keep seeing this picture in my mind when we were overseas, at the hostel, during our third day together. It was morning. We had showered after some serious lovemaking. It was love for me back then, you know. I suppose it wasn't anything for you. We walked downstairs, but I forgot something in my room, so I ran back up to get whatever it was, my subway pass, I think, and as I bolted back down there were these patterned, decorative holes in the brickwork. As I passed the bricks, I saw you standing below me on the sidewalk. The sight of you made me stop, like I was seeing you for the first time all over again. You shook me to my core, and I could feel all those things they say happen in love stories—the fluttery chest, the butterfly stomach, the foggy eyes that ache to be rubbed out because you can't believe what you're seeing. I knew you were the one. As I made it downstairs, you turned around, smiled at me, and extended your hand. When we touched, it was an affirmation of all the beauty in the world. It was love. It's difficult for me to accept it wasn't. We grasped for each other every chance we had. We walked down the street giving off this energy to everyone who passed us, and I would periodically follow their gaze to see if they knew it too, and I believe they did. Their faces said so. Surely, they must have sensed what they were seeing was arcane—two people gripped by an epic love, destined to walk together. What we had then is talked about everywhere, sometimes seen in myths, rarely experienced. But that was all in my head. I lived it all by myself. You didn't see it, because if you had, there is no way I would have found you like I did that morning. Instead of living out our story, our spectrum of love, I'm drowning in this monochromatic abyss. I wish I'd never met you. You're the reason fairytales had to be invented, because you make reality into a monster. You break the universe's heart with every breath.

    Your soon to be ex-husband,
    Liam

~ * ~

You said I was a fling, a one-night stand gone wrong. Yet, you stayed. You claimed love was imaginary, yet you married me. It makes no sense. We made no sense.

~ * ~

If fairytales ran like life, they'd go like this:
Once upon a time there was a princess who was tired of meeting bland princes. It was always the same: they'd show up with gifts, tell her how pretty she was, profess their love, and speak to her father about marriage. The princes would bid a dowry—such as vast sums of gold or land—for the princess's hand. Naturally, the king would accept, but then the princess would run away for a week, or until the façade had blown over. Of course, the king was angry, but what could he do? He had to wait for the next prince. The king was a patient man, hopeful his daughter would settle. The princess, however, yearned for her true prince to come. One day, her true prince finally arrived at the castle in shining armor, riding a virile white stallion. He knew instantly that she was his princess, his soulmate, his one. The princess sized him up as another hollow suitor, and then locked herself in her room to plot her escape. The next morning, with the princess gone, the king broke the news to the prince. The poor prince rode away heartbroken, confused, and with a sweltering bitterness. Having lost his true love, the prince rode off a deadly cliff, damning both him and his horse to an eternity of torment in the underworld. A week later, the princess returned home to wait for her true prince in her dimly cobbled room. She waited her whole life until she died alone, calloused, old, and ugly. The End.

Part Four: Nothing Lasts Forever

Fifteen

Gabby

The ocean is the two-face of the earth, the Jekyll and Hyde of the planet. It's gentle in the mornings when every ounce of water gifts the world some long lost conch or hermit crab. Yet, after sunset, when the moon rises and drags the water back, the waves roar in protest. Days at the beach are like the sweetest dreams, but other times are spiked nightmares. My childhood memories revolve around the Pacific Ocean—ironically named, since it's an abysmal, raging body whose thunderous waves batter the shore. I was born near the Pacific and walked its shores with my father, who was born there, as he also did with his father. The water was the source of the most phantasmal slumber. When the waves were no longer visible, when all light had vanished, the crunching of earth resonated in my child imagination. Each clap was a terrific footstep descending upon the sand. While I slept, the echoes of a distant god's stride seemed to ravage the planet. Sometimes, when I stalked crabs and starfish, the Pacific's cool waters dared my feet to step deeper into the vastness, until my father warned me, "Don't get closer or you'll go under." The water tempted me at times when the waves spoke gently, massaging the speckled rocks and shells up the beach, placing them within my grasp. On days like this, the beach was a place of healing.

~ * ~

Miami had been kind to me, and months had passed since I'd left Briana. One day there was a package in my mailbox addressed from my uncle in Texas. There was no letter or explanation, but none was needed. Inside was my wedding ring with the engraved *B 4 L, Briana for Liam*. The *4* meant *forever*—that we belonged together forever. I figured my uncle had taken pity on her (he'd always been a pushover) and mailed the ring to me. I was agitated but figured this was an isolated incident, so I let it go. There was no anger as I held the ring, only a dull ache. Briana wore our emblem of love the morning I found her with naked Mandy. The ring was the ultimate witness to heartbreak and destruction. I set it aside for a while, but it gradually began making appearances on my dining table, bathroom counter, and nightstand. I pondered over the tragic symbolism of the metal. Hypnotized, I marveled at its ironic circularity.

Eventually, it found its way into my pocket, and I began carrying it everywhere. I made a necklace for it, for fear of losing it, and hid it under my shirt as a reminder of that morning. I don't know why I tortured myself, but it hung around my neck long enough that I stopped feeling it…its presence tattooed on my skin. The ring was my last connection to Briana, and it rested on my chest as an extension of her, as an invisible emotional appendage. The first time I found myself alone with another woman, the ring was there as witness for me as it was for Briana. Her name was Gabby, and she was married, too. We were lying in bed, in her house, while her husband worked.

"Why do you wear that?"

I was unsure of how to respond.

"Tell me what happened, *amor*."

She was on her side, a powerful Latina with Native American hair, facing me, nestled in my left arm, caressing my left cheek, while

I was on my back staring into the swirly patterns on her white ceiling. The sunlight sneaked through shuttered blinds and hit her wall. The shadowy effect transformed the sheetrock clumps into mini-icicles dangling on ledges, ready to drip on us at the slightest bump. The illusion gave me a headache.

"Tell me," she said again. "*Por favor.*"

I wasn't ready to answer her question. She wanted to know more about me, but I didn't know what I wanted.

"I haven't told anyone except an uncle," I said, cheating her out of my history.

Speaking about it felt too cumbersome. She must have sensed something was wrong because, she dropped the subject.

"Sorry," she said as she rested her hand on my chest and fondled my ring.

A sharp feeling of disgust came over me, and I said, "Don't touch it, okay?"

She let it go without protest and never brought up the ring again. I didn't know how to explain it anyway.

I wasn't much into Latin women, but Gabby was the exception. Not because I was irresistibly attracted to her, but because she appreciated boundaries and distance. She didn't get attached and was more experienced. I wasn't her first mister, which didn't bother me at all. She was my first mistress, however, and she relished this status…as if she was obligated to indoctrinate me into this ancient ritual practice. Gabby may not have counted as a mistress but was the closest thing since, technically, I was still married. Surprisingly, she didn't want to ruin her marriage, at least not outwardly. Of course, lying naked in bed with me meant she'd done enough damage. Nevertheless, she wanted to maintain the façade and keep her family together if possible.

"Sex is the wrecking ball of all human relationships," she told me once, yet still couldn't give up her double life with me.

"How long do we have?" I said.

"An hour, but I'll tell you when it's time."

"Why do you do this, Gabby?" I said as I got up and began to dress.

"For the same reasons you do, *mi amor*," she responded.

I recalled when her accent first stood out, like she was trying to talk with a quarter in her mouth. Now, I barely heard it.

"No," I said. "I want to know why *you* do this."

"Get back in bed," she said. "If I tell you, you have to tell me your reasons."

I obeyed but wasn't completely honest with her. I fed her a watered-down version of my past, but she understood what I'd been through.

"I've seen this before," she said. "This sickness of love. You're a shadow of yourself, and I wish I could have known that other you who loved a woman so deeply."

Her accent felt edged and pointed, like a shank knife.

"That doesn't help, Gabby," I said, trying to shift our conversation.

"Nothing can help you," she said. "She's a fool for abandoning and ruining something so rare."

Me or the love?

"I'm the damn idiot for believing it meant something," I said, "but it really wasn't that amazing. Love is the darkest place."

"I meant you, *amor*," she said in the most final way. "You're the thing that's been lost to her, to the world, to everything. And all is lost to you, too, isn't it?"

"Things have always been lost," I said. "I think in Spanish it's called *entropia*. Entropy. The collapse of all things. It's a law of the universe."

"It's not the law of love, *amor*."

"Yes, even love."

Our confessions revealed how easy it was to find ourselves in her bed. I was deceived and broken-hearted, while she enjoyed the thrill of deceiving without breaking hearts. She did it out of neglect and boredom, for the sexual ecstasy and pure adrenaline rush. I did it out of guilt and rejection.

The idea of pitying her husband vanished when I realized he deserved it for being naïve enough to believe that marriage and love were sacred, for denying that human nature trumps all. He would never understand that both those things were relics. From the way Gabby spoke of him, I gathered he was a simpleton, a jerk who fumbled through life in a panic. He was broke, and full of regret, and wasn't entitled to any kind of fidelity.

Gabby's story was common. By eighteen, she got pregnant and was forced to marry the donor, her new fling and future husband at the time. Her belligerent, Catholic father did the forcing. The machismo for his daughter ran deep, along with the double standard and hypocrisy that clotted the veins of the old Latin culture. Now, she was the lonely, dejected housewife of a blue-collar misogynist who left her alone with three kids 50 hours a week. His appeal, Gabby said, was in his predictability. He was like a badger, home every evening for his dinner, beer, and television, unless he had to travel for the rare high paying construction job.

At twenty, the marriage had suffocated her, and by twenty-two, when she met me, she was the one doing the suffocating. We met while I was working as a substitute teacher for continuing education programs run by community outreach facilities for the underserved in Hialeah, all subsidized by the government, of course. Many of these "non-profits" paid as much or more for part-timers than the major colleges or universities with the same outreach programs, but with half the workload and a fraction of the competition. It was an easy way to make rent without having a graduate degree.

One day, I was called to this rough part of Miami, where illegal immigrants could complete language, culture, GED, and citizenship courses without being questioned for paperwork. Gabby was an undocumented ball of fire. Her rounded curves and long legs were befitting a professional salsa dancer, thus attracting many men. In whatever room she sat, she was always the woman in red, or was perceived as the black widow who other women shied away from for fear of losing their caballeros. She stayed after I dismissed the class and watched me erase the day's notes on the whiteboard. I wondered what she wanted as she sat in the front row staring at me. When it became too awkward, she packed up.

As she strapped into her backpack, she said, "Are you married?" Her English was unclear, piggybacking heavily on her native Cuban accent so that she sounded more like, "Or jew moreed?"

I wasn't offended, or put off, and reflexively answered, "Yes, I'm married. Why do you ask?"

"Does she make you happy?" she said, ignoring my question. Her blood-red lipstick made her white teeth stand out as her face set into a beaten, yet alluring, smile. Her lips belonged on a Maybelline advert.

"We are in love," I lied.

"Then where is your ring?" she said.

My bare finger didn't have a tan line anymore. All traces of my marriage had vanished to the outside world. She knew I was lying.

"I don't need to wear a ring to be married," I said defensively.

"True," she said, "but if I was your wife, you wouldn't leave home without a ring."

I didn't know what to say in response.

Gabby then walked up to me, shoved a piece of paper into my hand, and said, *"Cuando quieres." Whenever you want.*

As she walked out, I read the phone number scribbled on the paper, and the name *Gabby* next to it. I called her the next day, and we met in a parking lot by an abandoned fifty-cent carwash in the middle of nowhere, the kind that surely had a bag of illicit drugs hidden behind the split cracked concrete somewhere. She wanted to dive in, but I hesitated and left her sitting in her heavily tinted white SUV with her pants halfway down and her bra dangling from the steering wheel. She was persistent and blew up my phone for a couple days until she sent me a text that said, It's okay, *amor*. I'll be patient. *Te espero*—I'll wait for you.

I still felt guilty, like I belonged to Briana, but it was time to move on. A few days later, she messaged me her address and a time. She was trying to make it easy for me. Gabby knew I would cave as all men did for her, but this time I didn't stop to think. The loneliness had become unbearable. As we lay in her bed, she assured me that it would become easier with time, that being with other women was a good thing.

For three months, we were together once or twice a week. She had been grooming me, sweetly ushering me into this new stage of my life. Gabby was a risk taker. Her motto and turn-on were the same: Don't get caught. Yet, she loved to take it to the limit, wanting to come as close as possible to being caught, like a mountain climber who's scaling the edge of a cliff with frayed rope, who knows the next step could kill her. Gabby relished the high. I suspected our end was near when we began to meet closer and closer to when her husband would be home, and she would see me out the back of her house as he was walking in. The stakes were too high for me to keep going, yet they weren't high enough for her.

Once, we met at a park late in the afternoon, and Gabby jumped into my car and unbuttoned my pants with one hand as she removed her panties from under her dress with the other. She was talented. There were a few fit couples running, teenagers chatting, some children swinging—all within fifty yards of us.

"Do we have to do this here?" I said.

"*Amor*, do you believe anybody is thinking that they will catch people doing the dirty mambo at the park, let alone in this car? *No lo creas,*"—don't believe it. "Plus, your car is tinted."

She rolled her eyes as she said this and ignored my concerns. People kept running and buzzing around the park, and not one person noticed us. Nobody looked in our direction. Gabby was like a siren with a voracious hunger for sex and blood.

Afterwards, as we were lulled by the hypnotic pace of rush hour traffic, she said, "My husband drives by this park at five-thirty every day. If he sees my car here, he'll probably kill us both."

It was 5:28pm. I kicked her out and peeled out of there.

Another time, she convinced me he was out of town, and that I should come over at 2am. I couldn't go inside because her children might see me and tell their father some strange man had slept in his bed and made mama scream in the night. Gabby met me in the back alley where she parked her SUV. We climbed in. It was more spacious than my sedan. There was enough light from the Cheshire moon leering down at us that I could see she wore a cream colored, silky pajama dress and nothing else. She was barefoot and still warm from being in bed.

"I'm glad it's dark," she said, "because I have no makeup on."

"You're a MILF either way," I said.

She slapped me on the shoulder, and her voice cracked a little from amusement. "You don't have to hit on me anymore to get under my dress."

As we finished, and as she covered her legs with her silky gown, a light came on in one of the rooms of the house, and she scrambled, "Shit, it's my husband."

"What?" I said in a panic.

"Get out and go now," she said as she opened her door and ran back inside the house.

This is how we spent our three months—always on the verge of being caught.

"What do you think would really happen if your husband caught us?" I said naively one day.

"Papi, what do you think would happen? I've told you. He may be an idiot, but he's still a man. He'd shoot you in the dick and then shoot me dead. I wasn't joking about that."

Her sex was wrecking me. But it all ended one day without warning. She messaged me and said, *Don't contact me anymore. Husband is too close to finding out. Have a good life, amor.* The risk had peaked. I wasn't worth any more sacrifice. So, she held on to her secret, and we never spoke again. More than likely, she'd found her next guy, someone who could provide a better high, and this was her way of saying goodbye. Our sex was easy enough to cast aside.

Without realizing it, out of some debauched hope, I'd wanted to meet someone like Gabby, someone indifferent to my vows, to help ruin me, to show me how shattered I was, and to help dissolve the cataclysm that comes with heartbreak. I didn't have another path to take. I was brittle. My love for Briana was all consuming and homicidal. It was damning.

Sixteen

Erin

After our meal and bland conversation, we stood in the parking lot under the pale spring sun. Her skin was translucent, and I doubted if she ever ventured out long enough to tan.

"I had fun," she said and politely flashed her teeth at me.

"Me, too," I said, trying to fake my way out of the situation as smoothly as possible, "it was nice."

I had no intention of seeing her again, since we didn't connect beyond the pad thai we'd eaten. If she liked me, she didn't show it. Her presence, and the fact that she was willing to sit down and have a meal with an older man, should have been clue enough that she was into me. But I was dense about Erin's intentions. She climbed into her car, turned the key, and then a baleful howl filled the parking lot before the motor died. The engine wouldn't turn, so I waited in case she needed help. It was feigned chivalry on my part. Her face was flushed when she got back out.

"That's not a fun noise," I said, trying to make her feel less self-conscious while playing off my discomfort.

"My car hates me," she said nervously. "It's my dad's old Ford Taurus, my sixteenth birthday present."

I did the math when she said this. Roughly thirty-six months ago—that's when she was sixteen. I felt red with embarrassment. Our age difference, her being in college, my being long out of college, were major barriers between us.

Her white sedan had tufts of paint falling off in some areas and was at least fifteen years old.

"It may be time for a new one. I prefer Hondas," I said, and pointed at a red Civic two cars over. "Can you call someone?"

"Yeah, my dad," she responded with cell phone in hand.

Erin leaned against the side of her car. Her vampire complexion made her slender legs white as ivory, and her pristinely painted toenails, a bloody red, stood out because of the scandalous white shorts she wore. Her bright blonde hair and sparkling blue eyes befitted some California valley rather than Cuban Miami. After a few minutes, she gave up calling. Erin dressed like a teenage superstar but was a hippy at heart. It wasn't surprising to see a half hippie, half valley girl in Miami since anything gaudy, including character, was rule of the land.

"Damn voicemail. I can't get ahold of him," she whined, without meaning to. There was a pause before she asked, "Would it be weird if you gave me a ride home?"

I hesitated but felt obliged, "Of course not," I lied, "I'll take you."

We drove for ten minutes until we arrived at the front of a large, two-story, beige house built in the 90s.

"I kinda still live with my parents," she said reluctantly. "But once I find a job, I'll get my own place and some roommates."

"That's good," I said, feeling awkward at how little we had in common. The years that separated us suddenly weighed on my conscience again. *When I was eighteen, she was still playing dress up.*

"You should come in for a minute, and let me fix you something to drink," she said as she exited my car. The passenger window was down, and she leaned in with an enticing, "Please. It's the least I can do for how nice you've been."

I didn't want to go in because I imagined her parents demanding to know why I was out with their daughter. The last thing I wanted was to be confronted with the people who had birthed this delicious, yellow-haired creature.

"Can I take a raincheck?" I said, not intending to cash it if she said yes.

Erin surprised me with a mocking, "Huh, so people really do say things like, *Can I take a raincheck?*"

She put on a gruff voice as she imitated me. Then she snickered to herself before saying, "Come in. Nobody's home."

She bit her lip in anticipation and, in a flash, I saw how easy it would be to fall for her. Fall into bed with her. Fall apart over her. And fall to my death from heartbreak because of her.

Another barrier, oppressive guilt, was squashed with her invitation. I repressed my ambivalence, turned off the car, and followed her inside. She offered me some powdered lemonade mix, which I reluctantly sipped, so I wouldn't come off as rude. We had very different ideas of what a "drink" entailed and sat next to one another on a white leather sofa in a living room fashioned with the latest 21st century computer, flat screen, modem, game consoles, and remotes. Fancy china and actual silverware adorned a large oak display in one corner.

Erin was privileged, but I couldn't figure out why she was so hippie with her mannerism, until she said, "Oh, I want to show you something." She ran off momentarily and returned with a deck of tarot cards. "My mother reads fortunes. You want to see what yours says?"

"Yes, please. Is your mother a psychic or something?" I said as she tossed the box on the coffee table in front of us and began to shuffle the deck.

"More like a secret gypsy with money."

"And your dad?"

"He's a software engineer. And a biker. He loves his hog."

It made sense now. Biker-nerd plus gypsy-narcissist equals hippie-beauty queen.

"Touch the cards," she responded, so I ran my hand across the top of the stack. Then she began to organize my destiny into rows.

The tarot box cover said *The Magician* on it, and I mulled over what it meant. "Why do they put 'The Magician' on the box?" I said.

"Oh, I know this one," she said excitedly as she picked up the box. "You see the infinity symbol above his head? It stands for the eternal cycling of things, like life and death on a loop."

"What about the number one?" I said pointing above the infinity symbol.

"It means new beginnings, I guess, because he's the one who has the power to change fate."

"Is that really what it means?" I said.

"I think it does," she responded.

There was a chalice on the table next to The Magician. "What's the cup for?"

"Hold on a sec," she said and snatched the instruction manual from the box. She was still very green at reading cards. "Okay, the chalice holds water, and it is a symbol of the soul."

"What else does it say?" I said, surprised at the deeply meaningful symbolism in this one picture.

"It talks a lot about alchemy, but it's mainly a history. Do you want to read it?" she said as she tried to hand me the booklet.

"No," I said. "I'll stick with your explanation."

Erin sat biting her lip for a minute. Her eyes darted up and down the cards she had laid out for me.

"Are you going to reveal my destiny, or what?"

"Well," she paused before continuing, "I don't know how to read all the cards, so I was going to make something up."

I decided to play along. "I don't mind," I responded with a playful grin. Her juvenile flirting technique exuded charm. "What's my fortune?"

Her face brightened at my openness. "Aw, you're too nice. My mom reads the cards, but I'm still learning. I barely know how to lay them out."

"That's fine," I said, wondering what she would invent. "Tell me what you think it says anyway."

Then a devious grin spread across her face. "It says you should come upstairs with me and let me show you the rest of the house."

I was uncertain if I'd heard her correctly, but before I could respond, she mashed her face into mine. It was a terrified kiss from the lips of a girl who hadn't been kissed much. Her lips were rigid and wouldn't give, so I gave in for us.

We kissed for a while on her sofa, until she paused and inhaled sharply as if to confess something, but she didn't say a word. After staring into me for ages, she stood and grabbed my hand. We went upstairs, and she pointed out her parents' room, her older sister's room, and then ushered me into hers. It was surprisingly undecorated with impeccable carpeting and a fluffy white goose down comforter.

"This is it," she said as she plopped backward onto her bed. "My mom picks out all this stuff." Facing up, she patted the empty space next to her with her left hand. "Come lie next to me."

We had overcome yet another barrier: fear of rejection.

I kicked my shoes off and climbed in. We were shoulder to shoulder. "I like your room," I said. I wasn't lying. It was a comfortable space.

"There haven't been many guys in this room or in my bed," she said.

I wasn't sure why she'd told me that. All that came out of my mouth was, "I shouldn't be here."

The guilt was creeping on me again.

Erin put me at ease when she turned her head to face me and said, "I want you to be here. My last boyfriend was an asshole, you know. I told my mom and dad he was homeless because of junkie parents and asked if he could move in with us. Then we pretended to be engaged so he could sleep in my bed, and they were fine with it. For a year, he said he loved me in front of people, but every day in this room he told me that I was the luckiest, ugliest girl because I had him. The pathetic part is that I believed it all because I loved him."

"That's terrible," I said. "He was wrong. You're stunning."

She had a devastating Chloe Grace Moretz style about her but didn't know it.

"Thank you," she said, her cheeks a hot pink. "It means a lot to hear you say that." She paused before continuing, as if confessing to a crime. "One weekend when my parents were gone, he hit me. When they got back and saw the bruises, I had to tell them what happened. They kicked him out, and I never saw him again. I didn't know he was so messed up until he messed me up. Stupid, huh?"

"It wasn't your fault. I can't believe your parents let him live here," I said.

"Yeah, but they trusted me, and I lied. He was older than what I told my parents, and he'd been dishonorably discharged from the military for fighting and drugs. What happened was my fault. I'm the one who asked my parents to let him stay here. I was dumb to let him manipulate me. He didn't love me but was using me for shelter and sex. Mostly bad sex."

She was about to sob but didn't. Instead, she cleared her throat and said, "He was my first."

"How long ago did this happen, Erin?"

"I was seventeen, so it's been a while."

Twenty-four months is like twenty minutes in adult years, and twenty years in teeny time.

"And how old was he?" I said.

"Thirty."

"Your parents are irresponsible."

"Totally, but their neglect is the reason you're lying next to me now," she said frankly.

"Huh, true," I said.

I had misjudged her. Love was bleak for Erin. Life had begun to pummel her spirit much too early.

A couple teardrops bulged on their way down the side of Erin's eye. I felt bad for drudging up old feelings.

"I'm sorry," I said, "I should go," and began to slide off the bed.

She wiped her face and said, "Don't. It's not like it was any of your fault."

"I know, but—"

"It's broiling in here," she interrupted, and jumped off the bed to turn on her ceiling fan.

Then she did something that caught me off-guard. Before climbing back in with me, she said, "I hope you don't mind," and removed her t-shirt in one graceful motion. Then she slowly crawled over me, dragging her legs across my thighs, and took her place again. When she was on her back next to me, she unclipped her white bra and threw it down on the pristine beige carpet.

Not knowing where to place my eyes, I abruptly turned my head back toward the ceiling.

She knew I felt awkward. "Don't freak out," she said. "It's okay."

My voice cracked, "I'm trying not to." I cleared my throat and still didn't turn toward her but waited to see what she'd do next. It seemed she was merely being a free-spirited, next generation, hippie-gypsy exercising her right to lie nude with a strange guy. Nothing more. It was too easy to want her, and I wasn't sure how much she wanted me to see.

I was wrong, of course. There was more. Erin wanted me to see everything. She was aching to dispel the ghost of her ex-fiancé. Without saying anything else, she kicked her pants off, sat up, and began to undress me.

~ * ~

We were two wreckages of adulthood sprawled on her unusually large bed under a heavy comforter, staring up at her ceiling fan humming and clicking rhythmically at high speed. The fan was doing a poor job of drying us as we glistened and dripped sweat on the bed. Our legs were pretzeled together, and she kept running her fingers over my nose and lips. My eyes began to dry out, so I turned on my side to face her. She was smiling.

"Are you glad you stayed?"

"I am," I said, and gave her a quick reassuring kiss on her bright pink lips. Her long, blonde hair fell in strands down her chest and onto the bed. She was like a fallen seraph with her milky skin.

"Me, too," she said, and sighed before adding, "I feel like I've had the plague for the last two years. I didn't want anyone near me. I guess I've been avoiding this."

"Well, I won't let you avoid this anymore," I said jokingly.

"Can I pretend *this* was my first time with a man?"

"Absolutely," I said as I slid onto her. She filled the room with gleeful laughter, and we role-played to her heart's content.

We developed a routine at her parents' house. We'd meet there after her classes on Mondays and Wednesdays, after eating our pad thai.

"I love our sexy fun routine," she said one Wednesday afternoon. "I don't think I can eat noodles without getting turned on." We joked around for a bit. *I'm going to use my noodle handcuffs to tie you up and screw you into unconsciousness. I'm getting you a noodle choke collar for your birthday. Noodle soup with extra special sauce, please!* She continued, "I want to do this next week, and the week after that, and the week after that one."

Erin was obsessed with the future because the past had treated her badly. She never asked about my past either, and I was happy to avoid the subject.

"I'm trying to find my place with someone," she told me one day in the sincerest way. "I want someone who will have me forever." Her body was still adolescent, but her ambition was middle aged. "I want to come home to the same person every day, to our house, and to our life." Even if I'd wanted it, her wonderful vision of the future didn't include me. I knew when she imagined a partner it wasn't me she had in mind. I didn't pursue her beyond what we had, didn't speak of myself in the future tense around her, nor suggest plans beyond our weekly pad thai sex rendezvous. It made our affair easier to dissolve when we spoke on the phone one day.

"Hey, gorgeous, how's your day going?" I said. "Are we meeting up as usual?"

"Someone asked me out on a date," she said matter-of-factly, almost solemnly, while ignoring my question. Usually, she was eager to meet and was lively in conversation, but not this day. I knew things were about to change between us.

"I'm not surprised," I said in a low, serious tone. I tried to swallow, but a knot in my throat forced me to cough.

She continued, "I want to know what you think I should say."

This was our goodbye.

"Erin," I began, and then briefly paused before uttering, "say yes."

A crackled sniff and a lengthy exhalation scratched the phone on her end. She was crying, but it was because our friendship was ending. Though we'd miss the sexually charged pseudo-therapeutic sessions in her bed, we would mostly miss the simplicity of being together.

"I hope you figure things out. Take care of yourself," she said and hung up.

There was a chance I was wrong again. She might have wanted me to say no, to ask her to stay with me, but it wouldn't have been fair to her. Erin knew I was lost, running from my injuries, and that she could never heal me. Instead, she did the next best thing…she healed herself and moved forward. Erin was a warm wave of goodness. Being with her was almost too damning. Because afterward, a numbness swallowed me whole.

Seventeen

Stacy

    The brittle plastic of our rear bumpers let out a crunching sound followed by a forceful interruption in our momentum. There was a thud as my head jerked forward from the impact and smacked the steering wheel. A sharp pinch shot up the back of my neck. I felt adrenaline surge through me, and I looked up and saw that my rearview mirror contained a warped, bent figure who was walking toward my door. She lurched forward like a hunchback but, before I exited to assess the damage, I realized it was an illusion caused by my twisted mirror and the awkward angle from her approach. She stopped by my door as I stepped out, blocking it, like an asshole cop.
    She could have passed for an Egyptian, a chunky Nefertiti of sorts, but she was not ugly in the face or body, yet. She carried an extra twenty pounds well, but in twenty years, she'd be facing the horrors of botched surgery in a futile attempt to reverse the ravages of middle-age. Her crackly, screechy voice scratched at my eardrums when she spoke.
    "Oh…my…goodness," she said slowly and dramatically. "I'm so sorry. I didn't see you in time. Are you okay?"
    Eventually, I'd grow mildly accustomed to her voice, but now her voice came off as a falsetto with congestion. She had many flaws, and despite her best efforts, her handicaps would prevent us from

venturing out in public too often. In fact, our relationship would initially sprout in the front seat of her car and then casually blossom in the back.

"I'll live," I said rubbing the back of my neck, remaining as composed as possible. Had she been more pathetic, I might have been irate.

As if on cue, she began to cry. Her face covered by her hands, she said, "I'm so, so stupid. I don't have insurance." She paused the dramatics momentarily and scanned for other witnesses before continuing her wailing. "I've never been in a wreck before."

"I wouldn't say this is a wreck," I said as I walked back to check on my bumper. There wasn't any damage on mine, but hers had an awful dent. "There's isn't a scratch on my end," I said as I bent down and rubbed out some scuff from her shiny, red, Chevy Malibu. "You know, it's illegal to drive around without insurance."

She knew that, but I wanted to remind her of my advantage.

As she bit furiously into her nubby index fingernail, she said, "Are you going to call the police?" She didn't care that her bumper looked like someone had taken a sledgehammer to it.

Her large hazel eyes were puffy and cracked pink as she mumbled. It was hard to tell if she was being genuine because of her exaggerated body language, but then her teeth began to chatter from fright. This girl was prey.

"I don't know," I said. "We could figure something out."

"Aw, you'd do that for me?" she said and exhaled with a series of irregular sobs.

She didn't hesitate to punch my phone number into her cell. I grinned at her and said, "Call me, and we can talk about this more over lunch whenever you're free."

I jotted her license plate number and driver license information mainly for show, in case she had doubts about contacting me.

~ * ~

It was two days later, on a Saturday, when I awoke to her text. *Hey, it's Stacy from the wreck. Do you eat sushi?*

"I love sushi," I said as I dropped a dollop of wasabi and a strip of pink ginger into my tiny soy sauce bowl, and calmly stirred.

"Aw, we have that in common," she said as she jabbed her roll with a fork and began scarfing it down. "Sushi is the bomb."

I frowned in disapproval, but she wasn't paying attention.

There was rice clinging to her teeth as she spoke, "So why didn't you call the cops when I hit you?" Chunks of eel and avocado fell out of her mouth, and she squinted as if apologizing with her eyes. She was a goofy exaggeration of an anime doll. "Excuse me," she said and then shoved the fallen dregs back into her mouth. There is nothing worse than a cute, gross girl—like the beauty in school who happens to eat her boogers when nobody's paying attention.

I secretly vowed never to eat with her again. I was still not used to her shrilly voice, so I began to speak as much as possible to prevent her from making more noise. Dealing with the disparity between her relative appeal and her repulsive mannerisms was exhausting.

I continued with the fakery. "You're a nice girl and didn't want to get you in trouble."

Her voice cut into a piercing "Aw, I like you." She accidentally dropped her fork on the floor as she reached for her ice water and, with a quickness, grabbed the chopsticks to snatch up the once delicate and colorful caterpillar roll she had ordered. Her accuracy was disturbing. "You like me, don't you?" she spat.

"Of course," I lied, trying to anticipate where she was going with her statement. "I wouldn't be here if I didn't."

Stacy was crude, but I appreciated how she wanted to get to the meat of things.

"Do you want to go out again?" she said as she wiped her face clean and gulped her water again. A few rice kernels were bobbing on the surface. "We should."

"Yes," I said, "Let's go out again." *But not to a place that serves food.*

Unbelievably, she had hit *my* car, and then asked *me* to lunch, yet I still ended up paying for the meal. But I would make her pay for these things a hundred times over through the emotional wreckage I would unleash on her over the course of two months.

~ * ~

We were parked behind a dingy, abandoned restaurant building in one of Miami's barrios in Little Havana, out of sight from the dimly lit mercantile road some yards away. A *paletero* cycled by on his pushcart while ringing a kid's bell, advertising frozen coconut and cacao ice-lollies. *Who the hell buys popsicles off the street at 10pm?*

"Is it usually busy here?"

"Pretty much," said Stacy.

This was our first time being alone. We had gone out many times. Not to eat, of course, but to walk in the park at odd hours, loiter in seedy parts of Miami to see if we could witness something interesting or illegal, explore bookstores on the brink of ruin, and go to midnight showings of unpopular movies. Normally, we met up in those parts, but today was different. Stacy had me pick her up and take her to drop off something to a friend. She didn't want to drive alone, so I escorted her.

Stacy's self-esteem was as rundown as the roads and buildings, and she didn't care how ungentlemanly I treated her. We still hadn't sexed because I didn't want her knowing where I lived, and she wanted more privacy before we did anything…like a room with a bed. But if I ever revealed my address, she was the type of gal who would appear and reappear at my doorstep like a wounded feline.

"Let's go to your place," she cawed for the hundredth time.

"I told you," I snapped, "let's not rush into anything."

"Okay, fine. I'm sorry," she said, instantly surrendering. "I get it."

She had nothing to be sorry for, but I let her apologize anyway. *Damn, now she won't want to fool around*, I thought before mentally berating myself for being tactless. After all, she had already agreed to hang out in the forsaken lot. I was practically in.

"What's on your mind?" I said, suspecting she'd caught on to my subpar companionship.

"I have to tell you something," she said as she faced me. "But maybe I shouldn't."

"Tell me," I said.

"Okay," she complied with goofy concern in her voice, "but don't judge me."

"Fine, no judging," I lied. I was constantly judging her.

She covered her face and spoke into her hands, "I'm still a virgin."

She didn't come out of hiding until I said, "You're joking."

"You said no judging," she whined as she folded her arms tightly in front of her.

"Who's judging? I'm just surprised."

"I'm not playing. I am."

"You're twenty-two, for god's sake," I taunted her, more from excitement than surprise. "How is that possible? Does it smell, or something?"

"Shut up, dick." She couldn't find the words to answer me, so we eyed one another. "Why does age matter?" she said finally.

"I guess it doesn't, but your sexting is filthy. I never would have guessed." I never suspected anything less than a seasoned sex object. "You don't talk like a virgin," I joked.

She didn't want to kid around. It was serious for her.

"It never happened. I mean, I had a boyfriend in high school, but we didn't do very much," she said and began to nibble her fingernails.

"What did you do with him?" I asked, partly from curiosity and partly to force her to speak of things she wanted to forget.

She hesitated.

"What?" I said in a mildly annoyed tone. "Don't tell me you're a born-again virgin, or something, because that's bogus. There is no such thing. You can't take back sex no matter how much you pray or dunk your head in water." I was purposely being mean.

"No, it's nothing like that. We did do stuff, but he was weird. He wouldn't let me go down on him, but he would go down on me."

"Oh, so you did have sex," I said. "Liar."

"No," she squealed and shoved me, "he was never inside me. Ok, listen, on our senior prom night we got a room, and I knew he wanted to have sex, but I didn't want to go that far yet and was afraid to say no. We were naked in bed, and I was on top of him, like a cowgirl, but he wasn't in me. His dick was flat and rubbing on the outside. I swear it never went inside."

"Man, you're filthy," I said. "You may as well have fucked him. Poor guy probably exploded from the blue balls you gave him."

She still wasn't ready for jokes.

"I'm glad I didn't," she said, maintaining her serious face. "He wasn't the one."

"Who is the one?" I said trying to see how much she'd reveal.

But she didn't answer my question. Instead, she said, "Everything else I know is from watching porn." She hid her face again in shame. "I text you stuff I've seen online." She paused so I could process her response. Then she said, "Are you mad?"

"I can't believe what you're telling me," I said, trying to sound betrayed rather than surprised that she cared so much about how I saw her. I figured I'd work the angle and selfishly redirect things back to me. I turned away from her, crossed my arms, and slumped in my seat. What I was doing suddenly hit me, and I deliberated over my intentions—whether I could go through with ruining this girl or not. I hadn't planned on warping a virgin. My damage was mainly intended for someone more experienced, someone who could still wrestle life as an emotionally gnarled human being. Messing with a virgin made me feel criminal, but Stacy never gave me the chance to back out.

"I'm so sorry I didn't tell you sooner, but I knew it would freak you out," she said. "Are you going to split up with me?"

It was unclear what we'd be splitting from. Her face was strained from anxiety, in anticipation of my answer. I sensed her desperation to keep our absurd non-relationship intact.

Then a lame cliché sealed her fate. I pecked her on the mouth and said, "Listen, what you have is special, and whoever you decide is worthy of this gift will be the luckiest man on Earth." I heard myself saying these asinine things and surmised that it was all emanating from some abysmal place within me.

She screeched, "Aw, you always know what to say to me."

After leaning in for a long hug, Stacy kissed me harder than she had ever done. She unbuttoned my polo, though our angles and the tightness of the car space didn't allow for much maneuvering. Her hand slid slowly up to my crotch, but my steering wheel blocked her access. I was letting her do what she wanted, which didn't amount to much. The burden of manipulation was on her at this point. I simply went along with it all.

She surprised me yet again when she said excitedly, "Let's get in the back."

Without waiting for my response, she climbed over and impatiently began to yank me across.

"Do you really want to do this?" I said as I stumbled into the back seat.

Stacy was such easy work, that it left me speechless and momentarily powerless to act. The impact of awful parenting and years of neglect had left her with no way to combat my evils.

"Don't you?" she said as she tried to stuff my hand down her pants.

There was no need to respond. After taking my hand back, I simply wrapped my arms around her waist and made her mount me.

"Tell me what to do," she said, and continued to smother me with her mouth.

~ * ~

Stacy plopped down next to me in the backseat in her bra and panties. She let out a gasp and then panted. It hadn't been that great, but she had no way of knowing better. I pulled my briefs and pants back up and absorbed the dreary surroundings of the empty lot. My shirt was drenched, but I was relieved I hadn't impulsively taken it off, or else she would have spotted my wedding ring, and then I'd have to explain things. Instead of ruminating on the seedy way this girl had lost her virginity, Briana came to mind, and I wondered exactly what she had been doing while I was inside Stacy. This didn't last long because the corrosive glow of Little Havana flooded my view as some previously unlit street lamps spontaneously began to flicker. The tufts of unkempt grass peeking through the gaps in the concrete slabs made the area seem post-apocalyptic and depressing. I tried to think of an excuse to leave and shower off the filth, but I was stuck until she was ready. Stacy breathed deeply with her eyes closed, quietly reflecting on what we had done. My necklace had absorbed copious amounts of our sweat and clung to my chest like a fat slug. I wanted to take it off and clean it but couldn't risk exposing it to her. Another stream of sweat made its way down my neck and chest, drowning the wedding band in our waste. The ring was witness to my third transgression.

Stacy's after-sex permeated the air. It was pungent and old smelling, making the air weigh heavily with each breath. She broke the silence with her annoying voice, distracting me from the funk that enveloped us.

"I can't believe I lost it in my car," she cackled. I didn't respond. "It didn't hurt too badly," she added as if I'd asked. "And no blood. Is that normal? Was I okay? How did I do?" She was dying for validation.

"It was fine," I said in a blasé tone. "We can work on it together." My acting was improving.

"Aw, I like you so much."

"You ready to go?" I urged her through a mawkish smirk as I climbed into the driver's seat.

"Whatever you want is fine with me," she said through her musky afterglow.

~ * ~

"Do a threesome with me," I commanded, many dejected sexual encounters later.

"You can't be serious," she said and stared wild-eyed at me. I stared back blankly, waiting for her to change her mind.

Stacy didn't notice that I hardly tried while she exerted herself. Her rewards included a string of crude, colorless responses from me at the end of our sex. "Good job," I'd say. Or, "You've been studying porn this week, huh? Did you learn that from a video?" Of course, it's impossible to get good at sex in the back of a Civic, or any car for that matter. When she blurted out "I love you" during one of our sessions, I didn't reciprocate. Instead, I abruptly stopped mid thrust and said, "Don't say things like that to me unless you're ready to prove it." Her eyes widened from terror when she saw my murderous expression.

Coincidentally, I was about to make her prove it.

She was hurt by my threesome question. "Am I not enough or something?" she responded. She would never be enough for anybody, but I didn't tell her that.

"You said you loved me. But if you didn't mean—"

"I'd do anything for you," she interrupted and grabbed for my hand, but I brushed her off. She pursed her lips and frowned before continuing. "But does a threesome mean that I have to be with the girl. Would I have to touch her?" she said with disgust in her voice.

"Of course, you'd have to do stuff with the girl," I said, as if this was a given in all threesomes. "You should study up this week online."

"Would it make you happy if I did that?" she said hoping it wouldn't, or that I was joking with her.

"Yes, it'd make me happy," I lied, snatching her wet hand back and squeezing as I sank my deceptively adoring eyes into hers. Being with Stacy didn't make me happy at all. What brought me pleasure was testing her limits and teasing her with the possibility that every step forward was part of a naturally budding love. Yet, every compromise was driving her further away into a personally desolate state of no return. Convincing her was easy if I mentioned that it would bring us closer together.

"Do you know who it would be?" she said.

"Not yet," I said, "but I'll take care of all that."

Stacy so lusted after a star-crossed love that she was willing to give everything and anything. I'd seen this disease before. Liz had it while we were together, and it crippled her. It struck me that Briana, who was my own fractured version of Juliet, believed that no matter how much a person sacrificed, it was never enough for love. Giving was futile, and so love for her was a taking enterprise. For me, it was a parasite that turned people into frail, hollowed out, versions of themselves...and the damage was for life. Stacy would never realize this and, after she somewhat recovered from our experience, she would simply bounce between crude, selfish, unappreciative men, always thinking that this was the way things worked between romantic couples. She had me to thank for setting the precedent.

~ * ~

It's surprisingly difficult to find a female who will entertain the idea of being the no-strings-attached third for a couple. Apparently, this kind of endeavor comes with a level of emotional and physical entanglement, something normal people would rather avoid. I gave up after a week of failed online posts and chats, and thus began the toughest compromise for Stacy.

We sat at a park bench eating sandwiches she'd made for us. I was tearing mine apart and throwing the bits at pigeons. "I love this sandwich," I said as I tossed it to the birds.

"Why don't we ever go out to eat anymore?" she said as she gobbled her peanut butter and jelly sandwich on a stale crescent. It was snowing from her mouth as she spoke, breadcrumbs popping out of her hole like crazy. "I don't think we've been out to a restaurant since we first met at the sushi place."

She was correct. But nobody wants to take a hungry hippo to eat fancy food. "I love our time alone," I said, not knowing what else to make up, but she was satisfied with my weak answer. I figured out that if I used the word *love* a lot in conversation with a girl who wanted me to say it, then all she heard was the love part and nothing else. It was as good as saying it without saying it.

Secretly, she hoped I had given up on the whole idea of a threesome.

"We're going to need a prostitute," I said to an unsuspecting Stacy, who immediately choked on a cracker she'd gotten from the lunch bag.

She spat it out on the sidewalk in front of us. The pigeons frantically cleaned it up. "Seriously? A hooker? Is that safe?" Her shrill was in full effect.

"It's safe if we make it safe," I said, aggravated by her questions.

"I'm kind of scared to do that," she said. "What if she has a disease or something? I mean, you'll be protected, but what am I supposed to do?" She put the food aside and began wringing her hands. I pretzeled my arms and posed defensively. Then she said, "I don't want to do this. Please, don't make me."

Her concerns were totally valid and should have been addressed. In fact, this was the most mature thing that had ever come out of her gross mouth, but with some quick thinking I squashed her mild resistance.

"Do you trust me, or not?" I said in a stern voice. "Because if you don't trust me, then what the hell's the point of us being together?" I was giving her my best act. She glanced my way momentarily but avoided my eyes so as not to upset me further. It was imperative that she understand my implied ultimatum, so I stood and said, "I'm going to go, okay? Hopefully, one day you'll grow up, and we can be together. I think it's obvious I love being with you more than you love being with me." What she heard was, *I think it's obvious I love you more than you love me.*

Her hand reached out and grabbed me before I could walk off. She tugged at me to sit down again, and I obliged. "That's not true and, yes, I trust you," she said in a low, defeated voice. Stacy sat for some time, eyes shooting nervously around the park, with her twitchy tics making her spasm periodically, as if expecting someone, a hero perchance. She stood to throw away her food and listlessly sat back down as if beaten. "Tell me what to do," she whispered as her bottom lip quivered.

I squeezed her hand to give her a false sense of comfort. "You're going to love this, and I promise I won't let anything hurt you," I said. "I care about you. Whoever I find will be safe."

"And how would you know?" she said after regaining her composure a bit. I sensed her apprehension creeping back.

But I could lie through my hands like no other, so I squeezed some more.

"I'm going to have her take all the necessary medical tests and won't bring her around unless she is completely clean."

"Aw, you would do that?" she said, relieved that I had a solution, no matter how unrealistic it was.

"Yes," I said in a calm voice. "Anything to keep you safe and pure for me."

"Can you find someone pretty?" she said through grieving eyes.

"Of course," I joked to lighten the mood. "Nobody wants to pay for an ugly hooker."

"Good point," she said flatly.

My hunt continued, but finding the hooker was easy. I had chosen a twenty-four-year-old blonde, blue-eyed, slender woman named Lady Ecstasy who specialized in "classy close encounters" with "gentlemanly generous businessmen" who could expect "relief from tension" from a "5'8, ex-gymnast dancer," and who was also "new to town and not fake in any way. All natural and available for incalls or outcalls. Backdoor open for extra fifty. GFE available." GFE stood for the Girl-Friend Experience, if I wanted to pay for Lady to pretend to be my girl. I paid the extra fifty, but not for any backdoor access. Explaining to her that we were lying to my girlfriend through a staged encounter was a whole other amenity, and so she required more cash to keep her mouth shut about the medical test she had supposedly taken and passed, though she assured me she wasn't skanky and always played safe. Secrets are expensive to keep, but we worked it out, and she agreed to all my terms. Then, I set up the hotel room, date, and time for us to meet.

Stacy was nervous and had been a diligent student all week. Sadly, she'd been developing performance anxiety over how to arouse a woman, so I told her to get online and explore porn sites for help. Unfortunately, the week we were preparing for our venture, she had several tests at the university. I had to give her another ultimatum about what was more important—a class or three that she could bounce back from if she missed one measly test, or her devoted boyfriend who needed her to be present and ready for this once in a lifetime opportunity to solidify our potentially lifelong bond. She chose me and, as a result, would fail one of those classes and barely recover from the other two.

We checked into the hotel room at 2pm on Saturday. I was a bit nervous about making this work. Stacy could have backed out and stranded me with the pro, who was prepaid for, but Lady was seasoned (five years in the business) and knew how to put Stacy at ease. Plus, I had been priming her to follow Lady's instructions all week. Stacy had one purpose: do what me or Lady Ecstasy instructed her to do. It wasn't until an hour and a half later—after Stacy was trembling in the nude from all the filthy orders I'd been barking and whatever else Lady added to tease Stacy's limits—that she saw I was still fully dressed. I sat on a chair spectating with beer in hand while her and Lady were resting on the bed, panting and hydrating before the next round, their sleek legs dangling off the edge like rosy honeysuckles.

"Hey," she said and sat up. "Why aren't you in here with us?"

Lady settled in for the show.

"I wanted to surprise you, babe," I said. "I'm not joining. I'm observing. It's just you and Lady Ecstasy today."

Stacy wasn't happy with my response.

"What in the hell?" she croaked. "Are you serious?"

I said nothing and only leered, waiting for her to absorb everything.

She began to shake all over, her plump thighs jiggling like prime gelatin, perhaps from fatigue or adrenaline. Stacy had come a long way from the panicked chunky Nefertiti I'd met. Now, she was an enraged Nefertiti. "This was supposed to be for both of us. I didn't want to do this shit." She jumped out of bed and began to dress. "How could you do this to me?" she sobbed.

Lady E. was composed, almost stoic, and erotically sprawled on the bed with her cigarette burning the air around us. She suddenly rolled onto her belly as if this would give her a better view of Stacy's breakdown. Lady's legs were bent in ninety-degree angles and swung frantically back and forth like a manic pendulum—her body the most industrial thing in the room. I remained in the chair as Stacy ran around the room hysterically gathering her stuff. "Oh, god," she kept repeating. I deliberated over the potential legal action that Stacy could take against me, but I was giving her too much credit. She exited the room in shambles, the door slamming behind her. It was the most cathartic instance of her life.

Lady had earned her pay and added yet another satisfied customer to her résumé. "What's next, hon?" she said and patted the sweat-stained sheets next to her, signaling for me to make a move. "This shit is a turn on."

I brushed off the ash on the sheets and jumped in since she was already paid for.

~ * ~

Stacy messaged me all week, but I hadn't decided if I ever wanted to see her again. After all, the damage was done, and there was no way to move beyond this together.

Monday's lunch time text from Stacy: *Let's meet. We need to talk.* I didn't reply.

Tuesday morning: *Why aren't you texting back? I need to speak to you!* I still didn't reply, but her jarring voice seemed to burst through the text.

Wednesday morning: *This isn't fair!! I didn't do anything to deserve this!!* I considered blocking her number but then stopped myself when she texted again Wednesday afternoon. *I can't stop crying. Please, talk to me.*

Thursday at 4am: *I'm sorry, okay? Forgive me and please, please, please say something to me. I'm dying here!!!*

I was asleep when Thursday's text came in, but it entertained me during breakfast—over coffee, bacon and eggs. It dawned on me how hasty I had been with Stacy. She deserved a proper heart wrenching, yet calloused, breakup. Ignoring her would be too easy and could possibly give her time to sort through the tidal wave of emotions drowning her. If I gave her too much space, there was a chance she would reflect on everything, and rightfully lay blame on me. There was still a glimmer of hope behind her words, as if, at any instant, I would text back and make it all better. I couldn't have that.

Friday, 11am: *I hate myself. Nobody wants me, and I'm lonely. I'm so disgusted by my own emptiness. I would do anything to have you back. I love you.*

Her words told me it was time to step in, but I didn't respond until the next day. A week after the Lady incident, I wrote Stacy back. It was 9:30am on Saturday: *Stacy, I obviously misjudged you. I've been hurting, too. Let's meet.*

I was careful to avoid apologizing for the situation. I needed her to feel as if she had to burden herself with at least half, or more, of the responsibility. She texted back and agreed to meet at her favorite sushi place. Considering our ending was near, it felt appropriate to violate my vow this once. Food has the amazing ability to thin a person's guard. It's programmed in us from our caveman days, a behavioral relic exploited in the modern world. This is the reason people share meals when they are first getting to know one another: they want in. We had lunch at 2:30pm, so the place would be empty.

It was gross to witness her gobbling down the crabmeat, tuna, and salmon. It was like watching a chinchilla file down its teeth on roughage. She attempted to utter something a few times during the meal, but I squeezed her hand and assured her we had plenty of time to speak about things afterwards. This was deception at its height. That's why, despite how horrible I'd been to her, she sat across from me in denial about being sexually invaded, probed, licked, and prodded in every imaginable way by a prostitute. She continued to stuff her big face, completely unaware that she had been emotionally and spiritually desecrated.

Stacy wiped her mouth, and bits of rice sprinkled onto her lap without her noticing. Her face was morose, her eyes were hopeful, and she hadn't slept much since she stormed out of the hotel room the week before. Then she said, "I'm so sorry I left you in the room. Are you mad?"

I loved how easy she made things for me. She was testing the waters.

"I'm not mad," I said calmly, "but I *am* done."

My arms were folded defensively, and the table between us was a husky wasteland of shrimp shells, tails, and seaweed, a true testament to the entropic nature of all things, especially love. She would never appreciate the symbolism.

Her eyes welled up with fear. Hope dripped down her cheekbones, leaving salty trails on her skin. "Please," she said, "don't do this." Her lips trembled out an, "I love you," and then through a pathetic howl she finished her declaration. "So, so much." Her hands trembled as she ran them through her hair. Bits of sticky rice dangled off the ends of her fingertips.

"Stacy," I said as I unfolded my arms and leaned into her, "this isn't love, and I'm not in love with you."

Tears streamed down her face as she stuttered in disbelief, "I-I don't understand," she said. "You don't love me?"

"No, I don't."

"What's wrong with me?" she said, as she covered face and sobbed for a bit.

I waited a moment before saying, "Is that a rhetorical question?"

"No," she dropped her hands on the table and began to raise her voice, "Why don't you love me? Tell me. I can change. I'll do whatever you need me to do." There was a pause. "Make this feeling go away," she quaked. "Fix this, please." Begging made her uglier.

"That's not how all of this works," I said. "Sometimes things don't work out."

She ignored what I said. "Please, tell me what to do," she said as she reached out for my hand. I immediately yanked it away from the table. My repulsion sent her into a quiet whining. I half expected her to break into a yowl, like the way small dogs do when run over by something.

"There isn't anything to fix, Stacy. I don't want to be with you."

"Don't leave me," she whispered, her voice sounding unusually normal as she slumped her head down onto her folded arms. She didn't move for a minute, as if she had fainted. The restaurant felt too empty, too forlorn, but perhaps it was just the vacuity in the hearts of all lovers.

I stood up and slipped into my dark blue windbreaker as she wallowed in rejection at the sushi table.

"Goodbye, Stacy," I said, as I began to head for the exit. I almost left money for the meal, but I figured she owed me this much for hitting my car, for being so foolish and reckless. For being so goddamn naïve. It was a cruel lesson, and she would bear the despair for life. Before I stepped outside, I realized how much our experience had thinned her out, and how she sat like a cheap fixture—transparent and brittle—as if the slightest movement would make her crack.

Eighteen

Laura

We all have darkness to dispel. Sometimes we pass it to others, and other times it's passed to us. There's a big fat cake of darkness somewhere out in the universe being partitioned and gifted to anyone with motive. There was mail from Briana in my box. Her letter was deceptively wrapped inside an envelope addressed from my uncle in Texas. A surge of anger froze me in place. He wasn't supposed to put me in contact with her, but Briana was suave and could have her way with any man and woman. She had proven that already. For the time being, she didn't have my address. Clearly, she had conned him into sending me the letter. First, the wedding ring, and now this. He was breaching our agreement. I was anxious about what it might say, and I squeezed anxiously at the ring, repeatedly pinching it between my thumb and index finger. It still hung faithfully around my neck. *Read it or throw it away?* I asked myself.

Two days later, I mustered the courage to read Briana's letter. It was more of a short note, really, and its pitiful length didn't surprise me. It was her style to be concise, to hurry through everything meaningful. As I tore the paper, her scent bit my lungs, making me shiver like I was caught in a heavy winter rain, and her words made me turn away for an instant as if my eyeballs had been scorched by fire.

Darling,

I'm sorry. Forgive me. I need my husband back. I hate myself for what I've done. Come back to me. You are my gravity. Remember: B4L.

Your wife,
Briana

My stomach tightened as I studied the shape of her writing. I read it over and over, her voice subvocalized in my mind. My insides swarmed with her sounds, so I decided to burn the paper. A part of me singed with the ink.

I focused on what I'd done since I'd left, which could be summed up through a short list of women: Gabby the disaffected wife, Erin the hopeless romantic, and Stacy the toy. Then there was Laura, the lovely tragic princess. She was in love but not with me. Coincidentally, she was encumbered by a similar heartache to mine. Laura was engaged to a hollow man, and with this engagement came the burden of a soul-wrenching hopeless affection, the kind that often ended in violent death or suicide. Unfortunately, he loved her, too, but his somber past translated into emotional, mental, and physical chaos for those around him. Laura was ensnared in the middle stages of this man's abysmal collapse.

We met in a cooking class. It was for couples, but I showed up alone with the excuse that my significant other was sick and couldn't make it. This class fit perfectly around my work schedule, and I decided it was worth the awkwardness. Laura, too, was alone, stood up by her fiancé, so we were paired up after a rushed introduction from the instructor.

She was gentle and slow with her words, and under other circumstances, I would have fallen in love with her at first sight. Laura glanced at me with doleful green eyes and inviting lips occasionally accented by perfectly maintained teeth when she spoke. Her long brown hair smelled of a spicy lilac. Anytime she was near enough, a hint of watermelon would escape her breath. She was an elegant twenty-five-year old accountant. Her sylphlike runner's figure was the product of five-day-a-week jogs. She was a southern-mannered girl whose empathic disposition made her persona radiate. Virtually impeccable, her biggest flaw was falling in love with someone incapable of appreciating her grace. She was a dream girl caught in the worst of princess nightmares.

There was a cooking cheat-sheet, and we both reached out for it. Her hand bumped into mine, and she went rosy-cheeked from embarrassment. I tried to alleviate some of the awkwardness by stating the obvious: "Hell of a coincidence that both of our counterparts didn't show." Laura was genuinely embarrassed that she had been stood up. Her freckled cheeks instantly bloomed crimson at my comment. "Sorry," I said, "I didn't mean to say that."

"It's all right," she said. "So, where's your partner?"

"Oh, funny story," I said, "I caught her in bed with two other people." Laura's eyes widened, and her mouth slowly dropped open as I added, "She couldn't make it."

"I-I'm s-sorry," she said turning away from me. I needed more tact with her.

The class began, and we followed all the instructions. Laura didn't say much, but I sensed a mutual curiosity whenever our eyes met. We worked in silence, and I told myself that, surely, we had produced the tastiest fajitas in the class. My attention was on Laura throughout the session, absorbing her movements and mannerisms. She was next, my fourth, but my uncouth statement had put her off. A change of tactic was in order.

The class ended, and she rushed off, literally disappearing from my side within seconds of dismissal. I sprinted to catch up with her in the parking lot and slowed my approach to a suave walk when she was within sight. It was barely 3pm on a Saturday, and the sun was ablaze.

"Hey, Laura?" I shouted.

She turned around and said, "Yes," pursing her lips in anticipating of what I would say next.

"Listen, I'm sorry about what I said earlier, and I hope I didn't make a bad impression on you."

"Oh, n-no. You're fine. I should apologize to you for being so antisocial the entire class. I had a lot on my mind and wasn't all there." It was barely noticeable, but she had an endearing stutter.

"Why did you stay?" I said.

"Well," she said gently, "you were alone, I was alone, and I would have felt b-bad abandoning you there."

"You stayed for me?" I said jokingly.

She blushed at my comment, "Well, that may be taking it out of context, but you helped me decide."

I leaned in closer for a whisper. Fragrant watermelon filled my lungs. "Honestly, she was never coming," I said. "I signed up for the class by myself and lied about having a partner."

Laura expelled a soft laugh and covered her mouth in embarrassment. "Were you lying about finding her with two people?"

"No," I said. "That part was true, but it happened a while back."

Her face went serious, as if I'd struck a nerve. "I understand," she said, and she did understand. She wasn't merely saying it out of politeness. "Do you want to get some coffee with me?"

"Yes, please," I responded eagerly.

~ * ~

Laura sat snuggly across the booth from me and sighed, "It's kind of weird to be having coffee at four o'clock. Don't you think so? There must be an appropriate cut-off time, maybe three o'clock."

I nodded in agreement. "For me, it's five. If I drink caffeine after that, I can't sleep." She nodded back.

Once the java arrived, she touched her lips to the hot mug and said, "Can I ask you a strange question?"

"Ask away," I said.

She closed her eyes for an instant before she spoke. Whatever she had to say had been on her mind for a while.

"Have you ever wanted to say anything without consequences? I mean, say exactly what's on your mind to someone and not worry about being judged or s-scaring them away?"

I briefly pondered her question. "It sounds liberating, that is, if you could find a person like that. But everyone passes judgment."

Her face brightened as she said excitedly, "Do you want to do it with me? I promise I w-won't judge. Tell me anything, anything at all. I promise I won't leave. And no matter what you say to me now, you will see me again."

I was stumped and tempted. I could have walked out and avoided plummeting into the void with Laura, but then I'd never see her again. Yet, revealing some of the things I'd done was risky, regardless of how considerate she appeared. I assumed she wanted to exchange shameful and regretful stories—the most haunting experiences—since we were both jaded by our past.

"How do we start?"

"I can go first, if you want," she said, "but you have to promise me the same thing. Stay, no matter what I say, and that I can see you again."

Laura was precise and charming, and easily swayed me. "Okay, I promise," I responded, genuinely intrigued. "Go."

Her finger pointed at a long blemish near her lower jawline. "Do you see this scar?" I nodded. "My fiancé, when he was my b-boyfriend, crashed his car into a pole, because I wanted to leave him after I discovered he was running around with other girls. I broke my jaw, nose, leg and hip, fractured my skull and lost several teeth. I also punctured an eye, which miraculously recovered."

"Jesus Christ," I said covering my mouth. "I'm so sorry. That's some crazy *Vanilla Sky* shit." Once she pointed those details out to me, I noticed the numerous other scars left from the accident. Her face was pocked by the events of her past. Somehow, I had overlooked everything except her delicate symmetry.

"Good m-movie," she said, "but don't be sorry. I chose this. I love him, and we ended up together. He put me through hell, and we still made it."

"Made it where? I don't get it," I said. "You *love* him? As in presently love him?"

"Yes," she said. "We are still together. After the—"

"But why?" I interrupted, my eyes wide in disbelief.

Laura bowed her head, expecting the judgment to be brutal, but I stopped myself before breaking our agreement.

"Sorry, go ahead," I said. It was hard not to judge. There was a chance she was crazier than her fiancé.

"After the wreck," she continued, "he changed so much. He cared for *me*. He'd never done that before, and since he only had a sprained ankle, a couple broken fingers, and a mild concussion, I was the one he focused on for once. I'm telling you, one of us should have died in that wreck. It was bad, but we made it. I had my jaw wired shut for six weeks, and he cooked me soup every day. He bathed me and dressed me and brought me back to life. I could barely move, so he devoted himself to me. I was missing teeth, for god's sake, and must have looked hideous, but he didn't leave my side for a year. He would spend thirty minutes a day brushing my hair, and I felt loved by the one person who mattered to me."

"But Laura, it was all his fault," I growled at her in frustration.

"I know, I know," she said. "He did it out of desperation to keep me, but I don't care. It was wonderful afterward, at least for a while."

"He's the reason you were hurt in the first place. I don't get you."

Laura saddened as she continued, "It sounds crazy, but it renewed my hope for us, even if it was the worst of him that brought it out."

"I don't understand how you can stay with him. He sounds insane." Hearing these questions from a strange man didn't help in any way, but it was all I could do to keep from blowing up and shaking her free of delusion.

"I didn't get to ch-choose who to love," she snapped and then paused to breathe. What she said was difficult to comprehend. "It chose me," she continued, certain that love was like that. "But I'm frail now. I've been hollowed out by everything." Her eyes welled up, but she was strong and instantly composed herself. Then she said something tragic: "I don't think I could ever leave him."

Her suffering was polarizing, and I couldn't help but squeeze her hand. I was uncertain if she wanted me to do that or if she would shun me. They were soft and slightly wet from sweat. She squeezed back.

"I'm old and used," she added.

"You aren't those things," I said. "You're an angel, and he's an asshole for not treating you the way you deserve."

She blushed and lowered her head, keeping her hand in mine, and began to rub my skin with her thumb. The contact gave me a rush. Her heavy-heartedness was seductive.

I knew I had immunity. We were still playing the game, and anything could be said without consequence. "I could kiss you forever," I said. A couple rogue drops fell off her face, so I grabbed a napkin with my free hand and leaned in to dry her off. I imagined being her fiancé, but less of an asshole, and I sensed she saw me as him, the good bizarro version, if only for a moment.

She cleared her throat and then continued to speak freely. "I love your eyes. They're wounded. I felt it when I first saw you and knew if I could talk to you, you would get me. But I chickened out. I was running away from that class. I'm not b-brave like you."

She was like a mirror reflecting my own torment. "I'm not that brave," I said, "but I'm happy you stopped to talk." My chest felt heavy and I knew it was my turn. I had to tell her something about myself. "You're the brave one for telling me secrets after knowing me for only three hours. You took a chance and that takes guts." She smiled at my compliment. I then reached into my shirt and revealed my necklace. "Open your hand," I said, removing it and settling it into her palm. My throat tightened so I gulped down my lukewarm coffee to distract myself, to dilute the bitterness of letting go.

Laura moved the ring through her fingers, taking in every detail. She noted the *B4L* engraved in the white gold but didn't ask about it. "Is this a wedding ring?" she said.

"Yes, a gift from the woman I loved," I said, feeling shredded as I began my confession. "We were married, and then it ended, but I'm not that person anymore," is all I could utter in preemptive defense.

"It's okay," she said. "I understand."

It felt strange to say aloud what had happened with Briana, but Laura was the first person to truly empathize with my story. I told her everything from the beginning. She cried but it wasn't because of my sad story. She was feeling through me what her fiancé had put her through for years. We shared the wounds of disenchanted love.

She was unassuming as she held the ring in her hands. "Why d-do you still wear it?"

I'd been evading this question for a long time. I didn't want to answer it, because I was afraid of what I'd discover, but I couldn't hold it back any longer. My eyes filled with shame and guilt in front of this strange woman, and my hands shot up to hide from her. Laura had the power to bring almost any man to his knees. Tragically, her fiancé was immune to her ability.

"I can't do this here," I said. "Let's go."

Laura stood with me, put my necklace on, and grabbed her bag. "Where to?" she said.

I paused for a moment, somewhat shocked at seeing the band hanging from someone else's neck, but in another universe, that wedding ring belonged to her anyway.

Laura blinked excitedly at me, wild-eyed, expecting something monumental to happen. I snapped out of my trance and said, "Trust me," as I dumped a bunch of money on the table. Then I grabbed her hand and led her away.

~ * ~

Oceans are dangerous places once the sun vanishes, and the roar of the tide slamming into the earth made us uneasy. We were at the point when the sunset was ushering in the darkness, just after magic hour, around the time when the suns of distant galaxies begin to pock the night. We sat next to one another, shoulder to shoulder, while I attempted to bury our bare feet in the sand. They touched as the mound grew. Without thinking, I moved my foot and lost Laura's. Her toes wriggled frantically in the sand, but once they reconnected with mine again, she relaxed. Our eyes adjusted, and we could see the edge of the water was at a safe distance from us. We wouldn't be drowned any time soon.

Finally, at ease, she leaned into me and rested her head on my left shoulder. Her warmth was soothing. "It's incredible," she said as she inhaled profoundly, "and terrifying. Thank you for bringing me here."

After a while, our breathing synchronized with the hypnotizing cadence of the waves, and I continued my confession. "The water speaks to me," I said to her. We both directed our words straight ahead into the abyss as we spoke. As the waves retreated, it was as if we sat at the edge of the universe, at the pivotal crevice, the exact precipice where reality jumped off into the vacuum of space.

In her gentle voice, she said, "What d-does it say?"

"That I can't ever go back to the way things were," I said. "Once you're in too deep, there comes a point when there is no shore to ever get back to. It's too far gone, too far behind you." I hated the words pouring out of me. I hated how true they were. "And the weight of the water keeps dragging you further into the emptiness. One day you wake up drowning in misery, wondering how things got to be so bleak."

"Everything you say breaks my heart," she said. "Your sadness pulls me under." I considered what she said for a while, not knowing how to react. Then she added, "Would you really want to go back?"

"I would give anything for another chance to fix things, to escape the quicksand. If I could have one do-over—" I retracted my answer. "Not to fix everything, but to at least make a different choice—one that wouldn't lead me to this point in time."

"But without those choices, you wouldn't be where you are," Laura said. "You're here with me, now, and this is amazing. This is the only beautiful thing that's happened to me in a long time." I turned toward her, leaned in, and kissed her. Her lips and words were gentle. There was love in our embrace, but it wasn't ours.

Laura backed away from me, ran her fingers over her bottom lip and said, "Is that how you kiss her?"

Embarrassed, I responded, "No. Yes. I don't know," but she knew the truth.

"You'll never stop loving her."

"I don't think I can," I agreed.

"Does she kiss you back like that?" she said.

"Yes," I said again. "At least, the last time we kissed, I believe she did."

"Then you are d-doomed," she said.

We fell backward onto the sand and bellowed into the chasm above us, rudely mocking the heavens. But our voices were absorbed by the roar of the waves below us, and I thought of my wedding band around Laura's neck. Then I said, almost grimly, "That ring is the last of her."

"Love keeps you terrified, doesn't it?" she said as she removed the necklace and handed it back to me.

"Ever since I met her, yes," I added. A silky calm swept over me as it settled onto my chest. I squeezed the ring and tried to imagine what Briana might be doing at that moment, or if she was thinking of me.

We lay on our backs for a while, entranced by the vastness of space. It had been overcast when we arrived, but now our view was infinite, and there was no difference between the body of the ocean and the expansive sky. One melded with the other, bound forever. In the sun's absence, oblivion held everything in place. I tried to remove my desolation from the equation, I erased the deception and lies, I sutured all wounds, and what was left was my love for Briana. That's what united us. My love was our skin. But the respite didn't last, and a massive hopelessness crushed me as I wept on the sand. Anger and resentment was replaced by fear and despair.

Without warning, Laura turned toward me, propped herself on her elbow, kissed me and said, "I want to do something for you."

"What?"

"Let me be her for tonight."

And so I let her. We made love under the flickering of distant suns and near the threat of a monstrous ocean. The darkness was our connective tissue which also served as the expanse keeping us apart. For an instant, we belonged to the people we loved, an immaculate connection through borrowed bodies. We were cleansing ourselves through ritual, preparing to delve back into perilous destinies. Everything seemed driven by the pulses of design. We weren't two strangers who had met by chance, but the leading sufferers of parallel love stories.

~ * ~

Laura lasted three short months. Our time was warped. We had created for ourselves a bizarre *kairos*, a distorted unreality. Ours was a convincing role play where we could live out the fairytales we deserved. But it ended abruptly one day, at the very coffee shop where it had all begun, when Laura said, "I'm m-moving."

"How far are you going?" I said in hopes that her answer would be *closer to you*. But it wasn't. "I'm leaving Florida and taking a job in New York."

"That's great," I lied, feigning happiness. "I guess there's a need for accountants up there." I paused to absorb the reality of our situation before I continued.

"Come with me. Let's s-start over together," she suddenly said as she reached across the table, grabbed me, and kissed me furiously. I reciprocated, not because I accepted her proposal, but because it was our last kiss. My heart broke from the sorrow in her lips, and I could barely lay eyes on her angelic symmetry. She wanted validation from me, but there was none. Laura couldn't start over in New York any more than I could begin anew in Florida.

Tears ballooned and ran down her cheeks as my answer never came, the silence growing thick like a fog between us. She wiped her face, settled back to her composed self again, and said, "I'm s-sorry for saying that. I don't know what came over me."

"It's fine," I said as I reached for her hand and squeezed one last time. She had simply asked the wrong man to accompany her. I tried to put her back on track. "What about—" I stopped my sentence, unable to say her fiancé's name. "Will he follow you there, if you ask him to?"

"Yes," she said. "We need this change." But she was lying to herself. He would treat her as terribly in New York as he had in Florida, but I couldn't squash her hope. She needed to believe in something. We both did.

"Will you miss *us*?" I said, trying not to think of our ending.

"I'm terrified of *us*," she said, "but not as terrified as I am of losing him." As apprehensive as we both were, we danced on the threshold of another tragic love story, one that wouldn't end happily because we still belonged to other people. Unless those ties were severed, there was no hope for us. Laura left as gracefully as she had entered my life. She slowly slid out of the booth, grabbed her coat, placed money on the table, and stopped to smile at me one more time before walking away forever. Her last words were, "Be brave. Go to her. You deserve to be happy."

"So do you," I said quietly to myself, after she had already vanished.

Nineteen

Karen and Larry

Another note from Briana:
Dear Husband,
I know you are reading this. I know this because I know you. I won't give this up. You can throw it in my face for the rest of our days, so long as I can spend those days with you. We deserve another chance. It's worth finding out if it could have gone further, to the end. I'm willing to go as far as you will let us. I wish you'd let the past go. I am no longer that person. I want a future with you. Send me a response. Call me. Anything. Let me know what's going on with you.
Faithfully Yours,
Briana

It was comical the way she had written *Faithfully Yours* as if that were a possibility between us. Of course, there was no mention of love—no *I love you to the moon and back, darling,* or *You are the love of my life,* or *Please come back to me, my love.* That word simply had no place in her vocabulary. But I didn't burn this one. I kept it, carrying it with me as a reminder, like my ring, that nothing in this world is forever.

I indulged in her fantasy. I tried to imagine what it would be like to go back to Briana. Each time I invented a scenario, I couldn't live with myself for long. I'd leave her over and over, or, if I stayed, I'd become a villainous version of myself, a sexually impulsive cheater. I imagined a decade or more going by. We'd both moved on and remarried, and had children, and careers, and countless lovers during our midlife crises. Then we'd meet up, but the mostly scabbed over wound hadn't fully closed and would burst open again at the sight of her. There would be hints of gray in her hair and new lines of wear on her forehead and mouth. And I would break all over again. There wasn't any scenario where I wasn't collapsing from the weight of her deception. Whenever I began to feel anything, I simply read over Briana's latest note, and a sizeable wave of disgust washed over me, anchoring me again to the past. There was a brief period when I couldn't move on anymore, to any other woman. I was a somnambulist in my own life. Then one day, tired of the loneliness, I ventured out to see the world again—ring around my neck and note in hand, just in case.

I met Karen outside a movie theater. She was my Emma Bovary, my cruel madam. It was a Friday at dusk, and she'd been abandoned by her date. As he walked away, she looked about, unclear of what to do next. Her feet were laced in gold strappy sandals, and she donned a short, aqua, cotton skirt whose trim rested a few inches above her knees. It was windy so her white blouse waved like an unfurled flag whenever the gusts blew against her. I could see her long, curly, dirty blonde hair was dyed. Two inches of brown roots sprouted from her scalp. As the wind picked up, her long strands lifted like puppet arms as if waving to passersby. Her baby face was framed in an athletic body. It was the opening day for *500 Days of Summer*; a sad film about a poetic introvert in love with a licentious woman who mistreats him as if he were a diseased leper.

I felt particularly bold on that day when I approached her from the side and said, "Excuse me, miss?" She turned toward me with intense light-brown eyes, full lips colored with murderous ruby lipstick, and a sloping freckled nose layered with light foundation. Karen was a natural beauty.

"Can I help you?" she said with a scowl. She was noticeably defensive and, evidently, an expert scrutinizer.

"Was the movie any good?" I said as I pointed at a poster with *500 Days* advertised on it. "Was it worth it, or was it a waste of time?"

"You're at a theater," she said coldly. "The whole point is to go in and waste time."

I disregarded her response and said, "Are you okay? I don't mean to bother you. I mean, it's none of my business, but are you lost?"

She sighed as a throng of people were forced to go around us to reach the ticket counter. She was analyzing the situation, still unsure of her next move. "Yeah, it's none of your business," she said as she grabbed two cigarettes from her brown leather purse. Surprisingly, she offered me one, but I politely turned it down. As she lit hers, she said, "Never trust a man who won't die a little for a lady in distress."

"And who made up that rule?" I said, but she didn't answer and, instead, exhaled puffs of smoke downwind. I grabbed the cigarette from her hand before she placed it back in her purse. I stared at its thin, white paper and brown filter. I put it to my nose to see if I still remembered the tobacco smell. The wind kept blowing around us, making it colder than hell. Then I said, "I haven't smoked one of these since high school." I put the unlit stick in my mouth and waited for her to light me up, but then she snatched it from me and placed hers in my mouth instead. She lit my one and began to smoke. I could taste the bitterness of her lipstick on the filter, but I didn't mind since it was our disembodied first kiss.

Her face softened as I began to inhale, but she remained apprehensive. After a few deep breaths, she said, "My guy decided to leave, and now I have to either catch a bus or call a friend."

"Call someone. The buses are shit and littered with nasty hobos."

"Okay, captain obvious," she said. "Thanks for the unsolicited advice."

Her words had bite, but I disregarded her sarcasm, paused after a few drags, and saw she was already a third through the cigarette. I considered walking away, but then I'd be the jerk who'd abandoned her on the sidewalk. Instead, I added, "I would offer you a ride, but I don't want to come off as creepy."

"I'll pass on the ride with the charming stranger for now," she said, scanning my face. I couldn't finish the cigarette and when she flicked hers to the curb, I did the same, but not before admiring the imprinted creases of her ruby lips on the filter. She reached out toward me, and I flinched. "Hold on. You have some lipstick on you. Don't move." I relaxed, and she rubbed my bottom lip with her thumb. She then winked and said, "You pull off that red beautifully."

"Thanks," I said, startled by her touch. "I'm sure I'd make a handsome woman, but the color is perfect on you."

"Why are you being so nice to me?" she said. "Have we met before?"

"No," I said. "I think I'd remember meeting you. I happened to see you coming out of the theater as I was about to go in."

"And why are you at the movies alone?" she said. "There's nothing creepier than a person alone at a theater, you know," she said. "Where's your date?"

"No date for me," I said. "I recently got out of a relationship."

"Of course, you did," she said suspiciously and paused to scrutinize me with her eyes. "So, you saw what happened," she continued. "Well, the man you saw walking off was my boyfriend, or ex-boyfriend now. And the reason I'm hesitating here is because I don't want to call my husband."

I was astonished by her response. "Oh," I said, "I'm sorry for being intrusive. I didn't mean to—"

"Yes, you did," she cut in and folded her arms. The enchanting effect of our shared cigarette was wearing off. "This isn't a coincidence. I'm not stupid. You saw me standing here alone, and now here you are. You're transparent, you know that? Is this how you pick up girls? And does it normally work?"

"Okay, okay," I said trying to put her at ease, "you caught me. I saw a gorgeous woman who was upset, and I swooped in for the kill like a ravenous vulture."

One of her eyebrows curved upward at my response, and she dropped her guard and said, "That's much better. You don't scare off easily. Anyway, I doubt you're some desperate scavenger. You're not the type. Predatory, maybe, but no scavenger."

"I'm not either of those things," I reassured her, lying to myself. "And it's not my habit to hit on women at theaters." The next show had obviously started since the bustle and roar of the crowd had died down. The front of the theater was occupied by a handful of disheveled stragglers who'd been stood up by their dates. "So, you don't want to ride the bus, you can't call your husband, and you don't want to get in my ice cream truck."

"Funny," she said, glaring at me.

"How about we get something to drink? You pick the place, and we stay on crowded sidewalks, and I won't try to vulture you away."

"Huh," she said and bit her lower lip as she weighed her options. "And you don't care about husbands?"

"Not if you don't," I said.

"You promise you're not some creeper?" she said in a serious tone. "Because I will Tae Bo you in the face if I have to."

"Sounds painful," I said as I stepped closer and whispered, "I'm not a weirdo. I promise."

She squinted in tense consideration for a few seconds and then caved.

"Okay, charmer, a drink sounds good."

As she turned to go, she threaded her arm around mine and dragged me along. She walked with confidence, with larger than life strides, all the way to an Irish pub named The Five-Leaf Clover three blocks away.

We sat at the bar, and she ordered for us. "Hope you don't mind," she said, not really caring if I minded or not, and turned to command the bar tender. "Two Murphys."

"You got it, Karen," said the middle-aged man standing behind the bar.

"They know you in here," I said somewhat amused she'd brought me to one of her haunts.

She cracked a couple of peanuts from the complimentary snack tray, and said, "I come here to think a lot."

"Just to think?" I said.

She glanced my way and saw I wasn't naïve. "Charming and intuitive," she said. "You caught *me* this time. Sometimes I come here to think and meet interesting people. It's my thinking rock."

"Or your hunting grounds?" I said.

She squinted her eyes at me and pursed her lips. Before she could say anything about my comment, two frothy beers were shoved in front of our faces. I drank mindlessly to ease some of the friction between us, but the syrupy texture put me off.

"Wow, this beer is heavy," I said. "It's like a liquefied anvil. I can't believe you drink this."

"Beer is good and good for you," she said and put the glass to her lips. "It's how my European ancestors survived the black plague. Cheers," she smirked and clinked my mug before asking, "You never told me your name, charmer."

I slapped myself on the forehead and said, "Sorry, I'm Liam." I tapped her mug and then the table before I drank again. She drank with me. "We didn't toast to anything," I said. "We're breaking custom."

"Who the hell cares about custom?" she said and kept drinking. "I'm Karen."

"Nice to meet you, Karen," I said, grinning behind my glass. We sipped the thick syrup a while as I admired the definition in her arms and calves. She was slender but toned. "You work out," I said, not knowing where else to take our conversation.

"You would have made a great detective," she said sarcastically.

"Yes, I lift."

"Lift weights?" I said, impressed by her hobby. "I've never met a female weight lifter. I mean, I've seen them on the internet and TV and stuff, but they're kind of like mythical creatures. You never see them around."

She nodded, amused at my reaction. "Well, I'm glad to be your first."

"Why lifting?" I said. "Don't women prefer cardio and light sculpting instead of heavy weights? You don't see too many women who want to hulk out."

"I started a few months ago and can't get enough. Brute strength is invigorating. It's so raw and primal. That's my main reason," she said through teeth so bleached, straight, and polished they were like stacked Chiclets. "I enjoy feeling powerful."

"And before the weightlifting? What gave you power?" I said.

She swigged the stout beer and then said matter-of-factly, "Cheating on my husband."

Her response made me choke down a few gulps before I said, "So, yeah, you have a husband. What's that all about?"

She leered at my nervous response, and said, "Indeed I do, but barely."

"How is he barely your husband?" I said. "You can't discolor matrimony, you know. There aren't gray areas in marriage."

"Maybe not for you, but we have this role-reversal complex where he acts like a woman going through menopause, and I act like I don't give a shit," she responded defensively, already halfway through her drink.

"Okay, fine," I said, accepting defeat, and not wanting to overstep boundaries any more than I had to on our first outing. After absorbing what she said, I joked, "I've never seen a woman down a beer this thick without any problem."

"You've never met a woman like me," she said and kept drinking. How right she was.

I sipped the beer again. It tasted like dirt and sludge in my throat.

"All women say that about themselves," I chuckled, then coughed to get the syrupy brew out of my larynx.

"Yeah, yeah, I know," she responded, "but I can prove it."

"How will you do that?" I said.

"You'll see, but you'll never see it coming," she said, the words echoing into her near empty glass.

"We'll see about that, I suppose. So, why stay with him if you can get more manly boyfriends? Why not leave him and get yourself some beefy character who can muscle you around?"

"I don't let random guys muscle me around," she said firmly. "I like being the force to be reckoned with in my relationships, but it's harder to find a guy who can deal with that than to find a typical masculine beefcake. My husband deals with it but in a weak, old fashioned kind of way. It's fun keeping him around all heartbroken and weepy."

"That's the weirdest thing I've heard," I said jokingly, though it was. "I want to meet this flaccid husband of yours. Next round is on me, if you can keep this pace."

"This is hardly a pace," she mocked as she bared her teeth from the bitterness of the last bit of stout. She pounded on the table with her free hand, "I bet I can drink you under any one of these tables at the bar."

"Only one way to find out," I said, accepting her challenge. We drank and flirted for a couple hours before our inhibitions shed. Karen would lean in and bump me with her elbow or her shoulder or her knee. Sometimes she'd place her hand on me and push away when she was appalled by some lewd or ridiculous comment of mine. I suspected she wanted me to get close, to lay my hands on her and hold on. But I didn't. Being a power junkie meant she had to make all the moves.

We were evenly matched, which impressed me more than it impressed her, and after sharing our conquests over people we didn't love, who we'd hurt along the way, she blurted out, "Are you going to sleep with me, or what?"

I raised my glass to the clouds of smoke above us, in libation of her reckless comment, and, in my haze, I downed the last bit of my stout and said, "Here's to husbands and wives." I slammed my mug so hard on the counter it should have bottomed out, but it was fine with only some splashing on the bar—a good sign.

Karen set her drink down and walked off without a word. I threw a bunch of money on the counter and walked away with her. An hour later, we found ourselves sprawled, but fully clothed, on the bed of a cheap hotel we'd paid for with cash. The receptionist knew what we were there to do as we walked in drunk and asked for a room. The carpet design was as offensive as the moldy air, and none of the windows or glass doors had been washed in months, as evidenced by the dozens of handprints, adult and child alike, splattered all over. Wisps of pollution hung about here and there. The staff had been smoking in the reception area for decades. It was so stifling it felt like a gross castigation of our lungs, a punishment to customers who stubbornly refused to leave until a room was rented to them.

The pool, abandoned and putrid just outside large glass doors behind reception, was mostly empty except for a pile of mulchy leaves from seasons past mixed in with the current season's fallen sproutlings. This place was like a long forgotten 90's public service announcement. There was the stench of decay emanating from the swimming hole, and even the mouth of hell couldn't have stunk more. Among the once life-giving water turned to sewage, was a dead grackle, a small brown one, a female, a victim of rigor mortis. She was cast aside. It was nature's backlash: protein and greens all mixed in a concrete bowl of sloth and sludge. We could have afforded something better, something with a timed air freshener designed to fool our olfactory, but we didn't deserve better, and so we settled for the first thing we found.

"Single or double?" said the listless face at the counter. We jokingly told him we didn't care so long as it was a room with a lock, bed, and shower. He handed us a greasy keyring, and two minutes later we had sex in the crumpled and squeaky elevator on the way up to our third-floor room. Each thrust rumbled the box and creaked the cables hauling us up. We were bereft of any sense of decency, with nothing but the heavy stout and misdirected resentment to urge us forward. The elevator doors opened half a dozen times, yet we didn't stop. We didn't care because we were adrift. The bell kept ringing, signaling that our time was up, that we'd arrived, but we ignored it. In the end, we grew tired and numb, and so I zipped up my pants as she slid her skirt down around her waist again. Her underwear was still collared around her ankle, but she kicked it off and it landed near the opposite end of the elevator where she'd hastily unstrapped her sandals. Karen didn't stop to get her stuff as she walked out, so I bent and got them for her. Her strappy sandals hung over my shoulder like a rucksack, and her red panty was stuffed into my pocket like a handkerchief. We turned down a hall, found our room number, 333, and both collapsed on the bed too deflated and drunk to try for sex again. I snapped her underwear up toward the ceiling and she laughed for an unjustified amount of time when it came back down and landed on my face. I bunched it up and tossed it to the floor.

We lay there for a while with the light on. All I could see was the end of the bed, a television, plastic cups, a bucket for ice, and her bare feet. Aside from the polish that had rubbed off from the gold sandals and scuffed her heel, her feet were pedicured to perfection—

her toes painted in the same ruby color as her lips. She must have known I was staring at them because she began to wiggle them and said, "I pamper my feet."

"I can see that. They're works of art," I said. "Why do you do that?"

"Isn't it obvious? Feet are mistreated and neglected, but they're more important than any other limb on your body."

"And how did you come to that conclusion?" I said, thinking she was joking. She wasn't.

"They take you where you want to go, and without them you are a stuck blob of flesh, dependent on people or machines to take you places. They're the most human part of you. Wouldn't you agree?"

"Well, when you put it like that, yes," I said, a bit stunned at her complex view of feet.

"I start pampering there first and work my way up," she said.

"That's an interesting philosophy," I said, uncertain if it was a philosophy at all.

Then we slept, had more unruly clothed sex, and slept again.

~ * ~

Usually, the morning after a gross mistake, adults scurry to extreme ends of the room or car, or wherever they happen to wake up—as if space or distance will somehow save them from the ugliness. Then they speedily depart and try to erase the event from their minds by going back to their husbands or wives, or boyfriends and girlfriends, or friends with benefits, and sexing them that very day to cover up the putrid stench of the stranger's fuck marking. That's how the word *sloppy* came to be associated with casual sex, not because of gooiness, but because of the emotional fallout. But it wasn't like that with Karen. The next morning, we awoke on our sides facing one another in our smelly clothes, acting as if we had checked-in to a bed and breakfast for our honeymoon.

She casually rolled out of bed, rummaged through her purse, popped in a stick of gum, rolled back to face me, and said, "Has anyone ever told you that you look like sex?" through a cartoony smile. Blonde clusters spilled down her chest and onto the bed. Her hair smelled of flowers and cigarettes, accentuating the turmoil in every lock. She may have appeared threatening to others, but I found her alluring. She was the kind of beauty that makes a man want to murder.

I squeezed my eyes shut, and then batted my eyelashes to get some of the haze out of my sight. Unsure if I'd heard her correctly, I said "What?"

"You look like the incarnation of the dirty deed," she prolcaimed. "Everything about you screams *great lay*. Like a walking implication of screwing any girl to death." She whistled out the trajectory of an imaginary grenade and exploded it in midair before saying, "Shit, did I say that aloud?"

I lay there in disbelief, not at what she'd said to me, but at the staggering chances that those very words would be said to me twice in my life. "That's weird," I said. "Someone else told me the exact same thing when I was in high school. I was walking down the hall, and this random girl ran up, and said, *You look like sex.* She ran off and vanished before I could ask her what she meant."

"Well, I'm not that girl," she said, "but I can tell you she would have killed to be where I am now. Take it as the best compliment you could ever get from a chick."

I shook off my last yawn, and said, "Have you ever said that to anyone else?"

"Never," she said. "But what we did on the elevator, that fuck till you're numb feeling, that poor girl will never know." Karen leaned in to kiss me, and I, too, was reminded of what had occurred in the elevator hours before.

"What's next?" she said as she scooted away and sat up at the opposite edge of the bed with her back turned to me. "Breakfast?"

We hadn't closed the curtains and slept with the lights on all night. Outside, it was a rainy Saturday morning.

"I have nowhere to be," I said, "but isn't your husband going to be worried that you've been gone for so long? Call him if you want."

"He's probably bawling his eyes out, but he'll live," she said as she reached for a cigarette. "That man is a tear factory, the eternal weeping willow."

I sat up in the bed, and Karen tossed a stick of gum and a cigarette over her shoulder. They landed in front of me. I grabbed the gum. "Why treat him so cruelly?" I said. "Did he cheat on you first?"

She slithered into the only decent amenity of the stinking room: a 70's styled chair made of polyester, accented by swirls of senseless shapes and colors, next to the bed and near the window. She faced me again with her legs crossed and shifted uncomfortably, trying to find the perfect spot. There wasn't one.

She sucked on her cigarette for a long minute before she said, "This isn't some veneer for heartbreak." Karen puffed away, expelling ominous clouds into the ceiling. "I settled for him – Larry, my husband, I mean. He wasn't the one. The *one* saw me as disposable. I was nothing."

"But you're not noth—," I began.

"God damn right I'm not nothing," she snarled at me. "I refuse to be used." Her face grew fierce as if I were *the one*. "But it's okay," she continued, her face softening again as she inhaled death. "What he did changed me. He woke me up from the fairytale, and then Larry showed up, put me back together, and unleashed me back into the world."

"I used to think everyone deserved a fairytale ending," I added.

"Some do, I'm sure," she said, "but personally, I don't know anybody who has that."

"Have you noticed that movies today rarely end happily?" I said. "Stories of the twenty-first century are bleak and in constant need of repair."

"The stories are more lifelike," she said as her eyes welled up, not from sadness or anything, but from the realization that an absolute truth was revealing itself. "We've created antiheroes—the warriors of our pre-apocalyptic society—who are willing to kill for love. Heroes are more realistic nowadays with their flaws and failures, and nobody cares about who or why they save anymore, so long as they save themselves."

"You're totally right." I coughed from the thickening atmosphere.

"Even fiction weeps for us," she said as she sucked in secondhand smoke through her mouth, held it, and then blew it out through her nose. There was a high-pitched sound, like a miniature flute that pierced the air. She cleared her throat and said, half cackling, "Don't you hate when that happens? You try to breathe some life back into yourself, and then your nose begins a sad tune. Nose whistling should be an art form."

I tittered at how comical the timing was, and how such a tiny sound could dispel the weight of the conversation. "By why hurt Larry?" I said trying not to lose focus. "Isn't he an innocent bystander?"

"I married my collateral damage," she said. "He's dead asleep, still making his way in the world, a prince charming with no kingdom to roam. It didn't help that he found me in distress. I made it worse by letting him rescue me. He faded into the delusion as I was thrust out." She squashed her cigarette into the dusty ashtray before continuing, the last of the gray smoke pinching into nothingness like a puny ghost. "I want to love him despite his fairytale façade." She was unsure of what I'd say and scanned my face for any signs of judgment. There were none. "Suffering is the great measure of life and living, so I'm doing him a service."

She justified her sorrow with a devastating grin.

"How was he when you first met him?" I said.

"He was a flaccid noodle, and who the hell wants that? If he didn't want what I had to offer, he would have left by now. But he stays, hanging on for dear life."

"How do you know when the fairytale ends?" I said.

"Are you in pain?" she said.

"Constantly."

"Are you with her?"

"No."

"Why not?"

"She didn't want me and cheated with two people."

"Then it's done," she said matter-of-factly. "It's hard to forgive when you're in agony."

Karen examined my face, gauging the truth of my words, and when she was content, she stood and undressed in front of the bed. Her instant nakedness shocked me because I'd forgotten she had no underwear on. The slingshot panty was still lying on the floor. She placed her hands on her hips like a super naked heroine and said, "Let's shower." She was completely awake.

~ * ~

I walked into The Five-Leaf Clover expecting to see Karen sitting at her usual spot, up front by the bartender, but she wasn't there, and it was unusual for her to be late. She was a punctual woman, and when she wanted to meet, it meant at the designated time. It was our routine. We always had just enough time to have a drink, walk down the street to get a room, have some fun, and then depart. Sometimes, we had a bonus shower, though we stepped out of there filthier than we had entered. A few days later we would repeat the ritual. We did this for a couple months until Karen changed our game.

She sat in a booth at the back of the bar, and I spotted her long blonde, corkscrew hair from behind. It was wet, as if she'd recently bathed. Before I reached the table, she turned around and a man sitting across from her stood up to greet me. He was too smiley.

"Hello, Liam," he said. "I'm Karen's husband, Larry. She's told me so much about you."

It was one of those instances when people are dragged by time, a bizarre *kairos* again. It went slowly. I absorbed everything about him all at once. It was a primal reflex: scrutinize your enemy, know every detail, and then attack. Save yourself. But I had already attacked Larry. I had slept with his wife repeatedly without the slightest hint of guilt. He was a few inches taller than me: lanky, bony shoulders, brown hair, blue eyes, a surprisingly short neck and a receding jawline. He was so thin—like he was on some abominable diet—that his skin appeared rubbery. Not that he carried around less skin, or that his skin was tight from workouts, but that his bones were so long and alarmingly thin that they stretched everything else. I was certain I could take Larry, but that's not what Karen had planned for us. I placed my hand in his when he extended it and, when I squeezed, he didn't squeeze back. It was flaccid.

"Join us," he said and motioned me into the booth he'd been sitting in, so I could take his place.

As I squeezed in, he told Karen to scoot, and he wedged in next to her. She stared at me with liar's eyes, not needing to utter a word for me to understand what was happening. This entire event was her way of complimenting me. She was confident that my lying was good enough to sit here with her naïve husband and feign a friendship.

"Karen says you're an old friend from school?" he said.

"We were great friends," I said politely. "We were in band together."

"Band?" he said turning toward Karen, "Didn't you say you were in theater?"

"Yes," she responded as she fingered the straw through her ice water, "but the band and theater program were run by one instructor." She began to crunch ice as her primary method of distraction, so she could think between mouthfuls. The best lying was done in short bursts, in enough sequential space to allow an accomplice to continue the farce. Children learned to do this early in their education through games such as *Finish This Sentence!* The game goes something like this: *A little____poked her____around the____and suddenly spotted a _____.* Thanks to the naturally creative genius of children, the sentence ends up saying something like, *A little kitty poked her hammer around the spaceship and suddenly spotted a bumble-hippo.* Children become the best liars because of those games, and it's a good thing they had much practice growing up because lying is the fuel of all adult conversation.

"Band and theater were on the same block schedule," I added. "That's how we met."

"What did you play?" said Larry.

"Drums," I said. "You two want a more spirited drink besides water?" I interrupted as I ran out of lies and began the truth. "I'm dying of thirst." I waved a server over and placed our beer order.

"I've always wanted to play drums," he persisted. "There's power in that instrument. It's the oldest instrument of humanity."

"Perhaps," I said glancing at Karen, signaling her to try her hand in the next set of untruths.

"See," said Karen, "I knew you two would get along fine." She sat contentedly listening to our conversation.

"I've never met any of Karen's friends. You're the first," said Larry. He didn't appear to suspect his wife of infidelity but, then again, we were all great actors.

"Liam doesn't get out much," added Karen. "He's a bit of a middle-age recluse like you, Larry, but without the middle-age."

"How interesting," said Larry as he stared longingly at Karen. He turned back to me. "Don't I have a wonderful wife? Not many men get to marry the love of their lives," he gloated.

Resentment flushed through me. "Most people settle for shit," I blurted out.

Larry went from bubbly to serious in no seconds flat. "What do you mean by—" he began.

Karen jumped in, sensing danger, "Liam is an aspiring writer," she said, "He likes trying out lines on people. You'll get used to it. He's a bit of a wordsmith." She shuffled nervously for the first time since the meeting began, and then said, "Oh, the drinks are here, finally." She snatched hers as it hit the table and gulped it twice before Larry and I had taken one sip. It was amusing to see her wash the egg off the face of her own game. "Larry wants to write a book one day," she added as she sucked up the inch of foam around her Murphy's.

"That's why I wanted you two to meet. You have that much in common."

She was lying, of course. Her words were husks, empty castings hiding the long-gone meat.

Despite our fumbling, Larry was content to converse with me. An hour into the talk, Karen scooted out and bid us farewell. Our topic had taken on its own life, she had been phased out, and Larry and I were stricken by nostalgia—not our own, surprisingly. Instead, we dwelled on a general loss of innocence, a nostalgia for all people. It was very empathic of us.

I liked Larry, even more so when he pointed out, "Your skin is in its twenties, but your mind is on the verge of a midlife crisis. Trust me, I would know."

He was a genuinely good guy and, had I not defiled his wife, we might have been buddies. Oddly enough, I found myself thrust into an affair with a husband and wife—sexually with her, and intellectually with him.

~ * ~

"Boys are born into tragic stories. They pop into existence and fall in love with their mothers. Soon, they realize their mothers are in love with the father or some other guy, the first rivals, and then come years of brutal heart-dicing," said Larry.

"What's that mean?" I said. He reminded me of a gracefully aging Tom Selleck, pre-mustache.

"It's the bastard cousin of a heart breaking," he said as he sipped a merlot. It was the first time I'd ever seen anyone drink wine at a pub. I sipped a lager as he continued. "Normally, you would imagine there's a shattering of the heart, like there's nothing left but shards. People do what they can to replace the metaphorical parts, but that's not very accurate to the actual experience. Love is about dicing, a partitioning of oneself to pieces until it's gone, till all that's left are the dregs."

I imagined the flattened organ in a pie tray—a gruesome pastry—and each lover stepping up to take their slice. Then each piece would get diced up into smaller bits as it was passed around and consumed like a party favor. The ancient Incas ritualized the mangling of animal parts in hopes that their enemies' power would be diminished, exactly like love. The Incas also ate the dregs. I didn't mention any of this to Larry since he probably knew about it.

He paused to drink more, and then asked, "Do you believe in psychology?"

"You kind of have to nowadays," I said.

"Would you say you suffer from Peter Pan Syndrome?"

"Nope," I said sipping my beer, skeptical of where he was leading me. "I don't suffer from any syndrome." *Lie.* The carbonation popped in my mouth and stung my sinuses as I hid my discomfort. "I feel pretty damn grown up." *Lie.*

"And did you feel this way before or after you fell in love?" he continued.

"After, I guess," I said. "But falling out of love is a hard reboot, if you can move forward. Or else you're doomed to relive the details of that first tragedy over and over with many lovers."

"Some can't move forward," he said.

"True, but when new beginnings aren't a possibility, and you're left with a gaping hole where your soul used to be, and you can't pick up the pieces any longer, then you fill it with something else. Everything else."

"Like what?" said Larry. "What could there possibly be to replace the emptiness?"

"Sex," *with your wife*, I said loudly, forcefully. I chugged my beer to show prowess, to emphasize my careless point, and the fact that I'd no clue what to fill it with. *With your wife* was a side-thought, and if he could have read my mind, he might have stabbed me.

"You talk as if you've been been painfully in love all your life," said Larry.

"I have been," I said, unhappy that he'd easily discovered that about me.

"I've never had that," he said. "I never grew up in that sense because my mother wasn't in love with my father or any other man. She was in love with me. I had no clue at how unnatural it all was until I met my wife. With Karen, everything she did, good or bad, tore at me, but I'm grateful she's stuck around for this long, to dice it up for me. She's been ripping me apart from day one, since I laid eyes on her." He slammed his wine glass down, nearly shattering it, as he emphasized, "BUT, writers and turmoil go hand in hand, wouldn't you say?"

Larry was singed, as was I, but in polarizing ways. The truth had discolored him. Yet, he was a good guy, the kind of guy I wished I could be. For him, love was the dark matter of the soul. It was everywhere, but nobody knew why, and there was no shaking it off. He swam like a shark in the ocean of inevitability, while I struggled to wake from the nightmare that sucked me in and pulled me under.

"Larry," I said, "Do you know about Karen, what she does when she's gone?"

He looked grim, as if about to embark on a killing spree, "Of course I know," he said and raised his hands to his face. His instant anger, as unsettling as it was, was ephemeral, and he immediately collapsed into the grips of defeat. I could see some tiny drops squeeze through the cracks of his fingers. There was no fury in this man. "She's chopping me up as we speak, probably with another man or woman or both," he sobbed, then gasped.

There is nothing more pathetic than a man crying in front of another man, except for a man who cries to the asshole who's screwing his wife behind his back. He knew nothing about Karen and me and, because it had to stay that way, I reached across our booth and placed my hand on his shoulder, and said, "Listen, I know how you feel. I've been in love, and married, and deceived. It burns forever. There aren't enough pieces to a person that can make it hurt any less than it does."

I let him go, and he exhaled loudly as he released his face and waved his hands like he'd just washed them. I was witnessing a purging of sorts, a poignant baptism. He ran his thin cupped hands under both eyes and flicked his fingers, as if trying to dispense with the last bits of his soul. Again, he waved them, sending his tears—slices of himself—flying all over the table, the condiments, and me. Some drops landed on my cheek, and I hesitated to wipe them away for fear of committing some profound offense to his gaping heart. *Tear factory.* His hands trembled when he reached for his beer again, and he cleared his phlegmy throat.

"You ever heard of The Trolley Problem?" he asked, composed again, as if he weren't chopped to chunks. "I learned about it in philosophy, in an ethics class."

"Yes," I said. "Everybody learns that in philosophy."

"Then you know how stupid and unrealistic the scenario is," he said as he began to wave his arms in attempts to paint a picture in the air. "A trolley barrels down train tracks, and you're standing there next to the lever that can alter its course. There's one or two people, let's say, some children, on one side of the tracks, and then on the other side are five people, all gorgeous women. And they're all pregnant, if you want a challenge. You're standing there with all that power. Except that nobody has all that power in life. Nobody," he shouted. "If you shift the lever one way, the children die, and if you move it the other way, five hot messes die." He paused and drank, then laughed aloud, "What do you do, man?" His eyes were bugged out, and he was shaking his fists in the air in defiance.

"Drop philosophy class," I said sarcastically.

Larry was no longer animated. I'd deflated his rant as fast as he'd fallen victim to it. He dropped his arms, relaxed his eyes, and dropped his voice. "You throw yourself in front of the train," he said, totally serious now, staring down into his near empty beer glass. "That's never a choice in those studies, but you throw yourself into the madness anyway, knowing you can save them all by sacrificing yourself, or else you die slowly and in agony the rest of your days with the burden of two or five lives, or ten." Larry was the knight in shining armor. It was his nature.

"I would have sacrificed the children," I said without hesitation, without him needing to ask me. I could hear him in my head: *Why the children?* And then the response I never shared: *Because they can be made again. Save the women and save all future children.* He was as surprised at my response as I was at his, but he didn't want to hear my explanation. So we allowed our differences to permeate the space for a bit. Then I asked: "Where does Karen fit in that scenario?"

Larry's face twitched. "Karen's the one who put those fucking people on the tracks in the first place. She's the reason I must choose. This marriage with Karen has been hell from day one, but I don't care because I love her. It doesn't matter who she's with when she's not with me. I'm the one she comes back to. Every ugly thing she's done is mine. Every beautiful thing is mine too."

"What if she doesn't see it like you do?" I said. "What if she sees you as a coward?"

"Come on, Liam," he said waving some imaginary threat away, "she's fragile and running for her life. Who do you think she's running from? Me? Don't bet on it. We keep each other intact."

It's the strangest feeling to hear the other side of a story you believed to be complete. People tend to run on half stories, and they decide much of their lives with this half knowledge in mind. Karen wasn't all power like she'd led me to believe. Here was Larry, her knight, strong as hell and gracefully slicing his soul away bit by bit to save the love of his life and himself.

Then it struck me. Larry embodied the choice I'd made in some far-off universe where I'd remained with my wife, Briana. In this world, however, I'd failed to rescue her, fleeing with my fractured armor, rusty sword, cowardice, and shattered pride.

~ * ~

"You're leaving me?" said Karen. Somehow, we'd ended up in room 333 again, many dozens of impassioned rendezvous later.

"We weren't ever together," I said, lighting up my last cigarette with her pink Zippo. She was getting dressed slowly, as if her clothes weighed a ton. "There's nothing left. What else do you want from me? We can't keep on with this. I'm numb."

"Bullshit," she snarled as she buttoned her pants and slipped on her shoes. She stopped dressing, lit up—bare chest hanging in the air—and began sucking away and puffing with a fury. She placed her cigarette in the ashtray and juggled her blouse before finally putting it on. Then she stuffed her bra in her purse and said, "You're running again. That's what you do. You run. You're a goddamn coward."

She knew about Briana by the end, and knew about my ring, but didn't care. She knew how connected I was to that band, how I felt as if I'd crack open if I ever took it off. I didn't need to say those things for her to know because she saw right into my soul. Karen didn't ask too many questions, and I did not volunteer information. She had discovered everything along the way, as she decrypted my movements in bed. It didn't bother her when my wedding ring would hit her in the face in smooth, rhythmic bursts, sometimes to the beat of some lonesome 80's hair band who bellowed of one-night stands with the lusts of their lives. And when the sex was bad, I'd stop moving, stare down at her, then lower my necklace and ring like a fishing line and bait it into her mouth. She gladly took it into herself, and then would yank me down with her lockjaw, but I'd resist to make her work, because she loved the struggle. I knew it was time to give in when the string of the necklace was so taut around the back of my neck it felt as if my skin would split. She knew the gesture would instantly take the sex from bad to critical. Sometimes, as soon as her mouth shut on it, I'd cover her face with my left hand, so she'd have to claw for each breath. I used my free hand to base out for balance to prevent her from tossing me to the side when she bucked her hips in discomfort, urging me to move off or change my pace. Her body said no sometimes, but her eyes never acquiesced, so I'd keep pushing forward until she was completely still and numb from the battle, until I'd conquered, and her body had gone limp. She was exceptionally strong and would try to get away when my weight overwhelmed her, but I was stronger. I wasn't new to working out with weights. I'd been working out all my life. It's impossible to outrun someone who's been running forever.

Every time we met was like a one-night stand. Sometimes, it was me who was abused and used by Karen. I'd rent our room in high spirits, but she'd be smoking twice as fast as usual. That's how I knew she was about to unleash some horrible energy on me. She didn't have a ring necklace to fish around for pain, to make it a battle, but she had strong hands and used them to squeeze my face until I said, *Ow, damn it*—until her death grip almost made my molars pop out. That was her cue, whenever the agony brought me to words, and then she would lean into my throat, her forearm perpendicular to my trachea when she was on top. Karen would grind away with her body, as if sculpting a deformation of reality from a heap of ice or rocks. We never talked about how we changed, how we were depraved hulks, as if destructive sex would somehow transform us back into human again. We hoped our depravity would be lifted but it never was, and we never went back to who we were. Every time we finished, we were worse off, more damaged, madder than before and ready to rage upon the world the whirlpool of treacherous energy that we dragged out of the room with us. Each time was a primer for an angrier meeting days later. There was no ceiling to our torture. Afterwards, we feigned civility with the people of the world, our veneers used to disguise the ugly. After days of being in the foulest mood, scratching at folks, we would schedule our next meeting.

Then there was Briana's letter, the one where she wished the past would be exorcised from our future. I'd made the mistake of placing it in my bag on a Karen day. I was using the restroom and when I walked out she was facing me, nude, her defined body a testament to the weights she lifted all week. Her legs were open as if she'd completed half a star jump, and she held Briana's note in front of her with both hands. I froze at the threshold, expecting a berserker frenzy. Instead, she casually lowered the paper, so I could see the sinister unveil in her expression. Karen had the answers to questions she'd never asked, making the reasons I was in this room apparent. She saw in the letter what I couldn't tell her, what I couldn't admit to myself. Only four words were spoken between us that day. When I removed my shirt, her eyes immediately shot to where the ring rested on my chest, as if she was viewing it for the first time. Both the ring and Briana's words were now part of what we did. That day was brutal. Karen fought me, her anger from another place. It wasn't sourced from Briana's note, or my secrets. It was a primal rage she harbored against her own past. It was so overwhelming that it seeped into our present and would eventually boil over into her future. Karen wouldn't stop clawing at me, desperate to uncover something under my skin. Then out of nowhere she demanded, "Say her name!" She was riding me, and her chest was against mine, her face so close and aching that I thought she would bite me. When I wouldn't say it, she wrapped the necklace around her left hand, held me down with the other, and squeezed until it was so taut the knuckles in her hand went white from the pressure. The ring's edge felt as if it was lacerating my throat. A gurgling noise shot from me, and this was Karen's cue to grind harder with her hips. Every movement of her body demanded the name be said. My larynx felt raspy, as if I'd been screaming far too long and, at the height of our sex, I finally cried out "Briana!" in a worn voice. We never spoke of this day again, and every time after that was as desolate as any other.

When we weren't together, when there was distance, we didn't think of each other or what we did in those rooms. It was too difficult to face the brutality of our fantasies in the real world. Any hint of it would send us recoiling. But as soon as we crossed the rotted wood of the shabby threshold, we ripped through our clothes as if there were a horde of rabid cannibals at the door, and we had to choose to die in fear or in razor sharp ecstasy. We always chose the razor. She would bite the ring sometimes, interrupting the pendulum attack to her face when I was on top. There were scrape marks on the emergent yellowing of the metal from her carnivorous teeth. The tarnish was the result of neglect on my part. Apparently, this substance wasn't as everlasting or pure like the judge had told Briana and me on our wedding day. It had to be restored, dipped in molten gold every six months because of its tendency to fade.

Once, I'd tried to remove the necklace, as a courtesy, but she stopped me and shook her head with a furrowed brow, as if I were removing my arm or ear. I kept it on every time after that. It was part of our affair. But I'd grown tired, not so much of our apocalyptic sex, but of Larry's penetrative intellectualism. I couldn't let him into my head anymore and then be inside his wife two hours later.

It wasn't until we were ending things that Karen mentioned Briana. "Go back to her then," she demanded. "Stop dicking around and save her." She was hiding behind a cloud of smoke, the last cloud she'd ever puff off for me. "Save yourself, for fuck's sake."

"Will you be okay?" I said, standing in front of the door, ready to turn around and be gone forever.

"I'll be fine. You're not my first and won't be my last. I imagine you've had a lot of girls tell you to remember them forever, or to never forget them." She mashed the butt in the ashtray to drive her point. "But this isn't a movie, is it?" she continued. "You go ahead and forget me because I'll be forgetting about you as soon as you walk out that door."

Karen wasn't mad I was leaving. She was mocking my uneventful departure. If anything, she was inconvenienced that she now had to find someone else to lure into the rotten hotel room with her.

"Fair enough," I said, suspecting this was her way of saying she would miss me.

I was in the hall when she said, "Wait," and I turned to face her again at the threshold. Strands of corkscrew dirty blond hung down her face and shoulders. The unit behind her clicked on, sending a quick burst of air through the room. "What about Larry? He'll wonder what happened to you."

Poor, heroic Larry. "Tell him I've gone to solve my trolley problem," I said. Karen was puzzled. "He'll know what I mean. Plus, you're a great deceiver. You'll figure it out." I admired her hair one last time as it flailed in my direction. "Goodbye," I waved and walked out.

Twenty

Michelle

"Who's calling you?" said Michelle.

"Hold on," I said as I peered down at my phone and sent the call to voicemail. *Goddamn it.* It was my uncle calling from Texas, but we were in a theater and the lights had dimmed.

"I'll call him back," I said.

"Good idea," said Michelle as she snuggled into me. The movie began.

Michelle loved tragic films. She said once that they were "true to life." I thought she meant life in general.

"You think life is tragic?" I had responded.

"No, I mean, that tragedy is at the core of every love story, and life is one long love tragedy." She paused. "Isn't it?"

She confessed during our first month together that before me she'd never felt an intense affinity for any one individual. "I think love has cast me aside, like the rough-draft of *Midsummer Night's Dream* Shakespeare threw out before the actual masterpiece was set to paper," she said jokingly."

With her, life was better. We found each other at a time when I'd tried to put all the ugliness of the past behind me. I didn't want to break hearts anymore and had no room to have mine tinkered with. Michelle didn't attempt to define *us*; she didn't ask me about children, or the future, she didn't try to understand my wounds. There was no *I love you*. She was ever-present. Her motto: "Now is perfect." I asked her once about her past scars. It was an inquiry full of presumptuous arrogance on my part. I assumed the whole world had been screwed over, needed screwing over, or was about to be screwed over. *Just you wait, World.* She stared at me bewildered, boggle-eyed, that I believed her to be part of the great hurt of humanity. I knew then that Michelle was my reset button.

We sat in the dingy dollar theater building which served as an Evangelical church on odd days, to watch *The Time Traveler's Wife*. Audrey Niffenegger is a genius storyteller. There's a part in the book that haunts me, when, without realizing it, Clare defines love for everyone who's ever loved by comparing it to living under water. Clare's desire for Henry is a perpetual sinking of spirit. For Clare, the *wait* of suffering is the *weight* of love. She persists through suffocating pressure and anguish, caged in a post-mortem state of longing. Love is muck. I'm not sure what's worse, uncontrollably bouncing in time while aging away from a chance at love, or being abandoned and anchored to a disjointed realm where time grinds against all momentum. Like love, time traveling is a slow assault—an oceanic drowning at the height of a storm. Love is absolutely damning.

Meeting Briana marked my life's mid-point, but we didn't make it beyond that. We'd abandoned one another. Secretly, I ached for another mid-point where we could meet unfettered from our past. Briana had come to me the first time. Our love was rooted in her bravery, not mine. She had taken the chance, not me. My return was an impossibility, however. I was too far gone. I'd lost my way. Now, we both tumbled through the labyrinth, surviving in our own distorted pockets of reality. Michelle was my respite for now.

Her head rested on my shoulder, our hands entangled. Michelle grasped me as if I were about to disappear. In a way, it was comforting that she was so vigilant. "You're *my* lost time-traveler," she whispered in my ear. She kissed my neck and continued viewing the film.

She'd asked me some time ago, "So tell me, what monsters keep you awake?"

Michelle knew there had been someone else I'd loved, who had made me into the emotional recluse that stood before her. But I wouldn't speak her name: Briana was my devil, and Michelle knew not to push for more.

~ * ~

She was a curvaceous, blue-eyed, strawberry blonde, the embodiment of a 1960's adman pinup model. I instantly knew we would go well together. On our first date, we played a game where we had to describe our first impressions. She referred to me as "aggressively mute," and "intellectually suave," with a "sprinkle of disastrous mystery." She was an intimidating wordsmith, and I reciprocated by describing her as "adamantly graceful," and "emotionally robust," as well as "charged with a magnetic levity." Though she romanticized my personality, she truly was those things.

Our first encounter was unextraordinary. We'd met at a training workshop for teachers. She was a twenty-four-year-old human resources administrator who'd already established herself in her department. She was driven to settle down and was a master of seeing the potential in things, including the potential in me. But potential is all it was. The reality of things was clear. I was damaged and emotionally unavailable. Michelle, on the other hand, didn't care to hear how impossible things would be because she chose possibility over all things.

I told her one day, "I'm a vacuous enterprise, babe. Use me and lose me."

She laughed and waited for me to join in, but quickly realized I wasn't joking. "Don't say that," she said sternly as she poked me in the chest to drive her point. "What you are," she began, "is mine.

You're not hers anymore." She had a way of bashing Briana, although she knew nothing of what happened, nor her name. Her intuition was uncanny. Undoubtedly, she saw it written all over me. Despite my flaws, Michelle was comforting and loyal. I sensed she hated Briana for what she'd done to me, whatever it was, and did her best to release the stranglehold by reassuring me that relationships didn't have to be chaotic and unpredictable—that a profound bond based on stability and predictability was possible, and that loyalty, unlike chivalry, wasn't dead. Michelle's practical philosophy was often lost on me. Still, it was evident that Briana had been a sullen madness, like the debilitating nervous disorder chorea, known as Saint Vitus's dance, which causes a person's reflexes to go haywire, their spasmodic movements resembling an epileptic attack. Michelle was the opposite. She was my slow dance. There was torment in one, and absolution in the other.

~ * ~

Michelle was passive-aggressive-possessive. It was an elusive trait at first, but it only took the wedding ring around my neck to expose the gentle lioness. Here's the gentle part. It happened on our first seductive evening together. We stood mouth to mouth in the darkness of my apartment, anticipating what was about to happen. The street lights from the parking lot were bright enough for us to see outlines yet dim enough for details to be lost in the contour. As my shirt came off, out popped my ring. It hit her in the face, as if acting in self-defense, causing her to step back a bit. "Ouch, my eye," she said. "What hit me?" She reached out with her hand to grope for the white gold dangling at my chest. Here's where I'd normally have to explain things, where she would unravel the tangled coils of my rotting spirit, but she wasn't having any of it. She merely asked, "Is this a ring?" Her tone was more curious than pressing for answers. Michelle had another piece to my broken puzzle. She ran the band around her fingers, turning it around and over like she'd discovered some cryptic talisman, her nails scraping my chest every few turns.

She then grasped it tightly as if to suffocate it and pulled down. The necklace dug into my skin so much that it nearly made me shove her away to alleviate the pressure on my neck. But the desperation making me want to get away also had me stuck in place.

"Take it off," she said.

"I can't."

"You can, and you will." She still had the ring in her hands and began to lift it off my chest and above my head, but I stopped her. It was reflexive. She stood in front of me, bewildered, admiring my resistance. Neither of us wanted to let go. We were love's witnesses.

"No," I said and began to lower the ring back down.

Michelle had finally discovered the exact physical source of my agony, and she competed with the ring to possess me. She sustained her grip.

"Who's ring is this?"

"It's mine."

"No. Who bought this ring? You or her?"

"Her."

"Then it should make things easier."

"Nothing about this is easy for me," I said.

"It's her ring, not yours."

"It was ours and she just—"

"This is her pain."

"But there's so much of it," I said.

Though Michelle couldn't see the tears running down my cheek, they were there; heavy, ugly bits of my soul pouring out of me.

"She's had you long enough."

"It wasn't supposed to be like this," I said.

"Let it go."

"I can't," I cried.

"You will."

She waited patiently for what I'd do or say next. But I had nothing. Gently, Michelle unveiled me of the forever and the never.

She lifted the ring off my body, leaving me feeling as if an organ had been reaped from me. Michelle remained by my side and held me together. The further away the ring, the closer she stood, until it was off me, and she was on me. It disappeared with a clink-clink as I felt the jerky aftershock of Michelle's arm. She'd thrown it, but she must have known where it landed or else she'd risk me finding it. And I did want to find it again. I wasn't exorcised quite yet. Our skin touched, and a shiver ran through me. I was freezing, teeth chattering and all. But she pressed into me, her warmth beginning at my ribs as a tiny spot and then growing into a blanket of protection. I shuddered in her embrace, fearing what she'd do with the ring, or if I'd ever see it again. Then something else struck me: this was Michelle's tragic love story playing out before me. I was *her* tragic lover. Perhaps, there was enough hurt in the world to go around after all. But there was faith in her love. There was redemption.

~ * ~

I was vexed at my uncle for sending another one of Briana's letters. I'd left him a colorful voicemail the day we saw *The Time Traveler's Wife*. Michelle had no idea I had the letter on me, at least not until we arrived home. Briana's words popped out of my pocket and landed at Michelle's feet as I undressed, almost as violently as the ring had popped her in the eye a couple months before. Luckily, this time the artifact had missed her completely. She was very casual about it, like it was some small grease fire that needed to be put out. "Rip it up," she said. "Why torture yourself?" But I knew it ticked her that I'd had it the whole time. She was unhappy I was leading a triple life. The one I led with her, the one in letters, and the ring. At least now, the ring was out of the picture. Only God knew what she'd done with it. I rummaged for the damned metal for many days after, hoping I'd "accidentally" stumble upon it, and *poof*! it would magically nestle itself around my neck again. Poor Michelle would have to come up with better sex and seduction to pry it from my clammy body again. Thankfully and regretfully, I never found it.

Good news for Michelle: one more life to squash and I'd be hers. She was not foolish. I, on the other hand, was very stupid. I was compelled to read Briana's letter, and Michelle insisted she be present when I did so. A big first for us. Couples anticipate good things like a first kiss, first orgasm, first trip together, first future plans, etc. For us, it was the first time she found out I was a fucked-up mess, first time I wouldn't let her in emotionally, and of course, the first time we tried to have sex it became this cathartic unveiling of my distorted past—ironically, tragically, a double first.

She didn't argue at all when I told her I couldn't rip it up, but she also didn't know that, for me, tearing that letter was as hard as splitting God in half. Maybe she suspected it, but all she said was, "Well, then, I might finally have a name for this demon." She never asked me about the name. Not directly. It's not that I held this information sacred. I just didn't want to have "Briana" thrown around in conversations or arguments, potentially tainting our breathing space. Putting a name to anything humanizes it too much, anyway. Of course, reading the letter was a stupid mistake, and we should've burned it together. We should have exorcized that last dybbuk rather than give it a full hearing. I read it aloud, as if it were a proclamation:

Husband,

Come back. You belong with me, and I know you feel this too. I will wait as long as I must for you. Give me another chance. Let me show you how things should be. Aren't we worth it? I would never hurt you again. Ever. Promise.

Your wife

Up to this point, Michelle had been gentle. Here's the lioness part. "Huh," she said, "no name." Briana's scent was all over the paper, and without hesitating I inhaled profoundly. It wasn't your average deep inhalation either. It was more of an *I'm surely drowning and am going to die, but sweet Lord here comes the breath that will save me!* kind of breath. Michelle witnessed this, snatched the note from me, and walked to the sink for a lighter. They were heavy footsteps, the kind that nobody would follow for fear of being crushed to death. She was a murderess destroying all evidence of the evilest doings. "You're not her husband," she said in a low growl, "and she's a lying, cheating bitch."

"Technically, I still am her husb—," I began. *Stupid, Stupid, Stupid.*

"Don't defend her," the lioness growled again. Her eyes were usually blue, but now they were a fiery set-to-kill mode. "You stopped being hers when she—". There was a hiccup as Michelle tried to word what had happened without any facts. But it was obvious, "when she spread her filthy legs for someone else. Because that's what she did, isn't it?" Again, my hesitation was answer enough. What she said stung, but she was dead on. I couldn't be mad at how impassioned she spoke. She was simply defending me. We let it burn in the sink and then fell into a bout of aggressive intimacy on the kitchen floor. The lioness was marking her territory. There were no more devils to come between us.

Afterwards, as we rested on the pile of clothes on the floor, Michelle spoke again, "You know, love doesn't erase all the terrible things others have done to you. If that person is damaged, then there is nothing in the world that can undo that. You end up loving the damage and all. It's enough to break a person." I couldn't argue that. "The universe speaks out about these awful things. It protests when you try to kill yourself," she continued. She was exactly that—my protest. Michelle sighed deeply and pressed into me as I contemplated what she'd said. She'd obviously been wanting to tell me these things for a while. Her voice dropped, making her words sadder to hear: "It's not fair. I get this tattered version of you while she keeps the best. We deserve better. You have *me*. Let her go."

~ * ~

We were in bed, and Michelle was dozing off while I mulled over *The Time Traveler's Wife* again. The book was more detailed than the film. Henry, the time traveler, dies at the end, kind of. He's seen the end, his end, like a grim reaper reaping his own soul, and he's gone so far into the future, he's visited Clare in old age. She's withered and always waiting for him to pop in and out of her lonely timeline. It's a geriatric finish. I'd read it three times, always ending with the feeling that I'd missed something crucial. That's how you know when a book is good...when long after you're done, you still can't believe what you've read, and so you find yourself re-reading it in case there is a new chapter that has suddenly appeared. Jorge Luis Borges's *The Book of Sand* is like this as well, always renewing itself, not permitting its reader to read anything twice. Borges wrote this as a lesson to those not present, to those who don't appreciate what is happening now. The protagonist of the story obsesses over the book until he realizes how monstrously infinite the damn thing is. The past is monstrous in this respect. People who are obsessed with the past are cursed with the impulse to flip back the pages of their lives, except that those pages are sand. Unfortunately, the present isn't much more solid than that. It's just mushy enough to be like quicksand. It's grainy muck.

Michelle was reassuring. The simple act of lying next to her made me feel safe. *Waiting is the bedrock of true love*, I told myself, and then wondered how Briana was handling the wait.

My phone lit up and angrily vibrated against the lampstand next to me.

"Who is it?" groaned Michelle as she reached over my chest to kill the noise.

"It's my uncle," I said, shaking her off. I jumped out of bed and walked into the other room to accept the call:

Me: *Hello?*

Uncle: *Liam, I'm sorry about sending the letters but—*

Me: *But I said no communication. (Michelle in background: Come back to bed!)*

Uncle: *Who's that?*

Me: *It's my girlfriend.*

Uncle: *I see. Listen, Liam, she knows where you are.*

Me: *How's that possible?*

Uncle: *She's been showing up here every other day since you left, asking about you, for any response to her letters. I invited her inside the other day and left her in the living room for a minute. When I came back, she was gone and had taken my address book. Your details were in there. Also, there was—*

Me: *Thanks for letting me know.* (Who keeps an address book in the 21st century? Old people, that's who.)

Uncle: *I was trying to help. Anyway, there was something else. Some mail.*

Me: *It doesn't matter. It's not your fault* (but I did blame him, secretly). *I gotta go.*

Uncle: *Wait, Liam—*

There was no reason to wait. I hung up and heard Michelle's voice as she got out of bed and came into the living room. "What's wrong?"

I didn't know what to say during the long pause between her question and the truth. Then Michelle blurted out, "Oh my god, she's dead. Tell me she's dead." She improvised a dance in the shadows of our apartment, her feet scuffling between the carpet and the linoleum kitchen floor next to me. Wishful thinking on her part.

"She's coming here."

Michelle froze when I said this. She sensed danger. "Backfire. Damn it. We need a plan."

"What? No. No plans."

"Tell me you're not considering seeing her?"

For the first time, Michelle's eyes welled up with fear. She knew there was only one way this could go. I'd have to face our demon.

~ * ~

We had no idea when Briana would show, but during the wait Michelle stood by me as if the world were about to end, like all life was about to expire. Except for when we had to work, we lived in anticipation of the ultimate apocalyptic wave, obliterating all we had. It was an ordinary day when it happened. I was sitting alone in the apartment when I received a text message:

Hey, it's me. I'm in Florida. I need to see you. Now.

Of course it was Briana, and hearing from her directly, in real time, reaching out to me, caused a surge of anxiety to wash over me. I resisted:

Let me live my life.

After a while, she responded: *I have something for you.* She was close.

The wait was ominous, and the air felt charged with static. The whole event paralyzed me, making me an unsheltered witness to bulging clouds rolling in at the birth of a storm, and all I could do was accept the inevitable. Then there was the brusque, invasive knock signaling Briana's arrival.

There were no words for a minute or so as we faced one another. Briana was faded, the damages of regret apparent and pronounced by her silence.

"May I come in?" she said. "Or are you coming out?" It had been a long time since I'd heard her British accent. I had missed it but hearing her speak teased my wounds.

"I'm good where I am," I said as I stood at the threshold, holding the door ajar with my left hand, ready to shut her out again.

"Let me in, darling."

I'd never imagined our next meeting, but this version was anticlimactic. My instincts said to shut the door but, without warning, she pushed through me and walked in as if owning the place. Then she threw her purse on the table and draped her jacket over a chair. Her back was to me, but she seemed shrunken, her shoulders smaller, as if she'd given up on something. Regardless, I still felt powerless to stop her. What could I say? *Get the hell out now and don't come back!* Nothing would work. She'd show up again and again. Briana was not many things, but she was persistent.

She turned around to face me, almost furiously, making everything she said sound threatening. "This is it. Time to come home with me." Briana reached into her purse and revealed the necklace. It was my ring, with the engraved *B4L* on the inside. Immediately, my eyes shot to her left ring finger. The other one, her half, the *L4B*, was securely bound to her hand. It was tragic that we only belonged together symbolically. She set mine on the table and then reached in her purse and produced a manila envelope.

I heard myself say, "How did you get that?" But I already knew the answer to my question. Michelle mailed the ring. She'd gotten my uncle's address from my phone. Whatever she had planned had backfired because here stood both of our nightmares, like Death herself come to scythe our lives to shreds.

"You didn't send this to me, did you?"

She began to scan for clues to see if she could spot the messenger.

Her arrogance infuriated me. "You don't get to walk in here and judge," I warned.

"Liam, wait."

"No. No more waiting."

Her face instantly went from arrogant to sullen. It sagged from the deepest sadness. Then, as she began to speak again, the lines of guilt faded from her face. "I can't undo my mistake. I didn't know what was happening to us." She reached out and tried to capture my left hand with hers, but her touch jolted me. My hand snapped away, and she pulled hers back to her side, shocked by my repulsion.

"Don't," I said as I folded my arms to avoid any more contact. "If I had done this to you, would you have forgiven me?"

She'd never considered it, yet her face said it all: *No.*

"It was too much for me. Forgive me," she said.

Briana was nothing but conditions, and her idle reasons made this apparent. She would never understand how much of myself I'd sacrificed for her. "You won't find forgiveness here." There was a rawness in my response, not at all what I imagined saying to her. I thought I'd beg for my life if I ever saw Briana again, but I knew it was Michelle who would heal me, who would haul me back to the shore and breathe life back into me repeatedly, forever, if she had to. Being with Briana, on the other hand, would consume me. I'd drown myself in her.

Her voice shook as she said, "Choose me." She pointed at the *B4L*. "That's us, forever us." Then her attention shifted to the manila envelope stuffed with our divorce papers. "This one," she choked up, "never happened."

But it did happen. All of it. And no amount of fiction would make things good again. As pathetic as it was, deep down, I wanted to be hers till the end. It was my last moment of weakness.

"Say it, Briana," I said, "Say the words and I'll tear up these papers and walk out of here with you." *I'm sorry Michelle. Forgive me.*

Nothing. Her mouth was sutured closed with some invisible thread. I couldn't wait forever so I handed Briana the manila envelope stuffed with signed papers, ring, signature, love, sorrow, and everything else that remained of us—and I shut the door after her. This was the last of us. I was finally done.

It was futile to divorce myself from something that didn't really exist. Yet, to cast off this love with its invisible pincers seemed near impossible. Ultimately, staying together wasn't a possibility, so we simply broke apart. There was no physical death to brood over, no sudden vanishing or sinister poisoning, no seductive suicide, no time traveling machine or genetic anomaly to set things anew, no rip in the fabric of space-time to take us back to the start, no forgiveness because of disease or cancer to absolve the past. There was no falling in love once more. There was nothing, just an ending.

Epilogue

Sounds of "Michelle" graze my ears. Notes blend with the breeze and quickly dissipate. All things are ephemeral near the ocean. I'm compelled to mouth the words, though I can't pronounce them correctly since my French is atrocious. The pulse of life is so tuned here. Howls of the Pacific drown out the music, and words rush in as the waves thin out. Sporadically, the wind is sucked back into the veins of the earth, then instantly manifests like a wraith. Everything synchronizes, and the cycle starts again. This is earth's song. The percussive nature of water slamming into the sand and rocks becomes an intrusive drum track, and the waves crash just as Michelle is called. My phone says there's a little over two-minutes left. Maybe the Beatles meant this love song to be heard near the waves. The ocean crashes into the song again. It blends perfectly. One verse passes, and the next one begins.

I close my eyes, and colors swirl about my mind until an alto voice cuts through everything and overtakes my ears. "Why does the song say Mama's name so much?" A four-year-old girl hovers over me. She's not quite real yet, because my eyes are adjusting, and I run knuckles over my eyes to exorcise the illusion. She's between the ocean and me, standing at three-and-a-half feet high with chocolate curly hair and blue eyes. The nose and eyelashes are petite versions of my own, yet hardly noticeable behind her speckled skin. She's an abstract work of art, and her skin is a beautiful canvas. Her legs are mine too, but her hands are her mother's. She speaks as gently as Mama but will assert a *leave me alone* like me when necessary. The girl smiles in anticipation, quietly guessing what it is I might say. *That's my smile*, and then my eyes drop to where her toes are digging into the sand like little hermit crabs. *My toes.*

"Because," I say as I reach out to caress her jawline, "Michelle is the name of the heroine in that song, and a sad man is calling her name over and over, so she will come to him."

"What's a heroine?"

"It's a hero, but better because she's a girl."

"Does he love her?"

"No, darling."

"But if he doesn't love her, then why would she come?" she says.

"Because," I say, "sometimes those kinds of people go well together."

Waves smash behind us and the girl abruptly turns her head and stands still for several moments, contemplating the commotion. She sees something near some large rocks and runs toward it—her question, and my answer, lost to the ether as her small feet kick up an alarming spray of sand into the air. *She runs like the wind.*

"Stay close," I shout as she sprints off. "You don't want to be pulled under."

The child frantically picks at the beach for a minute and runs back to me, excited to have discovered something new and yet so primordial.

"This one, Daddy, look at this one!"

She drops the object in my hand. It's a salty smelling starfish, the least tentacular of all sea monsters.

"It's a star," she says.

But there's no glimmer, and it's duller than expected, as if a shade has been permanently cast over a sad maroon. It seems cruel to suspend this bold animal out of its element, this ultimate survivor who's emerged from the ocean's stormy brushstrokes.

"Can we keep it?" she says.

"He can't live out here with us. He'll die. Let's throw him back."

I stand and reach down for her hand, then lead her along with me into the water. Walking on the beach this time of year is like balancing on the blade of a knife. We stop at the line where the ocean pricks our toes and then rolls back into the depths. There is a roar all around us as a fat wave rolls in and tries to knock us backward, but our feet are encased a couple inches into the quicksand. She doesn't panic but presses into me and hugs my left leg. We are stuck together at the edge of the world. This place runs differently. Time stops.

"You do it," she says, staring up at the star in my right hand. "You can throw it far."

I wind my arm back and launch the starfish into the expanse, as if aiming to stab at the heart of the earth. It skips a few times and sinks into the horizon, seemingly close to the bottom curve of the sun, directly to the west. Without warning, the sun's rays reach for my eyes, and I'm blinded. I turn away reflexively and drape my hands over her, pulling her closer. My eyes come into focus again, and the speckles that run along her spine pop out at me. We are harmoniously aligned with swirls of light. She's the love of my life, a little octopus tightly wrapped around my leg, and I'm grateful she won't let go. *Love is blinding and then unmercifully defines you*, I think to myself as the illusion fades yet again. I'll tell her that one day when she's ready to love beyond me.

"Will we ever find him again?" she says.

"I doubt it," I say, "but eventually someone will."

She's hopeful at my response and says, "I'll find him."

"I know you will, darling," I say and laugh lightly at her untainted optimism. There is a long pause as we are painted by the splash of waves. A tiny droplet of water stings my eye, and it makes me wince, but the sting is ephemeral, overshadowed by the salty air rolling into our lungs.

"These are the waters I played in when I was a child," I say automatically.

"Like me?" she says, "Where I'm playing now?"

"Right here, exactly like you," I respond and stroke the top of her hair. "This is as close as we can get to breathing the water," I say randomly, subconsciously.

She is smiling up at me when she says, "Silly daddy, people can't breathe water."

"You're so right, darling."

"Do you think it remembers you?" she says innocently.

"The water?"

"Yes," she says with wonder in the word.

"Probably not."

"Maybe if you speak to it, it'll remember you," she says matter-of-factly.

"But what if it doesn't speak back?" I say with playful concern in my voice.

"Just try, Daddy."

I inhale deeply in a futile attempt to hold in this moment indefinitely. But then I exhale, "I love you, Briana," and bend down to kiss the top of her head.

She squeezes my hand and kisses it long and hard, her tiny lips squishing onto my skin. Then, the words that have drowned me for eternity are spoken through a childish sigh: "I love you, too."

The air swirls all around us, as if the ocean is about to sing. Suddenly, she takes off again, racing away from me toward the unspeaking water, her words riding back with the wind, "Forever and ever!"

Meet R. F. Gonzalez

R.F. Gonzalez was born in a small town in the impoverished country of Nicaragua at the end of its revolution. He then immigrated with his paternal grandparents to Texas in the 80s. Soon after, he moved to Europe with his mother and father for six years. He traveled around the world and, at age nineteen, moved back to Dallas. In 2010, he earned a Ph.D. at the University of Texas at Dallas. Since then, he has been an entrepreneur, aspiring writer, and writing instructor. There are more interesting things to tell and, perhaps someday, he will write stories about it all.

You *can* make a difference!

Independent publishers like Wings ePress, Inc. do not have the financial or advertising clout of the larger publishing houses.

We depend upon another precious resource: our dedicated base of loyal readers. Please help us get the word out.

What can you do?

Take a few minutes and post a review on this book's Amazon page or you can post a review on our Wings ePress, Inc page at: *https://wingsepress.com/love-is-a-cheerleader-running/* by clicking on the User Reviews tab located in the Review section below the author biography.

Seriously, even a one-line review is helpful.

Thank you!

Visit Our Website
For The Full Inventory
Of Quality Books:

Wings ePress, Inc

Quality trade paperbacks and downloads
in multiple formats,
in genres ranging from light romantic comedy to general fiction and
horror.
Wings has something for every reader's taste.
Visit the website, then bookmark it.
We add new titles each month!

*Wings ePress Inc.
3000 N. Rock Road
Newton, KS 67114*

Made in the
USA
Monee, IL